MAGIC OF THE FAE

The Faeveil Saga - Book 1

J.E. Taylor

Magic of the Fae © 2025 J.E. Taylor

Case Cover Art by SG Designs

MAGIC OF THE FAE

Survival isn't guaranteed. Magic isn't eternal. And destiny isn't merciful.

Reya never asked for a crown. She never wanted to lead the remnants of a shattered kingdom. But when goblins raze her homeland, leaving nothing but embers and echoes of the past, escape is the only option. Her parents' final act opens a portal to Earth—a desperate bid for survival.

But Earth is no haven. It is a war-torn wasteland, where distrust reigns and magic withers. If the fae cannot reclaim their power, they will fall—not to goblins, but to the ruthless hands of mankind.

With Ashur at her side—the palace gardener turned reluctant protector—Reya must navigate the ruins of human civilization, forging alliances where betrayal lurks in every shadow. As the veil weakens, one question looms: Will humanity offer salvation, or spell their extinction?

Fate once dictated her path. Now, Reya will carve her own. And this time, destiny bows to her.

CHAPTER 1

SMOKE CHOKED REYA DAWN, thick and acrid, clawing at her throat as she stumbled across the uneven, soot-dusted floorboards to slam the window shut. Her hand trembled on the wooden frame, slick with condensation and grime. The icy draft cut through her skin, but it was the scene outside that froze her breath mid-gasp. The air was alive with the bitter tang of burning wood and metal, mingled with the sickly sweet stench of charred flesh.

Once, the view from this window had been a living canvas of vibrant green fields, rippling like silk under golden sunlight. Wildflowers had painted the landscape in dazzling bursts of color, their delicate fragrances carried on soft, playful breezes. Beyond them, the ice mountains had loomed like silent guardians, their pristine peaks glimmering with an ethereal radiance, whether drenched in sunlight or moonlight.

Now, all that beauty was swallowed by desolation. The fields were blackened wastelands, their fertile earth cracked and bleeding tar-like sludge. The floral rainbows had been obliterated, replaced by curling smoke that stung her eyes and turned the world gray. Even the majestic ice mountains bore the scars of destruction, their snow-packed faces smeared with streaks of toxic ash that hung heavy in the air.

No one dared venture far enough to measure the devastation, but rumors whispered that only their castle remained. The goblin horde left nothing untouched. Fields, forests, homes—it all fed their greedy appetite for ruin. These squat, gnarled beasts were relentless, their grotesque faces contorted into mockeries of glee as they burned, tore, and consumed. Their war cries were guttural, a sound that grated on her ears even through the thick stone walls of the castle. And their hunger? Insatiable. Every fae was either bled dry on their blades or roasted alive, the crackle of their flesh blending with the triumphant howls of their executioners. These monsters weren't just at the gates—they were an infestation, and they were almost here.

Reya slammed the shutters closed with a resounding thud, her chest heaving as though the smoke had invaded her lungs. The cold stone wall against her back offered little comfort as her heartbeat thundered in her ears. Precious few of her kin remained, huddled behind these battered walls. This was the last stronghold. They all knew it.

"Reya, your parents wanted you in the courtyard," Lily, her lady-in-waiting, chided, her voice edged with urgency as she packed bag after bag. The flickering torchlight cast restless shadows across her face, emphasizing the tightness in her expression. She clutched her hands together as if trying to steady herself, but the tremor in her fingers betrayed the fear threading through her heart.

Reya nodded, a careful, measured gesture, though inside, her thoughts churned like a raging storm. She had no intention of simply obeying. Not without speaking to them first. If they expected her to leave without question, they were sorely mistaken.

She inhaled sharply, the breath of earth rising from wet damp stone and melted wax mixed with the crisp night air. Her pulse quickened, a drumbeat urging her forward. She needed to see them. To look into their eyes and read the truth they wouldn't speak. Was there truly no other way? No escape, no loophole, no mercy?

Time slipped through her fingers like grains of sand, each second stretching impossibly long, yet vanishing too fast. The world seemed to tilt, the echo of expectation pressing against her chest.

She needed to act. Now.

She flung the bedchamber doors open and was instantly engulfed by the chaos of the corridor. Shouts echoed against the high ceilings. Every corner burst alive with movement. The guards barked commands, their voices sharp and urgent, while courtiers and attendants rushed past, their expressions hollow and pale. The flickering torchlight painted everything in a frantic dance of orange and shadow, lending an air of unreality to the scene.

Reya weaved through the crowd, her boots whispering over the cold, smooth flagstones. The air inside was almost as oppressive as the smoke outside—hot, stifling, and heavy with fear. The noise swelled and receded like waves in her ears, blending into a cacophony of despair.

When she pushed open the carved double doors of the throne room, the solemnity of the space hit her like a slap. The marble columns glinted coldly in the flickering light of the chandeliers, and the air was taut with dread. On the dais, her parents stood like statues of sorrow, their faces etched with the burden of countless lives. Reya stepped forward, her heart pounding not only from her frantic sprint but from the dread of what was to come.

"Reya, what are you doing here?" The king's voice cracked, raw and jagged, shattering the heavy silence of the room. His words reverberated against the cold stone walls like a hammer strike, pulling every set of eyes to her. The gravity of their stares pressed down on Reya like a leaden shroud, suffocating and relentless.

"There has to be another way to defeat the goblins, father." Her voice came out more fragile than she intended, trembling like a candle's flicker in a storm. The taste of smoke and fear clung to the back of her throat with unyielding bitterness.

The king's expression didn't falter, but there was a shadow behind his eyes—a grim acceptance, carved deep into the lines of his face. He shook his head, the motion slow and deliberate, like a man bearing the burden of a thousand invisible chains.

Without a word, his answer tilted her world. Pain spiraled outward from her heart as it broke under what had to be done.

Turning to his closest guards, the king's voice hardened, regaining its authority as he issued the order. "Bring the remaining fae into the interior courtyard." The guards nodded briskly and exited with sharp precision, their armored footsteps fading down the hall.

Then his gaze shifted back to Reya, and her heart lurched in her chest. "It's time."

The words struck her like a blow, robbing her of air. Terror coiled around her ribs, a venomous viper sinking its fangs deep into her chest. She stumbled back a step, her legs threatening to buckle beneath the stress of those two simple words. They had spoken of this plan in hushed tones many times before, their voices tinged with the hope that it would remain a distant hypothetical. But now, the hypothetical was an unrelenting reality.

The air in the room grew colder, as if death itself were creeping closer, drawn by the grim ritual about to unfold. Reya's gaze flicked to her parents, her mother standing tall despite the pallor of her cheeks, her lips set in a line of quiet resolve. The light from the chandeliers above seemed dimmer now, their once-proud brilliance dulled, casting eerie shadows that danced across the floor like specters.

It would take all of her parents' blood—every last drop spilled in sacrifice—to open the ancient portal to save the last of the fae. The thought clawed at her mind, leaving behind jagged trails of dread. The portal was a lifeline, yes, but it was also a finality. Once their lives faded, the door would close, sealing off this realm forever. The ancient texts had always said there would be no return, no reversal. A world left behind for ashes.

Reya's vision blurred as tears welled in her eyes. Her pulse pounded so loudly she could barely hear anything else. Her throat ached from the pressure of unshed screams. The thought of her parents—her mother's gentle hands, her father's steady voice—reduced to empty vessels, lifeless and cold, was a horror too great to hold. Yet there was no other way. The goblins were so close now that their guttural snarls and the screech of their blades echoed through the castle walls.

Her chest tightened further, as if the despair of the room was an invisible force crushing the breath from her lungs. Still, she straightened her back and met her father's gaze, desperate to cling to whatever strength she could summon.

Time had run out.

CHAPTER 2

ASHUR COLLINS RAKED THE brittle, yellowed grass in the interior courtyard. The dull scrape of the iron tines against the dry earth grated in his ears. The once lush lawn was patchy and sickly, reeking of decay, as if the land itself had resigned to the looming despair. His hands gripped the worn wooden handle of the rake, the rough texture biting into his calloused palms. Each pull sent up wisps of blackened dust that clung to his skin and settled in his throat, tasting of char and ash.

"What the hell am I doing here? I should be out there fighting," he muttered under his breath, his voice low and raspy, scarcely audible over the distant, ominous clang of the castle's warning bells. His father had insisted he take care of the courtyard today instead of taking up arms against the goblins.

The toxic air wrapped around him, thick and cloying, carrying with it the bitter tang of smoke and something far fouler—a metallic undercurrent that hinted at blood, though none had been spilled within the castle walls yet. The atmosphere pressed down on him, heavy and suffocating, as if the courtyard itself could feel what was to come.

A storm was building. It resonated in the unnatural stillness of the air, the way even the usual chirp of birds or rustle of leaves had vanished. He was a gardener by trade, not a warrior, even though he was competent with a sword, and he was certainly not privy to the royal family's plans, but the silence chilled him to the bone.

He raked harder, the physical exertion pulling at the muscles in his arms and shoulders, offering a fleeting distraction from the dread coiling in his gut. He could have waved a hand, letting his magic ripple out in a surge of green, effortlessly restoring the grass to its former vibrancy. But today, he needed the raw, physical strain to keep his hands from trembling.

When the princess stepped out into the courtyard, her presence sent a jolt through him. He froze, gripping the rake tightly as if it were a lifeline.

Her figure emerged from the murky gloom like a shard of light piercing the oppressive dark. But it wasn't her appearance that made his breath hitch—it was her eyes. The fear etched in her darting gaze was visceral, almost infectious, and it set his pulse racing. The princess, usually poised and unflinching, looked...lost.

She turned in a circle, her fingers weaving through her hair. The gesture was frantic. Her hand shook as it tangled in strands dulled by the mist hanging in the air. Her gown, once regal and immaculate, hung limply, smudged at the hem with dirt and soot. The sickly light filtering through the overcast sky cast her in pallid hues, draining the warmth from her features.

"Where is everyone?" she asked, her voice cutting through the stillness like a blade. It carried a sharp edge of desperation that made Ashur flinch.

Her eyes locked onto him, and his heart lurched in his chest, slamming against his ribs in a frantic rhythm. He opened his mouth to respond, but the words stuck, trapped behind the sudden dryness in his throat. Her gaze pinned him as surely as an arrow, and in that moment, the gulf between them seemed insurmountable. A lowly gardener with dirt under his nails and sweat dripping down his brow, faced with a princess bearing the fate of an entire kingdom's survival.

As if summoned by the princess's question, her lady-in-waiting emerged from the gloom, her slender frame bowed under the bulk of the heavy bags slung haphazardly over her shoulders. The straps dug into her skin, leaving red, angry marks, and her breathing came in labored gasps as she trudged forward, each step kicking up small puffs of dust from the dry courtyard ground. Behind her, at least two dozen fae followed, carrying bags of their own, their faces shadowed and hollow, their expressions tight with exhaustion and barely concealed dread.

Then came what was left of the royal guard, their polished armor dulled by the clinging ash and soot in the air, their boots striking the stones with a cold, rhythmic precision. At their center strode the King and Queen, their presence regal yet weighed down by the palpable despair surrounding them.

"You there," one of the guards barked, his voice slicing through the tense quiet as he pointed at Ashur.

Ashur froze. The rake slipped from his fingers and thudded to the ground. The sound was faint compared to the rapid thunder of his heart in his ears. He stepped forward reluctantly, the guard's steely gaze fixed on him like an iron clamp.

The guard shoved a dozen bags into Ashur's arms without ceremony. The rough leather pressed uncomfortably into his skin. Their weight nearly toppled him as he adjusted his grip, the straps sliding and cutting into his wrists. Before he could steady himself, the guard thrust a sword into his hands. The cold metal shocked him, its hilt coarse and unfamiliar against his calloused palms. The blade's weight was foreign, an anchor tethering him to a role he never sought.

"You are now tasked with protecting the princess," the guard growled, his hard stare drilling into Ashur as if daring him to protest. The words coiled around him like chains, heavy and suffocating. Ashur's stomach clenched, and the sour burn of bile rose in his throat.

Protect the princess? The absurdity of it stung like a slap—he was a gardener, not a warrior.

He adjusted the bags with trembling hands and awkwardly rested the sword on his shoulder. The blade's edge gleamed dully in the low light. The guard's eyes remained locked on him, sharp as a knife.

"Go stand by your charge," the guard ordered, his voice low and dangerous.

Ashur swallowed hard and obeyed, his legs as unsteady as a newborn fawn's. He stepped next to the princess's lady-in-waiting, her face etched with weariness as she struggled under her own burden.

The air seemed even heavier now, thick with fear and the scent of desperation. He tried to focus on the mass of the sword and the bags, hoping the physical discomfort would drown out the storm of emotions roaring inside him. But the truth loomed in the back of his mind, undeniable and chilling—he was no protector, and the storm wasn't coming.

It was already here.

CHAPTER 3

R EYA HUDDLED CLOSE TO Lily, seeking comfort in the calming scent of lavender that clung to Lily's cloak. The guards behind them shifted uneasily, their armor clinking with a discordant rhythm against the tense silence that hung in the air. The stench of steel and sweat tickled Reya's nose as she glanced at the sparse crowd and swallowed down her own dread.

Her gaze drifted to the man now standing on the other side of Lily. The edges of his white hair clung damply to his forehead, glistening under the tempered sunlight. A trickle of sweat rolled down his temple, catching the light like a fleeting star. The rosy hue of his cheeks stood out sharply against the pale, solemn faces around him, like a splash of warmth in a world of gray. His bright slate-colored eyes roamed the crowd, their piercing clarity igniting a flicker of something undefinable within Reya. Then they locked with hers. His lips curved into a smirk, a boyish expression that contrasted the grim heaviness of the moment. He shrugged, the motion causing the straps of his bags to creak softly as he adjusted the weight on his shoulders.

She tried to recall his name but couldn't. Still, he was memorable—how could he not be? She had noticed him tending the gardens, the sun warming his skin to a deep, golden bronze. There was something timeless about the way he moved, as though the earth itself responded to his presence.

Her parents crossed to the ancient archway ahead, their footsteps heavy against the worn stones. The crowd behind Reya sank to their knees in unison, the rustle of fabric and the whisper of prayers blending into a solemn chorus. The cold weight of expectation settled on her shoulders as the king, her father, turned to address the group.

"Rise," he commanded, his voice cutting through the tension like a razor. The authority in his tone sent a ripple of resolve through the gathered fae. His eyes, sharp as a hawk's, bore into Reya's as he spoke again. "Remember your destiny. Lead your people to the promised land and never forget that royal blood runs through your veins."

Reya's heart twisted. A dull ache radiated through her chest. She swallowed hard, forcing down the lump that rose in her throat. The sting of tears pricked her eyes, but she blinked rapidly, unwilling to let them fall.

Her mother stepped forward. The jeweled crown in her hand caught the sunlight and cast tiny rainbows across the stones. The clink of the metal echoed in Reya's ears as her mother placed the crown upon her head.

Its weight was suffocating with the implications of this moment. A moment she didn't believe would ever come to pass.

"Trust your heart," her mother whispered, her voice trembling with a rare vulnerability. The scent of her perfume—a blend of jasmine and something faintly citrus—lingered as she fastened her weapon belt around Reya's waist.

The queen's guard approached, his boots heavy against the stone, and handed over a quiver brimming with arrows and the gilded bow Reya had practiced with until the pads of her fingers turned from raw agony to calloused tools of precision. She slung the quiver over her shoulder, the strap biting into her skin, and adjusted it to ensure the arrows were within easy reach. Her mother's sad gaze met hers, the gravity of unshed words hanging between them.

The warmth of her mother's embrace enveloped Reya for a fleeting moment. The softness of her silk-clad arms and the familiar scent of home made the inevitability of their parting all the more unbearable.

"Be strong and choose your king wisely," her mother said, her voice both a plea and a command. She lingered for a heartbeat longer before stepping toward the archway.

Her father's arms encased her, a rare show of affection that made her chest tighten painfully. His grip was firm, his presence a bulwark against the storm that loomed ahead. When he released her, he handed over his crown and sword, signifying the passing of the throne to Reya in front of the remaining fae.

The jeweled blade was cool in her palm. Its weight nearly buckled her knees as she grasped it. The crown sparkled with an almost mocking brilliance. Together, they were heavy with far more than just metal—they carried the lives of her people, the legacy of her bloodline.

Reya straightened her spine, even as her chin quivered and her determination wavered.

He snapped his fingers; the sharp sound echoed through the still air like a crack of thunder. A page stepped forward, his boots scuffing against the stone floor, and placed a thick tome into the king's waiting hands. The book's leather cover was worn, its edges frayed and corners softened by time. A lingering trace of aged parchment wafted toward Reya as her father handed it to her.

"Our history." His voice was heavy with the expectations of generations.

Reya's fingers trembled as she accepted the tome, its surprising heft pressing into her palms. The leather was cool and smooth against her skin, except for the ridges of embossed symbols that seemed to pulse under her touch. She gulped down the lump in her throat, the motion tight and uncomfortable, and clutched the book to her chest.

"Know that we love you and will always be with you in spirit," her father whispered in her ear before he backed away.

He nodded, the movement slow and deliberate, before stepping toward the ancient archway. The stones hummed, as though anticipating the ritual. He drew a jeweled blade from his belt. The gems embedded in its hilt caught the dim light, scattering fractured rainbows across the walls. The sharp edge gleamed with a cold and unforgiving promise.

He held it out to her mother, the gesture solemn.

The queen hesitated, her hand hovering over the blade as if reluctant to touch it. Her chest rose with a deep inhale, the sound of her breath steadying Reya's own racing heart. When she finally grasped the knife, her fingers curled tightly around the hilt, knuckles whitening.

An ancient spell tumbled from her lips. The foreign words vibrated in the air like the low hum of a distant storm. With a swift, practiced motion, she raked the blade from the king's elbow to his palm. The cut was deep, and crimson welled up instantly, spilling over his skin in rivulets.

Reya's stomach churned as her father's jaw tightened, his teeth clenched against the pain. The sharp hiss of breath cut through the silence.

He took the blade from her mother and chanted the same spell. The words rolled off his tongue with a rhythmic cadence, each syllable carrying an almost tangible weight. The blade sliced through her mother's arm in a mirrored motion, the sound of steel against flesh sharp and visceral.

Reya's breath hitched as the queen's blood joined the king's, the mingling scents of iron and earth filling her nostrils.

Together, they turned to the archway, their faces pale but firm. The stones seemed to drink in the blood as they swiped their arms across the rough surface, leaving streaks of red that glistened in the dim light. The spell grew louder, their voices overlapping in a haunting harmony that sent shivers down Reya's spine.

They threaded their fingers together between them, letting their lifeblood fall to the earth. The crimson liquid dripped steadily, pooling at their feet and spreading outward, the dark liquid gleaming like molten rubies.

Reya's fingers tightened around the tome as if the book of their legacy could shield her from the ritual unfolding before her eyes. But nothing could have prepared her for the devastation rising in her soul.

CHAPTER 4

ASHUR'S EYES WIDENED AS crimson poured from the king and queen's arms, the thick, glistening streams pooling at their feet. The copper tang of blood filled the air, sharp and nauseating, making his stomach churn. His gaze darted to the princess, her face pale and drawn, a single tear carving a glistening path down her cheek. The silence was suffocating, broken only by the drip of blood hitting the stone floor. No one spoke. No one moved. The silence steeped in their inaction pressed down on Ashur like a physical force.

He opened his mouth to object, to cry out against the madness unfolding before him, but the archway shimmered. A soft, otherworldly hum filled the air, silencing him as if the sound itself had stolen his voice. The shimmering wall between the king and queen pulsed, its surface rippling like liquid silver.

The king and queen dropped their hands, their bloodied arms hanging limply at their sides. The king's commanding voice cut through the tension. "Go." His tone left no room for hesitation, even as he turned back to the ancient chant, his voice blending with the queen's in a haunting harmony.

Ashur's heart clenched as the princess swallowed audibly, the sound unnaturally loud in the oppressive quiet. Her shoulders squared, and she stepped forward, her movements deliberate yet hesitant. The shimmering wall seemed to part for her, its surface rippling as she passed through. Her lady-in-waiting followed closely, her steps quick and light, as though she feared the portal might close behind her. The rest of the people moved in unison, their collective footsteps a soft shuffle against the stone. One by one, they disappeared, their forms swallowed by the shimmering barrier until only Ashur remained.

He stood frozen, his gaze locked on the king and queen. Their faces were pale, their expressions resolute despite the blood that continued to drip from their arms. The air around them seemed heavier, charged with the significance of their sacrifice.

A sudden commotion behind him shattered his trance. The clash of steel and guttural snarls sent a jolt of adrenaline through his veins. He spun around, his breath catching at the sight of goblins breaching the courtyard. Their twisted forms moved with terrifying speed, their weapons glinting in the dim light. Without thinking, Ashur's feet propelled him forward, his boots pounding against the uneven ground.

He charged through the archway just as the whistle of a javelin cut through the air. The sickening thud of metal piercing flesh made him glance back, his heart plummeting as the king collapsed, the weapon protruding from his chest.

The queen's scream was drowned out by an explosion that rocked the space behind him. The force of it sent him sprawling, the ground beneath him rough and unforgiving. Dust and debris filled the air, stinging his eyes and clogging his throat as he scrambled to his feet. The magnitude of what he had just witnessed pressed heavily on his chest.

Ashur's gaze swept over the huddled crowd of fae, their expressions a mixture of fear and exhaustion. Faces smeared with soot and streaked with tears stared blankly at the ground, their postures slumped in defeat. The rustle of their tattered garments mingled with the soft, hollow sounds of their whispered prayers. Smoke clung to the air around them, an unrelenting reminder of the destruction they had fled.

He tore his eyes from the crowd and scanned the barren, blackened expanse that stretched endlessly before them. The landscape was a desolate sea of charred remnants, the skeletal remains of trees clawing at the sky like blackened fingers. Patches of scorched earth smoldered, sending thin tendrils of smoke spiraling upward. The air was heavy and dry, filling Ashur's throat with a bitterness that made him want to retch.

Jagged edges of broken stone dug into the soles of his boots. A dull orange glow hung on the horizon, casting long, distorted shadows across the wasteland. It wasn't the warm, golden hue of a sunrise; it was the eerie light of an ever-burning fire, a cruel mockery of life and warmth.

This isn't paradise.

The thought clenched like a vise around his chest, squeezing the air from his lungs. This wasn't the sanctuary they had been promised, the verdant landscape painted so vividly in the tales of old. This was a hellscape, blackened and lifeless, worse than the land they had abandoned. The fallout from the betrayal settled heavily on Ashur's shoulders as he tried to reconcile the stories with the harsh reality before him.

The silence pressed in, broken only by the low, mournful sigh of the wind as it swept across the wasteland. Ashur's fists clenched at his sides, the rough fabric of his sleeves brushing against his skin. His heart pounded in his chest. Each beat a drum of frustration and despair.

CHAPTER 5

REYA'S JAW SLACKENED, HER breath catching in her throat as her wide eyes took in their new world. A world that seemed to mock every promise she had been given. The air was thick with a strange, bitter odor, burning in her nostrils and scratching at the back of her throat. The grit of fine dust clung to her skin, carried by a hot wind that whispered like a warning across the desolate plain. The sun hung low in the sky, its harsh light casting everything in a washed-out glare that made her squint.

She turned just in time to see the gardener hurtling out of the portal. His limbs flailed as he was unceremoniously deposited onto the cracked earth. A cloud of fine mist trailed behind him.

The portal shimmered one final time, its luminous edges pulsed before disintegrating into a sparkling vapor that dissipated into nothing. The lingering scent of ozone marked its absence, a cruel reminder that they were now stranded, utterly and irreversibly. This inhospitable place seemed more like an exile than the salvation she had been promised.

Earth had been described as a land of abundance: lush vegetation carpeting the ground, rivers and lakes sparkling like jewels under a clear blue sky. Glittering cities rose in majestic spires, with mountains that kissed the heavens. She had imagined the soft, cool touch of its air, so clean and welcoming. A realm of bounty and vitality, untouched by the decay and oppression they had fled. But standing here now, the reality struck her like a blow.

"What the hell is this?" Quinn Moondove spoke, breaking the stunned silence. His glare pierced through her before he spun, taking in the bleak scenery.

She ignored the arrogant ass that had been saved by her parents' sacrifice and raised a trembling hand to shield her eyes. She scanned the horizon again, her heart sinking deeper with every passing moment. In the distance, a mountain range loomed, its jagged peaks almost obscured by a thick haze that clung to the landscape like a suffocating shroud. The mountains should have been majestic and inviting, but instead, they looked distant and forbidding, their outline distorted by the undulating waves of heat radiating off the scorched earth.

"I know it doesn't seem ideal, but perhaps we will find what we need in those mountains." She nodded toward the distant peaks poking toward the sky.

The ground beneath her boots was barren and cracked, each fissure a silent testimony to the land's lifelessness. Stray tufts of dry, brittle grass poked through the fractured soil, their brown, withered stalks bending feebly in the wind. The air itself seemed hostile, heavy with a dryness that sapped the moisture from her lips and left her tongue parched. Reya's fingers curled into fists around the book in her arms as a dull ache grew in her chest. Perhaps, she thought with desperate hope, they had simply landed in a forsaken corner of this world—an anomaly, not the true paradise she had read about in history books. That hope was a fragile shield against the wave of despair threatening to drown her.

Her gaze swept over the ragged group, each face worn with exhaustion and grief—except for Quinn. He stood apart, carrying himself with an air of superiority, as though his royal blood made him more sacred than the rest. His blatant arrogance grated on her.

The rest of the survivors huddled together, their once-pristine garments now torn and dust-streaked, clinging to their frames like ghosts of the lives they had left behind.

Reya's eyes locked on the gardener, his sun-bronzed skin smeared with ash and streaked with grime. His eyes glinted with a truth too raw to voice—a haunting knowledge that mirrored the ache in her own chest. As he navigated through the remnants of their people to stand at her side, the shuffle of his boots over the cracked ground seemed loud in the oppressive silence.

"My Queen." His steady voice lowered. He dipped his head in respect, but his gaze never wavered, anchoring hers in its unflinching intensity. The words resonated deep within Reya, vibrating in her bones like the aftermath of a powerful chord. His voice carried a warmth that cut through the cold desolation around them, stirring something in her soul—a fragile flicker of solace in stark opposition to the barren ruin encasing them.

Quinn scoffed at the gardener's display of respect.

"What shall I call you?" she asked without giving Quinn any attention to his audible slight.

His lips twitched into the barest ghost of a smile, a fleeting expression that tugged at her resolve.

"Ashur Collins, at your service." He executed a sweeping bow, the fluidity of the motion a stark contrast to the dull, exhausted movements of the others. The bags on his shoulders slipped and hit the scorched earth with a resounding thud, sending up a small puff of dust that settled almost as quickly as it rose.

When Ashur straightened, any trace of his smile had vanished. His expression hardened; the crushing force of responsibility pooled in the set of his jaw and the crease between his brows.

"I am sorry about your parents." His voice softened, yet was weighted with genuine sorrow.

Reya's throat tightened, but she forced herself to inhale deeply. The bitter air clawed at her lungs. Her gaze flickered to the others—each one avoiding her eyes, staring down at the cracked ground as if searching for answers in its jagged patterns.

"I am sorry we were not strong enough to safeguard our kingdom." The words were thick on her tongue and heavy in the charged air.

Another chuff from Quinn had Ashur sending a searing glare in his direction before he refocused on her with those steel-blue pools she could get lost in.

The truth anchored in her confession pressed down on her shoulders, but the subtle nods of acceptance from those around her offered a hollow kind of unity. Every bowed head acknowledged a truth too painful to deny. She shifted her gaze to the horizon, where a line of mountains rose in the distance, their jagged peaks blurred by a lingering haze.

She pointed beyond where the portal had spit them out, to the only semblance of hope she could see.

"It looks as though we have a journey ahead of us." Each word carried the hope of their fallen kingdom. "Perhaps we will find a more hospitable place to rest there."

She scanned the group, her sharp gaze piercing through the hazy light. Her nostrils flared, catching the musk of sweat and leather. They were moving sluggishly, their weariness etched into every stiff movement, every sluggish glance toward where she pointed. The men seemed preoccupied, their hands fumbling with straps as they saddled the bags—except for Lily. Her lady-in-waiting stood apart, shoulders stooped under an ungainly pile of satchels.

They would never make the trek with such uneven burdens.

"Even out the load," Reya commanded, her voice slicing through the morning stillness like a taut bowstring. She stepped forward and reached for one of the bags perched precariously on Lily's narrow shoulder, the coarse burlap rough against her fingers.

"No, Your Highness." Lily's sharp refusal startled Reya as the girl jerked away, her voice trembling with apprehension.

Reya's gaze hardened as she turned back to the group. The intensity of her stare seemed to press upon them, but none of them budged. A hot tide of frustration burned in her chest, mirrored by the flush of heat rising in her cheeks.

"Did you not hear me?" Her words carried an edge now. "We need to even out the load; otherwise, we will not make it to those mountains." She jabbed a finger toward the distant jagged peaks cloaked in mist, the sight of them looming like a promise of impending trial. "Those overwhelmed will drop from exhaustion before we reach our destination."

A wave of muttered grumbling rose in answer, a sound that bristled against her nerves. Quinn added an eye-roll as if her request was ludicrous.

"We don't know whether we will be met with hostile forces," she snapped, her tone cold now, as if daring them to defy her logic. "And we need to be able to react. Drop your bags right here so we can divvy them up."

Her words hung in the heavy air like arrows waiting to find their mark. For a moment, no one moved.

Then she drove her authority home. "Everyone needs to shoulder the responsibility. This is how we survive."

Grudgingly, the group stirred. Boots scuffed against dry soil as bags were shuffled forward, landing in a pile at her feet with dull thuds. The sour undertones of resentment lingered in the air, but she ignored them. She watched as they, including Ashur and Lily, obeyed, their reluctance palpable in their stiff movements.

Rea stabbed the earth with her father's sword and then bent down, the edges of her skirt brushing the ground as she grabbed a bag. The weight hit her shoulder with a familiar ache, but she adjusted it until it sat securely. She tucked the book and the crown inside, ensuring her bow and quiver remained unimpeded.

"Now, everyone take a bag." She barked the command with an authority that brooked no argument.

She straightened and reached for another, but Ashur stepped forward, his hand a steadying presence. "I can take your second bag, My Queen."

She exhaled, not quite a sigh, but a slow release of breath that echoed her weariness. "Another bag will not make a difference," she countered, her tone softening. She offered her father's ornate sword to him. "Why don't you take my father's sword instead? That way, I will have the latitude to use my bow if need be."

Ashur's eyebrows rose in surprise, his hesitation betrayed by the fleeting quirk of his lips. "I already have a sword."

“Then give it to one of the others,” she replied coolly, pressing the hilt toward him. “And take my father’s instead. You were assigned to protect the crown, so you will have the crown’s sword.”

CHAPTER 6

ASHUR STARED AT THE king's sword, the polished metal gleaming even in the muted light. The hilt was cool to the touch, its intricate carvings catching the amber glow of the sun. Then his gaze shifted upward, locking onto the queen's eyes—deep pools of blue with flecks of lavender that seemed to pierce through his thoughts.

He turned, the crunch of dry earth beneath his boots marking his movement, and handed his sword to the nearest man. The fae, his posture upright and measured, took the weapon with a brief nod. Ashur noted the man's wiry build and keen gaze, calculating that he seemed capable enough to wield it. His fingers flexed as if reluctant to let go, but then he turned back to accept the king's sword from Reya.

The blade's weight settled into his palm, heavier than the one the guard had thrust upon him, its balance familiar yet foreign. The scent of oil and leather lingered on the scabbard, mixing with the crisp tang of the morning air. The sword carried not just its physical heft, but the palpable history and authority it symbolized.

"Wait a minute. I should hold that," Quinn said, his voice sharp and entitled as he stepped forward, hand already reaching, as if the sword were his by right. His brazenness turned heads—but it was Ashur's attention he wanted, and got.

Reya moved without hesitation, planting herself between them like a drawn line in the sand. "My father gave that sword to me." Her voice carried her unwavering choice. "And it is *my* prerogative to give it to Ashur." She lifted her chin, defiance sparking in her eyes, daring him to press further.

Quinn halted, lips curling into a sneer. His gaze burned past her, locking onto Ashur with something between resentment and challenge. But Ashur didn't flinch—he simply shifted the sword onto his shoulder, the gesture careless, almost mocking, as a smirk tugged at his mouth.

Quinn huffed, his expression twisting in petulant displeasure, and stalked off with all the wounded pride of a child denied his favorite toy. Behind him, a few of the nearby fae exchanged glances, the corners of their mouths twitching as they struggled to smother their amusement.

Reya moved again, her skirt sweeping softly against the ground as she reached for another bag.

"No," Ashur said firmly, stepping forward and catching the strap of the bag mid-motion. The worn leather was rough against his fingers. "There are enough of us to carry the rest. You have a bow and quiver to handle." His calm voice brooked no argument. He eased the bag from her grip, the tension in her fingers releasing as he took it.

He slung the bag over his shoulder. The straps dug into his already sore muscles. His shoulders rolled instinctively, adjusting to the added weight, though compared to the crushing load he'd stumbled through the portal with, it felt almost manageable.

He gestured to the others with a sharp nod. "The rest of you, follow suit."

Grudging compliance rippled through the group. Ashur's sharp ears picked up the scrape of bags being hoisted, the labored breaths of men shifting their burdens. In the end, he bore the brunt of three bags, their combined weight settling like an old, familiar ache across his back. A handful of the others matched him, their movements steady yet strained, while the rest carried lighter loads. The grumble of dissatisfaction lingered in the air, but Ashur dismissed it. His gaze drifted briefly to Reya, standing tall despite the tension in her shoulders.

She had the bow and the mountains ahead to contend with—and that was enough.

CHAPTER 7

REYA LED THE PROCESSION across the barren wasteland, her boots crunching over jagged shards of blackened earth that crumbled with every step. The scent of burned soil clung to the air, filling her lungs with each shallow breath. A dull ache pulsed in her legs, each step a reminder of the strain on her muscles—tight, cramped, and on the verge of rebellion. Yet the deeper ache came from within, where repressed devastation gnawed at her resolve, threatening to drag her thoughts down like an undertow. She forced herself to focus on the steady rhythm of her footfalls, the sound distracting her from the chaos of her mind.

As the sun dipped low, its weary rays painted the landscape in shades of amber and rust. The ground beneath their feet shifted, the charred remnants giving way to softer, brown dust that clung to their boots in dry, powdery layers. The grit in the air lingered, creating a bitter tinge on her tongue with every exhale. The horizon grew gentler, the jagged peaks of the distant mountains drawing nearer, cloaked in shadows that deepened as daylight waned. Yet, despite their progress, the mountains were as unattainable as the comfort of rest—a destination still a day's grueling journey away.

Her pace slowed, then stilled. The silence of the wasteland enveloped her as she turned to face her people. Their faces mirrored her fatigue, shoulders sagging under burdens they carried without complaint.

"We will make camp here." Her voice was steady despite the weariness dragging at her tone.

Reya closed her eyes, shutting out the sight of their exhaustion as she drew in a slow breath. The air was dry, stinging her throat as it passed. She pictured rows of tents—one for each of the couples—envisioning a brief reprieve for them all. The familiar flicker of magic stirred deep, fragile but present. She waved her hand in a smooth arc, willing the vision into reality.

Half a dozen tents shimmered into existence, their muted tones blending into the dusky landscape. But the spark within her faltered— snuffed out like a candle caught in a sudden gust. A cold emptiness flooded her chest, hollow and aching, as her magic refused to answer her call. She tried again, clenching her jaw against the cloak of her exhaustion, but the effort was in vain. Her fae magic, once a boundless wellspring, felt as drained and frail as she did.

Reya ran her palm over her face, her skin brushing against the fine, dry grit that clung stubbornly from the journey. The sensation was coarse, a grimy reminder of the relentless hours under the sun and wind. When she glanced at her hand, streaked with the dust of their march, bitterness curled in her chest.

As a fae with royal blood, she was supposed to embody strength—grace under pressure, her power undeniable. But the magic that should have surged with the vitality of her lineage remained thin and fleeting, like the last gasp of a dying ember.

She swallowed hard, forcing down the bloom of fear clawing up her throat, its tendrils tightening around her resolve. "I seem to be more exhausted than I thought." Her voice wavered, a brittle edge betraying her disquiet. A nervous laugh escaped her lips, fragile and unconvincing, its sound foreign to her own ears.

Quinn and his sister Petal sneered at her as if she were not fit to rule this small band of fae. Before they could make a snide comment, Lily, ever the steadfast presence, didn't hesitate.

"We will make do," she said with quiet assurance, slipping an arm around Reya's waist. Her touch was firm yet gentle, a stabilizing anchor Reya hadn't realized she needed. Breath of lavender clung to Lily's hair, a rare, comforting note amidst the harshness of their surroundings.

Reya didn't resist as Lily guided her to the nearest tent, the canvas billowing in the evening breeze. Inside, the air was thick and still, tinged with the mustiness of fabric and earth. She dropped the heavy bags in a corner with a muffled thud, the sound punctuating her fatigue. Stripping the quiver and bow from her aching shoulder, she sighed as the tension in her muscles loosened just enough to notice the throbbing ache beneath.

Without a word, Reya stepped back outside, the cool air brushing against her flushed skin like a tentative balm. Ashur stood just outside the front of their tent, his broad silhouette outlined against the dimming horizon. He let his bag fall to the ground with a solid thump, the motion deliberate. When their eyes met, his steady gaze was a mixture of silent inquiry and unwavering support.

Quinn stood rigid in the entrance of one tent, arms crossed like a barricade, his icy stare fixed on the two fae clutching their bags, their indecision thick in the air like fog before a storm. His presence was more wall than man—unyielding, deliberate. Every fiber of his posture screamed that this ground, this shelter, belonged to him.

"What seems to be the problem?" Reya asked, striding up with a deliberate calm that failed to soften the razor edge in her voice. Her steps were measured, but her eyes burned with suppressed fury, scanning the scene like a hawk spotting prey.

The male fae squared his shoulders and shot a scathing look at Quinn, his voice taut with frustration. "He refuses to share the tent."

"I am of royal lineage," Quinn replied coolly, the corners of his lips curling downward, voice oozing contempt. "I don't share with peasants."

A heartbeat passed in silence. Then another. A collective breath was held. The tension didn't just hum; it howled beneath the silence. Reya's jaw tightened, a nerve twitching along her temple as her eyes locked on Quinn, glowing with restrained fire. She didn't blink.

Then she pivoted to the displaced fae, her tone clipped and sharp enough to cut silk. "What are your names?"

"Ari and Blaze Lightningsong, your majesty," Blaze replied after a hesitation, his voice thin and uncertain, his bow awkward. "We are cousins."

"You're welcome to stay in my tent." Her voice was as smooth as ice over a frozen lake. Her gaze snapped back to Quinn like a thrown blade, her stare daring him to object.

Blaze hesitated visibly torn, his fingers tightening around the straps of his bag. Panic flickered in his eyes—royalty and rebellion trapped in the same breath. "Oh no, My Queen. We cannot—"

"Ari can stay, but it would be highly inappropriate for Blaze to stay with us," came Lily's voice, sudden and sharp like a bell tolling in a quiet square. She stepped out from behind Reya, arms folded, her expression unreadable but her tone leaving no room for debate.

"He can stay with us," Tristan called from across the camp. His voice was steady, unflinching. He stood at the entrance to his tent, arms folded and jaw set, his offer spoken like an oath.

Quinn's lips curled into a slow, triumphant smirk, his eyes gleaming with something dark. "Then it is settled."

All around them, the camp had stilled. Shadows clustered in the flickering firelight, silent observers suspended mid-movement. Conversations faltered. The hush was heavy and coiled, like the last breath before lightning strikes. The confrontation had pierced the camp's rhythm—and Quinn basked in it, knowing the performance had landed precisely where he wanted it: center stage.

One by one, the rest of the fae looked to her for direction, their expectant stares heavy with both hope and doubt, like leaves trembling before a storm. Faces half-lit by firelight turned toward Reya, shadows dancing in their wide eyes, waiting—needing her to lead, to fix what was unraveling before it even began.

Reya licked her dry, cracked lips, the grit of dust catching on her tongue like ash from a dying flame. Every nerve in her body bristled with a veil of fear. The question clawed its way up her throat, rough and unwelcome, but it had to be asked.

"Did anyone bring food?"

A silence deeper than before swallowed the camp. Heads turned. Eyes shifted. No one stepped forward. The fire popped with a sharp crack, as if mocking her. Somewhere, a pot clanged hollow against a rock, the sound oddly final.

Blaze looked down, his jaw tight. Lily flinched as though slapped. Even Quinn, usually so smug, didn't speak—his smirk gone, replaced with something colder, darker.

Reya closed her eyes for a moment, the air thick around her like it might choke. Hunger gnawed at more than just their stomachs now. It crept into the cracks of their fragile unity, already fraying beneath the surface.

"We were told food would be abundant," Blaze finally said, his voice low and hollow, echoing the shared disappointment that graced every face.

That had been her understanding, too. But as she scanned the barren campsite, her vision blurring with exhaustion and hunger, no sign of provisions revealed itself. Her chin dipped, her resolve folding under the mounting weight of failure. The dull ache in her stomach joined the chorus of rumbling abdomens around her, a cruel reminder of the bleak reality they faced.

Ashur kneeled on the parched earth, his movements deliberate yet burdened by a quiet intensity. Reya's gaze lingered on the crease that deepened between his brows, as if the tension of unseen forces pressed heavily upon him. She watched as he took a slow, measured breath, his chest rising and falling with controlled precision. When he exhaled, the stream of air felt more profound than mere breath—there was purpose in its release, a tether between the natural world and the magic that pulsed within him.

The ground trembled beneath Reya's boots, a subtle, rippling vibration that sent a shiver up her spine. Her breath caught as the barren soil suddenly cracked, dark tendrils of vines curled forth with startling speed. They surged upward in graceful arcs, their emerald leaves glinting in the fading light. The ripe scent of berries filled the air, sweet and intoxicating, mingling with the sharper, earthy tang of fresh melons. The vines wove themselves into a living shield around the camp, their lush growth stark against the desolation beyond. It wasn't just food—it was life, a vibrant defiance against the wasteland that had plagued them.

Reya's brows shot upward, her chest tightening as she took in the abundance Ashur had conjured. It was more than enough to feed the entire entourage—a miracle given shape by his will. Yet her awe gave way to concern as she turned her gaze back to him. The flush of effort had drained from his cheeks, leaving his skin pale and almost ashen. Dark circles deepened beneath his eyes, shadows that spoke of an exhaustion far beyond the physical. When his hands rose from the earth, the tremor in his fingers was slight but undeniable.

He lifted his gaze to meet hers, and a shy smile curved his lips—a fleeting expression that barely masked his weariness. "I'm the gardener after all," he muttered, his voice soft and tinged with self-deprecation. The words carried an edge of humility that caught Reya off guard, as though he brushed off the magnitude of his gift as something trivial.

Ashur climbed to his feet with deliberate slowness, his movements weighted yet determined. Reya's heart ached at the sight of his effort, the toll it had taken evident in the heaviness of his posture. Without hesitation, he crossed to the lush vines, his fingers brushing lightly against the fresh growth as he harvested the spoils of his magic. Each motion was precise, almost reverent, as though he treated the fruits of his labor with the same care he had used to create them.

"My Queen," Tristan's voice carried through the camp, steady but tinged with a formality that made Reya turn her head. Her gaze landed on him—a tall figure with a sword cradled in his hands, the metal catching the dimming light and gleaming with a sharp, cold edge.

Before she could speak, Ashur abandoned the fruit he'd been gathering and moved swiftly to position himself in front of her. The pulse of silence tightened with his protective reflex. Tension radiated off his broad shoulders, his stance like that of a coiled spring. Her exasperation mingled with a warm bloom of affection. She leaned in close, catching the scent of pine mixed with sweat clinging to him. "I do not need protection from our people," she said, her words brushing against his ear.

Ashur's head turned, his gaze sliding back to meet hers over his shoulder. His eyes were sharp, laced with an edge of suspicion. "He carries a sword," he replied, his tone low, weighted as though the weapon alone was an imminent danger.

Her eyes flicked to the man as he halted, his boots scuffing the dirt beneath him. He followed Ashur's line of sight to the blade in his hand and raised it, the motion both hesitant and casual. "I do not have a scabbard for this," he explained with a shrug, his grip firm on the hilt despite his nonchalance. His gaze shifted to Reya, dark and direct. "I am Tristan Starfur."

"Tristan." Reya inclined her head, acknowledging him with a measured dip of her chin. She forced her voice to remain steady, her posture composed, even as her muscles tightened. "What can I do for you?"

"While the fruit your guard provided is plentiful, we are also in need of water."

Reya's stomach dropped, the sudden weight of his words pressing against the fragile scaffolding of her composure. Her throat tightened as she reached for the magic within her, only to find emptiness—a hollow void where her strength should have been. Her fingers twitched at her sides, the movement an involuntary betrayal of her frustration.

"Do we have water magic holders in our midst?" she asked, her voice calm, though inside her nerves churned like a restless sea.

Four fae raised their hands, the gesture hesitant, as if the acknowledgment came with a hidden weight. Their expressions mirrored her unease, with lines of exhaustion and doubt etched into their features.

"Can one of you produce some water for us to drink?" Reya asked, her tone gentle but edged with urgency. The silence that followed was thick, pressing down on her like an oppressive fog. When the others exchanged quizzical glances, their hesitation grated against her skin, sharp and irritating, like the relentless crawl of insects across her flesh. She swallowed the rising discomfort and offered a conciliatory smile, her lips cracking as they stretched. "I have exhausted myself."

A pretty woman with soft, delicate features stepped forward. "I can create some water if someone creates a clay pot to hold it," she volunteered.

From the edge of the camp, near the third tent, a man waved his hand. The ground shifted, the dry dirt giving way to the smooth rise of a clay trough. The magic flickered in the air, its faint hum resonating in her bones. The man's face paled visibly as the spell took its toll, leaving him swaying before he steadied himself.

The air grew heavier as the woman concentrated, the invisible threads of her magic weaving into the space around them. The mystical energy vibrated in her chest, a sensation both foreign and familiar. Water appeared in the trough, the liquid pooling slowly at first before rising steadily toward the rim. The sound of it filling—a soft, rhythmic trickle—was almost soothing, a brief reprieve from the tension gripping the camp.

CHAPTER 8

ASHUR MOVED BACK TO the vines, the earthy scent of freshly grown fruit filling his lungs as he crouched low. The soft, pliant skin of the berries yielded easily to his touch, their coolness a contrast to the warmth of his calloused fingers. He used his shirt as a makeshift bowl; the fabric stretched under the load of his harvest until he could carry no more. The sweet tang of the fruit lingered in the air, teasing his senses and mingling with the musty undertone of the camp.

When he returned to the queen's tent, his steps slowed, his gaze drawn to her as if by some unseen force. Reya stood with her back straight, her presence commanding even in her weariness.

The soft light of the setting sun caught in her hair, turning it into a cascade of molten gold that framed her face. He placed the bounty at her feet, the fruit tumbling softly onto the ground. "For you, My Queen."

Her reaction was immediate and unguarded. The way her lips parted into a small, surprised 'O' sent a flicker of warmth through his chest, a sensation both unfamiliar and disarming. A grin tugged at his lips before he could stop it. The sight of her blinking rapidly and fussing with her hands stirred something deeper within him.

She nodded at last, her voice soft but measured. "I was waiting until everyone had their fill." Every ounce of her quiet dignity laced her words.

Ashur's grin widened, though he quickly tempered it. "You are the queen. You should be fed first." His words came out firmer than he had intended, with a subtle edge of protectiveness threading through them. He didn't wait for her response, knowing she might protest. Instead, he turned away, his hunger gnawing at him like a restless beast. The effort of pulling the plants from the earth had drained him, leaving his body aching and his stomach hollow. It was time to gather what remained and sate the hunger that clawed at him.

Yet, as he walked away, his thoughts lingered on Reya. The memory of her expression—vulnerable yet composed—etched itself into his mind. There was a strength in her that drew him, a quiet resilience that made him want to stand by her side, to shield her from the shadow cast by countless expectations. The realization unsettled him, but he didn't push it away. Instead, he let it settle, like the roots of the vines he had summoned, growing deeper with each passing moment.

CHAPTER 9

NIGHT ENVELOPED THE CAMP in a suffocating blackness, the kind that pressed against Reya's skin and seeped into her thoughts. She lay still, staring into the void, her eyes tracing the outlines of the tent's fabric as it shifted with the breeze. Beside her, Ari and Lily's soft snores broke the silence, rhythmic and unbothered, a shadow set against the glow of the storm raging within Reya. Memories surged forward, relentless and vivid, each one a dagger twisting in her chest. The faces of her parents, their laughter, their warmth—gone. The screams of her people echoed in her mind, a cacophony of anguish that refused to fade.

The blanket Lily had packed was heavy and stifling against her skin. With a sharp motion, she threw it off, the cool night air rushing to meet her as she stepped outside. The camp stretched before her, bathed in the silver glow of starlight. The sky above was a canvas of endless stars, their light cold and distant, offering no solace.

Her gaze fell on Ashur, curled up near the tent's entrance. His broad frame was relaxed, his breathing steady and deep, the rise and fall of his chest almost hypnotic. Sleep had claimed him despite the chill in the air. His face softened in repose. The sight of him lying on the dirt sent a pang through her chest, a sharp ache that deepened the well of sadness threatening to consume her. He deserved better than this.

Reya turned away, her steps carrying her to the edge of the vine barricade. The sweet, heady scent of berries filled her nostrils, a fleeting reminder of Ashur's earlier efforts. She inhaled deeply, the fragrance mingling with the dry, earthy tang of the wasteland beyond. Her shoulders sagged as the strong façade she had worn all day crumbled, piece by piece.

Her world was gone.

Her parents were dead.

Everyone she had ever known, save for Lily, had been slaughtered by the goblins.

And here she was, stranded in this inhospitable world, her magic drained to nothing but an empty, mocking void.

Her breath hitched, the sound sharp and raw in the stillness. She pressed a trembling hand to her mouth, stifling the keening cry that clawed its way up her throat. The ache of her grief was unbearable, a crushing force that threatened to bring her to her knees.

A rustle behind her snapped her out of her spiraling thoughts. She spun around, her heart lurching, her fingers instinctively reaching for the quiver that was no longer on her back. Her pulse thundered in her ears as her eyes locked onto Ashur. He stood there wide-eyed, her father's sword gripped tightly in his hand. The blade caught the starlight, its edge gleaming like a silent promise.

"My Queen?" His voice was soft, hesitant, the question laced with concern.

Her vision blurred as tears spilled over, hot and unrelenting. The world around her dissolved into a haze of sorrow and exhaustion. Without a word, Ashur stabbed the sword into the ground and stepped closer, his movements slow and deliberate. He reached for her, his arms steady and sure as he drew her into his chest. The warmth of him, the solidness of his presence, broke the last of her defenses. She clung to him. Her fingers curled into the fabric of his shirt as she silently wept. Her tears soaked through the material, but he didn't flinch or pull away. He simply held her, offering his quiet strength as her grief poured out in waves.

Reya stayed there, cradled in Ashur's arms as the torrent of her grief ebbed into soft, trembling breaths. His heartbeat was a steady rhythm beneath her cheek, grounding her in the present, even as her mind wrestled with the past. The warmth of his embrace dulled her anguish, though it couldn't erase the void inside her.

She wasn't sure how long she stood there, letting the tears soak into his shirt, but for the first time that day, she felt the toll of her burden shift—just enough to breathe.

When she finally pulled back, her hands remained on his chest, unwilling to sever the connection entirely. Her gaze lifted to meet his, and in the dim starlight, she saw the quiet understanding in his eyes. There was no judgment, no demand for her to explain herself— just the steady presence of someone who would stand with her, no matter the cost.

"I'm sorry," she whispered, her voice raw and rasping from the strain of her sobs.

"For what?" he asked softly, his brow furrowing. "For being normal? For mourning all you've lost? My Queen, you owe no apology for feeling." His words were gentle but firm, and they reached a part of her she hadn't realized was still clinging to guilt for breaking down.

Reya took a shaky breath, her fingers curling into his shirt before she let her hands drop to her sides. "I—I've always been the strong one. For my people. For my parents. Even for Lily. I don't know how to be anything else."

"You can still be strong and let yourself grieve," Ashur replied. There was a weight to his words, as though he spoke not just to her, but from a place of his own pain. "Even the strongest among us have moments when we need to let the weight fall."

Her throat tightened again, not from grief this time, but from something softer, something fragile. Gratitude, perhaps. Or relief.

She nodded, her gaze drifting briefly over his features—the shadows under his eyes, the firm set of his jaw, and the way the starlight caught in his white hair. Something stirred within her, subtle and unbidden, like the first hint of warmth after a long, bitter winter.

"I'll try," she said. It was all she could offer, and she hoped it was enough.

Ashur inclined his head, a small smile ghosting across his lips. "That's all anyone can ask."

He stepped back, releasing her fully, though his presence still loomed like a protective shield. Reya turned her head toward the vine barricade, the sweetness of berries still lingering on the cool night air. The silence stretched between them, not awkward, but companionable.

"Go back to sleep, My Queen," Ashur said gently, his voice steady. "I'll keep watch."

She hesitated, her feet rooted to the earth for a moment longer. But the exhaustion that had been gnawing at her all day pulled her back toward the tent. "Thank you, Ashur." Her voice hardly reached a whisper.

He nodded once, already turning to face the horizon, his posture straight and alert. Reya lingered for a second more before retreating into the shelter of the tent. Lily stirred briefly but didn't wake, her quiet snoring resuming in soft, even intervals. Reya lowered herself onto the makeshift bedding, the tension in her muscles slowly unwinding. Her grief hadn't disappeared, but it had found a place to rest, at least for the night.

As she closed her eyes, the memory of Ashur's warmth lingered. Since the collapse of everything familiar, something close to safety shielded her. It wasn't much—but it was enough to carry her through until morning.

CHAPTER 10

REYA STRETCHED, HER MUSCLES stiff and aching from the strain of the previous day. Her eyelids fluttered open, the bright interior of the tent momentarily blinding her. The sunlight filtered through the canvas, casting warm, golden patches on the ground that contrasted with the cool shadows lingering in the corners. The tinge of earth and fabric filled her nose, mingling with the lingering tang of sweat and dust clinging to her skin.

She glanced around the empty tent. Lily had packed up everything except the blanket draped over her. The soft, worn fabric seemed heavier than it should, as though it carried the strain of her restless dreams. Her bow and quiver lay neatly in the corner, the only items left for her to collect. Reya's chest tightened as fragments of her fitful dreams clawed at her memory—goblins, blood, and the echo of screams that still seemed to linger in the back of her mind.

She pushed herself to her feet and winced at the stiffness in her joints. Her fingers brushed against her clothing, and she grimaced at the gritty layer of dust that coated the fabric. She closed her eyes for a moment and wished for clean clothing. The air remained stale without the shift of magic. She blinked down at herself, her heart lurching as realization struck. Last night, she had clung to the hope that a meal and some rest would restore her magic, but the emptiness within her told a different story. At home, even a quick nap or a simple meal would have been enough to replenish her reserves. Here in this barren, unforgiving world, her magic remained stubbornly absent.

The thought sent a jolt of panic through her, and she launched herself outside, the cool morning air hitting her like a slap. The camp was quiet, with the rustle of the wind through the vines making the only sound. Her gaze darted around until it landed on Ashur. He was crouched near the edge of the camp, his broad shoulders hunched as he worked. The sight of him, solid and steady, should have been reassuring, but the urgency in her chest only grew.

She crossed the distance. "Can you produce more fruit?" she asked, her voice escaping in a breathless rush that made her cringe. She hated the desperation lacing her words, but she couldn't suppress it.

Ashur turned his head toward her, his expression calm but focused. He crouched lower, his fingers pressing into the dirt. Reya caught the crease that appeared between his brows, a telltale sign of his concentration. He exhaled slowly, the sound deliberate, and for a moment, the air around him seemed to hum with potential. A spark of magic flickered, faint and fleeting, before it fizzled out entirely.

Her stomach twisted as his eyes darted to hers, the apology in his gaze mirrored by the frantic panic coursing through her veins. Their shared helplessness pressed down on her, heavy and suffocating, as the reality of their situation settled deeper into her chest.

Reya's gaze lingered on the man and woman who had worked their magic to create the water holder the night before. The early sunlight glinted off the trough's rippling surface, and the crisp morning air carried the earthy tang of damp soil. "You two." She gestured toward them with a deliberate wave of her hand. Her voice, though steady, scarcely carried over the nervous rustle of Ashur and Lily behind her.

The pair stepped forward, their expressions expectant but wary under Reya's scrutinizing stare. The woman, graceful and delicate like a blossom on the verge of bloom, dipped into a practiced curtsy. "Opal Brambleshore, Your Highness." Her voice was light and melodious but tinged with a quiver.

The man, more angular in build, executed a bow with a sharpness that suggested discipline. "Rob Flickerthorn," he announced, his voice steady as stone.

"Opal. Rob," Reya repeated, her tone clipped yet considerate, nodding in acknowledgment. She glanced back at Ashur's weary face and parched lips, then turned her attention to the duo before her. "Can you create clay cups and fill them with water for everyone?"

The corners of their mouths lifted into tentative smiles, but their confidence soon wilted as Rob sank to one knee. Reya's sharp eyes tracked his every movement. She noticed the way his shoulders tightened and his brows furrowed in deep concentration. His fingers dug into the gritty soil, and his lips compressed into a thin, pale line. Then his head snapped up, his gaze catching hers, shadowed with trepidation. "I don't seem to be able to access my magic," he confessed, his voice cracking like dry wood.

A cold knot twisted in Reya's stomach. She pressed her fingers to her temple, closing her eyes to block out the disquieted whispers rippling through the crowd. She wiped her damp palms over her face and opened her eyes to Opal. "Can you top off the trough?" Reya asked, though the demand was heavier now, like a stone being passed hand to hand.

Opal mirrored Rob's efforts, crouching with poised determination. The tension in her jaw betrayed her fear as she extended her hands, palms downward. Moments passed, each one stretching taut like an overdrawn bowstring, but no magic surged forth. Her face crumpled in a silent, stricken plea, and Reya's chest tightened in a matching pang of despair.

The sense of futility hung heavy in the air as Reya turned to Ashur and exchanged a look weighted with trepidation. Her brittle voice addressed the group. "It appears this land does not rejuvenate our magic the way our realm did." The dry lump in her throat made swallowing a trial, but she forced herself to continue, her tone regaining its commanding edge. "Preserve your magic for such a time as absolutely necessary. Once we find a place to settle, I will find a solution that allows us full access to our magic."

Quinn's gaze narrowed in her direction, but she ignored his aggravated leer.

Reya drew in a deliberate breath, the crisp air colder against her lungs, and released it slowly. Her mind churned with snippets of her father's histories—fragments of tales, warnings, and lore that now felt like the thinnest of lifelines. She straightened her posture, steadying herself with sheer will, and cast her gaze across her people. Vulnerable or not, she vowed to herself, she would find a way to keep them safe.

CHAPTER 11

ASHUR'S JAW TIGHTENED AS he scanned the camp. A weight settled heavier in his chest with every passing moment. The vines he had coaxed from the dry earth still bore a few clusters of fruit, their waxy skins glistening in the weak morning light. Yet, the sight offered little comfort—those fruits wouldn't last through the morning, let alone sustain them for another day.

His gaze shifted to the trough, where the water sloshed sluggishly with every breeze that passed through the camp. It was barely half full, and the dull sheen of the water's surface mirrored the growing dread gnawing at him. The tang of sweat mixed with the musk of damp canvas and the tinny hint of fear that no one spoke aloud.

Ashur bit down on his lower lip as tension roiled in his gut. He glanced toward Reya, who stood a few paces away, her shoulders squared but visibly weighed by the silent burden she carried.

"Your Highness?" He pitched his voice low yet firm. He waited until she turned, her expression a mix of weariness and guarded resolve. "We need to assess what everyone brought. Considering our predicament, we need bags to carry what fruit is left and canisters to transport water. And we need to break down and move these tents and blankets." His hand swept toward the patchwork camp, where tents swayed gently in the cool breeze, their shadows stretching long across the uneven ground.

For a moment, her face flickered, the look in her eyes eerily similar to the startled prey Ashur had hunted in the dense forests back home— wide-eyed, vulnerable, frozen at the edge of flight. His stomach clenched, but then, to his relief, she stiffened her spine and nodded.

Reya's voice rose to meet the assembled crowd, though it trembled as it left her lips. "We need to pool our resources."

The slight crack in her voice echoed louder than any shout. It struck Ashur like a blade, a pang nesting deep in his chest. She ran her tongue over dry, dust-cracked lips—a small, unconscious motion that revealed far more than she intended. He ached to reach for her, to ground her with the warmth of his hand on her shoulder, to draw her close and promise they'd make it through. But he didn't. His fists clenched at his sides. It wasn't his place.

"What do you mean?" Quinn's voice sliced through the still air like a whip. Ashur's head snapped toward him, jaw tight. The arrogant fae stood with arms loosely folded, regard cold and calculating, as if Reya's authority were something to be questioned—something to be taken.

The sound of Quinn's voice alone ignited Ashur's blood, his pulse roaring in his ears like dry tinder set alight.

Wordlessly, Ashur stepped forward, placing himself beside Reya in a quiet but unmistakable show of support. The damp earth sucked at his boots, and behind him, bodies shifted with uncertain rustles—doubt rippling outward like disturbed water.

"With little to no magical reserves." His low voice edged with urgency. "We must conserve what we have and take it with us. Every bit of food, every drop of water counts now." He gestured to the wilting vines and meager trough. "We'll need sacks, containers—whatever can carry provisions. And we'll need to break down the tents. We move as one, or we don't survive."

"Who the hell are you to bark orders?" Quinn shot back, his words crackling through the charged air.

The camp tensed, all breath and bracing silence.

"He's the only one offering solutions," Reya snapped, turning to Quinn with a glare that could shatter bone. "He fed us when no one else could. That's more than you've done." She looked at

Ashur then, her voice softer but unwavering. "I'll be following his advisement."

Ashur gave a small nod, humbled but resolute. He turned to the crowd, gaze sweeping over each worn and wary face. Their fear was genuine—but so was their strength.

They would endure. For her, he would see to it.

Ashur shifted his weight as Reya turned to her lady-in-waiting. The cool breeze carried the heady scent of berries from the nearby foliage, but it did little to soften the tension that hung in the air like a storm waiting to break.

"Bring our bags and dump them here," Reya commanded, her voice sharp with urgency, as she gestured to the patch of grass at her feet.

Lily hesitated, the hem of her dress trembling in her grasp as she stalled. But Reya's determined stare was all it took to send the maid scurrying. Ashur's eyes followed her hurried movements as she began pulling bag after bag from the tents, dragging them toward the spot Reya had chosen. He took a step back, folded his arms tightly across his chest, and observed the spectacle unfold.

One by one, the contents spilled out— excessively frilly garments that looked as though they'd disintegrate under the weight of the dirt. Shimmering fabric caught the rays of sunlight and painted fleeting glimmers across the ground. Jewelry boxes, encrusted with gems that seemed to pulse like trapped stars, clattered onto the earth with dull thuds. Books bound in delicate leather stacked precariously beside glass bottles filled with shimmering liquids, their mysterious hues refracting colors that danced over Ashur's steely gaze. And finally, amidst the mess of regal opulence, the dull gleam of blades and royal weapons emerged from the last bags like buried treasures uncovered at last.

Reya turned to him, her voice cutting through the moment. "What do you suggest I keep?"

Ashur's brow furrowed as his gaze snapped to hers. Her question hung in the air for a moment too long, the challenge pressing against him. "Me?" he asked, incredulous, pointing a finger toward his chest.

"Yes, you." Her tone was firm, almost impatient, as she waved at the jumbled chaos before her. "You seem to be the practical one in the group. What can be useful to us in this…" She paused, pressing her lips into a thin line, then waved dismissively at the mess on the ground.

Ashur inhaled deeply, the mingled scents of rose oil, earth, and leather rising around him. He crouched down, his movements deliberate, the damp chill of the ground biting through his trousers as he sifted through the items. His fingers closed around a large glass bottle with a cork stopper. The liquid inside shimmered, a deep, rich purple that caught the light like crushed velvet. "What's in this?" he asked.

"That is Her Majesty's perfume," Lily snapped, lunging forward in an attempt to snatch the bottle from his grasp.

Ashur jerked back, raising his brows at her as Reya's sharp tone intervened. "Lily!" The single word halted the maid, who froze mid-reach, her cheeks coloring with indignation.

Ashur turned the bottle in his hands, his calloused fingers brushing the smooth glass as he met Reya's steady gaze. "Is there anything in this that could be deadly?" he asked, pulling the cork free with a muted pop. The aroma wafted into his senses—rich, floral, intoxicating. It triggered an ache deep within him, a reminder of home, of better days spent in the sunlit embrace of a thriving kingdom.

Reya shrugged. A small but telling gesture betrayed her weariness. "It is a combination of rose oils. Drinking it might make you sick to your stomach, but it won't kill you."

Without hesitation, Ashur tipped the bottle and emptied its contents onto the ground. The violet liquid seeped into the soil, its perfume lingering in the air as both Reya and Lily gasped in unison. "This can transport water," he said as he set the bottle next to him.

Ashur hefted one of the larger bags, its coarse fabric rough against his fingers, and extended it to Lily. "Fill this with the rest of the fruit on the vines, please." His calm voice carried firm authority.

Lily huffed audibly, her arms snapping across her chest as her brows furrowed in defiance. The sharpness of her reaction pricked at Ashur's nerves, but he remained silent, letting the power of Reya's authority carry the moment.

"Do as he says, Lily," Reya commanded, her voice cutting through the tension like the crack of a whip.

Lily's demeanor shifted, her rebellious scowl softening into reluctant compliance as she snatched the bag from Ashur's hand. The shuffle of her stomping feet faded as she trudged toward the vines.

Ashur let out a soft sigh, turning his attention back to the pile of belongings scattered around them. His eyes fell on an ornate metal bowl, its intricate engravings catching the light with a dull gleam. When he lifted it, the bowl was surprisingly heavy. The clinking within hinted at its contents, and when he pried it open, a cascade of jewels greeted him—a treasure trove of glimmering colors, their polished surfaces refracting the sunlight in dazzling sprays. The sight almost seemed absurd, its opulence at odds with the harsh reality surrounding them.

"Hand me that silk pouch." He pointed to a pink satchel resting atop a small heap of discarded items. The delicate shimmer of its fabric seemed almost mocking in its fragility. Reya handed it over, and Ashur pulled the drawstring loose, revealing a necklace nestled inside—a piece so exquisite it seemed crafted from liquid crystal, its flawless surface bending and scattering light into a soft rainbow. For a brief moment, he marveled at its craftsmanship before pouring the bowl's contents into the pouch, the jewels landing with soft clinks against one another. He set the bowl aside and glanced up at Reya, who was watching him with a curious tilt of her head. "Something to drink from," he explained, meeting her questioning gaze.

She raised an eyebrow, but before she could speak, Ashur held the silk bag aloft. "You should consolidate all your jewelry into this. It's big enough to carry all of them." He offered the pouch to her, noting the tension in her expression.

"Then we can use some of the bags that carried your jewels for the tent fabric."

Reya's lips pressed into a thin line, her hesitation clear. "Throwing them in one bag could make a tangled mess of them," she muttered, but she took the pouch, regardless. Under his watchful eyes, Reya scooped the jewelry into the bag, the jewels slipping from their ornate, gilded boxes like stolen stars abandoning their thrones. The discarded boxes clattered to the ground, a satisfying sound as practicality triumphed over extravagance.

"I'll help untangle them when we find our place here," he offered with a shadow of a smirk. The frown lingering on Reya's lips wavered, her exasperation giving way to a flicker of appreciation, though she said nothing.

Ashur returned his focus to the remaining items, his hands brushing against weathered leather and cold steel. "Weapons are necessary." He tested the heft of a dagger in his palm before setting it aside. His gaze shifted back to Reya. "Perhaps we can outfit the group with them instead of carrying these in bags?" His brow arched as he studied her reaction. His note of humor in his tone was his quiet attempt to cut through the tension that still hung in the air.

Ashur's gaze followed Reya as she lifted the King's crown, its gilded edges gleaming under the pale sunlight, along with the pink bag of jewels. The crown's intricate filigree caught the light in a dazzling display, while the soft satin of the pink bag muted the brilliance of its contents within.

"We can put this in the bag with the books." She turned her piercing gaze toward Ashur, and her finger jabbed at him in a clear, commanding gesture. "And you will be tasked with carrying it."

Ashur straightened, his boots digging into the damp earth beneath him. "It would be my honor," he replied, his voice steady, though his mind flickered briefly to the weight—not just physical, but symbolic—that this task would carry. His eyes shifted to the array of weapons scattered across the ground: blades of all kinds, their steel surfaces sharp and glinting like spilled shards of starlight. He gestured to them, his hand cutting through the air like a blade itself. "But what of the weapons?"

Reya turned toward the gathering of their people, who were talking softly in a huddled group while he and the queen rifled through the remnants of her belongings. Ashur's sharp gaze caught fleeting expressions of curiosity and apprehension as her subjects held tight to their belongings.

Her voice broke through their quiet din, steady and measured, like the strike of a gavel. "There are enough weapons here for everyone to be armed."

The statement hung in the air, grim and inevitable.

Ashur's eyes lingered on the reflection of sunlight dancing across the polished hilts and scabbards before him. Each blade was a relic of craftsmanship—some straight and utilitarian, others curved like a serpent's fang, all gleaming with lethality. The sharp scent of oiled leather and cold steel filled the air, mingling with the earthy aroma of damp soil.

Nearby, a large heap of clothing—crimson silks, sea-foam satins, brocade trimmed in fading gold thread—spilled from a toppled trunk, a garish reminder of opulence abandoned in haste. The garments fluttered in the wind, out of place in this grim landscape.

Without waiting for an invitation or instruction, Quinn sauntered forward, each step exuding the casual arrogance of someone long accustomed to bending rules. His hand reached for the king's sword, the one laid with reverence by Ashur's side—a weapon with a history, unmistakable in its craftsmanship, the grip wrapped in dark leather and embossed with the royal crest.

Ashur's hand clamped down on the hilt before Quinn's fingers could make contact, his glare heavy with warning. The message was unmistakable.

"That isn't up for choosing," Reya snapped, her tone as cutting as any blade in the pile. The air tensed around them, charged with challenge.

Quinn muttered something under his breath and turned, brushing invisible dust from his sleeve. Instead, he selected three other swords, each ostentatiously adorned with inset gems and gilded pommels—trophies more than tools. The audacious fae swung one experimentally, its jeweled hilt catching the light like a beacon.

Ashur watched him wordlessly, the thread woven through his thoughts settling on his shoulders like another layer of armor.

He turned back to Reya. "That leaves your clothing." The edge in his voice softened as he stared at the pile, the vivid colors muted and strangely lifeless against the dull browns of the surrounding landscape.

His jaw tightened, and he resisted the instinct to rifle through the private items himself. The mere thought felt intrusive, and he knew better than to overstep that boundary. He waited, his posture firm and poised, the strain of their predicament pressing against him like a relentless tide.

CHAPTER 12

REYA STOOD BEFORE THE towering pile of clothing with a knot of dread tightening in her stomach. The sheer magnitude of the task loomed before her, daunting and oppressive. Fabrics of every texture spilled over one another, silk and lace tangled with heavier brocades, their vibrant hues muted by dust and the dim light of the overcast sky. She crouched down and ran her fingers along the topmost garment—a soft, finely woven tunic—before plucking it free. The once-luxurious fabric against her fingertips seemed hollow, as though its charm had been stripped away by the harshness of their surroundings.

With deliberate movements, Reya sorted through the pile, making quick decisions as she sifted. The delicate rustle of silk and the occasional scrape of beads against leather filled her ears as she worked, while the earthy scent of damp soil mingled with the lingering perfume still clinging to some garments. She ignored the ache building in her knees as she sorted with quiet determination. By the end of her efforts, a modest stack emerged—soft, worn undergarments, a handful of sturdy outfits practical enough for the road, and two stunning dresses her mother had fashioned for her that she couldn't quite bring herself to abandon. Her heart tugged as she eyed the discarded remnants, their finery reduced to meaningless clutter beside the jewelry boxes and perfumes she'd already cast aside.

The pile she kept fit neatly into a single bag, its weight far less than the burden of excess she'd carried before. Reya rose to her feet, brushing dirt from her palms, and stood gripping the bag in one hand. Her shoulders were lighter, her breath steadier, as though shedding these unnecessary items had lifted an unseen weight pressing on her chest.

As Lily returned, a large bag of fruit cradled in her arms, she froze, her eyes wide with disbelief as she took in the sight of Reya's simplified belongings. "What are you doing?" Lily asked, her tone sharp and disapproving.

"Being practical." Reya's reply was curt, but unwavering. She turned to the rest of the group, her gaze sweeping over their uncertain expressions and overloaded bags.

"You will need to do the same with your belongings. See if there is anything that will hold water and fill it before you leave. The tents and blankets will need to replace the items that you leave behind.”

“You are out of your mind,” Quinn scoffed, stepping forward with a glare that could have curdled milk. “You want us to just abandon our gear? Half of this stuff we’ll need if we’re out more than a day.”

Reya didn’t flinch. “You’ll need water and shelter more than satin cloaks and scented oils.”

“That’s not all I packed,” Quinn shot back. “Some of us brought things that *matter*—maps, equipment, tools we can trade.”

“And some of you packed like you were heading to a royal banquet.” Reya crossed her arms. “If you think carrying jewels and brocade through a wasteland will serve you better than a full canteen and a dry place to sleep, be my guest. But I’m not dragging your frostbitten carcass out of a ravine when your ‘necessities’ weigh you down.”

Silence followed. A few members of the group exchanged glances, shifting awkwardly beneath the heaviness of their packs.

Quinn’s jaw worked as if chewing over a sharp retort, but it never came. Instead, he huffed, spun on his heel, and stormed back toward his bag. With exaggerated irritation, he began shoving items aside, muttering curses under his breath as he dug through his belongings.

“Tent. Blanket. Fine.” His voice was low, grumbling. “Let’s all live like bloody paupers now.”

Reya didn’t comment, but a flicker of satisfaction passed through her eyes. She turned back to the others.

"Anyone else want to argue, or are we done wasting daylight?"

The crowd murmured, their hesitation palpable as their eyes shifted between the sprawling pile of discarded luxuries and Reya's newly meager collection. The difference was stark, almost jarring—her reduced belongings now fit into three manageable bags as opposed to the nearly dozen and a half that had previously encumbered her. Slowly, they began their own task of narrowing down their items, the ambient noise of shifting fabric and muttered complaints filling the air.

Lily's sharp tone disrupted the rhythm of the group as she directed her ire at Ashur, who stood nearby. "What about you?" she snapped, tossing another handful of frilly dresses onto the growing junk pile.

"I have nothing but what you see on my back. I was pulled into being the queen's guard from tending to the garden." His gaze flicked down to the ground, and then his eyes met Reya's briefly. The quiet intensity in his look made her chest tighten, her pulse stuttering in an unfamiliar way.

Reya forced herself to redirect her attention, turning to Tristan, the only other male in the group who matched Ashur's build. "Tristan, do you have a spare pair of pants and a spare shirt that you can part with in your belongings?"

Tristan's jaw tightened as he hesitated. But finally, he dug through his belongings and produced a pair of faded slacks and a gauzy shirt. The muted hues spoke of simpler times, and Reya accepted them with a grateful nod. She tucked the garments into her bag alongside her own clothes.

Lily reached for the bag, her gesture brisk. "I'll add my things to the bag, and I will carry it," she offered.

Reya hesitated, her fingers brushing the coarse fabric of the bag as she weighed Lily's offer.

"You have the bow and quiver to carry," Ashur interjected, his voice a quiet authority as he strode toward the tent Reya had slept in.

She handed Lily the bag as her gaze tracked Ashur.

The scrape of leather boots against damp earth accompanied his movements as he picked up two empty duffel bags and began dismantling the tent. The tie-downs came free with sharp tugs, the anchors slipping from the soil with quiet pops before he dropped them into one of the bags. The heavy canvas of the tent and its blankets followed suit, folded with practiced efficiency into another bag, alongside the metal rods that had supported it.

Inspired by Ashur's calm efficiency, the others began dismantling the remaining tents, their hurried movements accompanied by the creak of ropes and the sharp snaps of fabric being folded. The disarray of their camp shifted into a semblance of order, the once-cluttered space transforming as piece by piece was packed away. When they finished, she stood among them, her chest lifting with a quiet sense of accomplishment. The women, each carrying a single bag now, moved with lighter steps, while the men bore two each, their burdens heavy but manageable.

As they set off, Reya's senses sharpened with the rhythm of their march. The ground beneath her boots was uneven and studded with loose stones, and the occasional snap of a twig echoed sharply in the stillness. The once-suffocating weight of unnecessary luxuries had been replaced by the practical heft of essential supplies—fruit and water nestled securely in their bags, a quiet assurance against the day's toil. The morning air held a crisp chill, invigorating her despite the ache in her muscles, and the tang of soil and greenery carried on the breeze, a subtle promise of better terrain ahead.

When they reached the base of the mountain, Reya stopped short, her breath catching as she took in the scene before her. The forest stretched wide and deep, its canopy a tapestry of vibrant greens and shimmering golds as the late-afternoon sun filtered through the leaves. The air hummed with life, the rustling of leaves and soft chirps of unseen birds blending into a symphony that was at once soothing and alien. The fading light bathed the landscape in warm golden hues, the horizon aglow with the sun's tender farewell.

She inhaled deeply, the rich scent of moss and wood filling her lungs. This place was so unlike the barren plains where they had spent the previous night. Here, the forest teemed with life— brambles heavy with berries, delicate flowers peeking through the underbrush, and the rustle of unseen creatures darting between the trees. Game, she realized, a flicker of hope kindling in her chest.

This oasis could sustain them. They had a chance here.

She straightened and tilted her head. The rush of nearby water reached her ears, and the thought of rinsing the travel dust from her body nearly had her falling to her knees. "We'll settle here," Reya said. Her pulse thrummed against her ribs. Her people needed her composure, her strength.

But as Reya surveyed the wilderness, a sliver of nerves wound its way through her thoughts. The beauty of the landscape held a deceptive quality, as though it concealed dangers unseen. She couldn't shake the impression that they were not the only ones drawn to this haven.

Apex predators. The term crossed her mind unbidden, sending a chill along her spine. The forest, for all its allure, was still untamed.

CHAPTER 13

ASHUR SURVEYED THE CAMP with a critical eye, noting the way the tents stood taut and sturdy against the gentle evening breeze. The freshly cut brush surrounding the perimeter gave off a crisp aroma of greenwood and sap, a subtle reassurance that they'd taken the necessary precautions for safety—though he knew it was no guarantee against danger. The dim light of the setting sun cast long shadows across the campsite, softening the harsher angles of their makeshift settlement.

He took a sip from his water flask, the cool liquid washing away the dryness in his throat, when movement at the edge of his vision drew his attention. Reya approached, her steps tentative and light against the uneven ground. Her posture was composed, as always, but there was something uncharacteristically soft about the way her gaze flitted past him without quite meeting his eyes. Ashur's brow furrowed, his grip tightening on the flask. It was rare to see Reya like this—hesitant, almost shy—and it stirred a quiet curiosity within him.

She stopped just a pace in front of him, the faintest flush warming her cheeks as she cleared her throat. "Will you keep watch while I bathe?" Her voice was barely above a whisper. The intimacy of the request caught him off guard.

Ashur's breath caught mid-sip, the water sliding down the wrong pipe like an icy dagger. His chest spasmed, and he sputtered violently, the liquid forcing its way out in a choking spray that landed unceremoniously on the nearest bush. He turned his head, coughing harshly as his lungs rebelled against the sudden onslaught. The sharp tang of the water lingered in his throat, accentuating his failed composure.

"You want me to what?" he finally managed, the words rasping out between shallow breaths. His voice was rough, a mix of disbelief and the remnants of his coughing fit. He blinked at her, his mind racing to reconcile the Reya he was used to—the fierce and unwavering leader—with the woman standing before him now, her expression calm but tinged with a flicker of amusement.

"Stand guard while I bathe," she repeated, her lips quirking upward ever so slightly. The hint of a dimple appeared in her cheek, a rare glimpse of something softer, almost playful, that set his heart pounding for reasons he didn't quite understand.

Ashur rubbed the back of his neck, the coarse texture of calloused fingertips brushing over damp skin. The heat creeping up his face was unbearable, as if it radiated outward to betray his thoughts. He swallowed hard, his throat tightening against the sickly sweet tang of adrenaline mingling with the lingering coolness of water on his tongue. His nod was stiff, almost mechanical.

"Of course." His voice wavered at first but found a firm edge as he forced composure into his tone. Yet, even as the words left his lips, his gaze clung to Reya. The flush blooming across her cheeks and the tremor of vulnerability woven into her voice disarmed him. It was a softness he hadn't anticipated. A glimpse of a side she guarded fiercely.

"I will do the same while you clean up." Her words brushed past him like the rustle of dry leaves in the breeze.

Ashur suppressed the grin tugging at his lips, redirecting his attention to the steady weight of his sword in his hand. He inclined his head in silent acknowledgment, watching as Reya turned with measured grace. She began gathering her things, her movements purposeful, but her fingers lingered for a moment too long on the strap of her satchel, betraying a flicker of hesitation. Lily padded faithfully at her side, her presence an assurance as they approached.

"We are going to bathe," Reya announced to the camp with practiced authority. Her voice cut through the buzz like the crisp snap of dry twigs underfoot. "When we come back, you may go in small groups as well." She didn't pause, didn't allow for discussion. Ashur noticed the subtle slackening of shoulders, the hushed sighs of relief that rippled through the camp as they absorbed her command.

The three of them moved along the camp's perimeter, skirts of grass brushing against their boots. The mountain loomed above them, its rocky face stark against the shifting hues of the sky. They navigated around its base, their path marked by the distant gurgle of water growing louder with every step. The air grew cooler, tinged with the earthy scent of moss and damp stone. Finally, an alcove revealed itself—a sanctuary draped in shadow. A cascade of water tumbled from the rocks above, its rhythmic roar blending with the softer babble of the pool below. Tendrils of mist curled lazily in the air, and the last rays of sunlight fractured through the canopy, dancing across the surface of the falls like liquid fire. Ashur's boots crunched on the pebbled shore as they drew closer, the sound grounding him amidst the tranquil beauty.

He stationed himself at the middle of the entrance to the pool, the rough stone beneath his boots grinding as he turned his back on Reya and Lily. The thunderous roar of the falls reverberated through his chest, almost drowning out the rustle of fabric as they undressed. The damp air, heavy with the odor of moss and the crisp scent of the falls, teased his senses. He clenched his fists and stamped down the urge to glance over his shoulder.

The splash of water reached his ears, sharp and sudden against the constant hum of the falls. Reya's gasp cut through the noise, her voice tinged with a shiver that sent a chill down his spine.

"It's cold." Her words trembled like the ripples in the pool.

"I can heat it up for you," Lily replied, her tone steady, almost teasing.

Magic bloomed around them, a palpable force that prickled against his skin. He turned his head just enough to catch a glimpse of his queen's bare backside. Her pale skin glowed in the misty light. She strode farther into the steaming water, her movements fluid and commanding. Heat that had nothing to do with the water brushed over him, a flush that crept up his neck and burned at the tips of his ears. He snapped his gaze in front of him and tightened his jaw as he stared at the jagged rocks ahead.

It was one thing to be attracted to his queen—a forbidden, quiet longing he had wrestled with in the solitude of his own thoughts. But to take visual liberties, to indulge in the fleeting temptation of a stolen glance, felt like a betrayal of everything he held himself to be. The consequences of his actions bore down on him like a leaden cloak, the shame twisting in his chest with an unforgiving grip.

Ashur silently berated himself for his lack of manners. He had been entrusted with her protection, sworn to uphold his duty with honor and vigilance. Yet here he stood, undone by a single moment of weakness. The image of her lingered in his mind, unbidden, weaving its way through his resolve like smoke that refused to disperse. He clenched his jaw, his nails biting into his palms as he fought to erase the memory—a battle against himself that left him raw and exposed.

The chill in the air seemed to mock his sudden heat, the roaring of the falls amplifying the tempest within him. How could he face her after this? The very thought made his throat tighten. He was meant to be an unwavering shield, not a man who faltered under the flame of his own desires.

CHAPTER 14

NOW THAT LILY HAD used her magic to heat the water, Reya stepped deeper into the pond, the warmth spreading up her legs and soothing the ache in her muscles. She dunked under, the water closing over her head in a muffled embrace, silencing the world for a brief, tranquil moment. When she surfaced, droplets clung to her lashes, and the misty air kissed her cheeks.

Lily handed her a small bar of soap, its lavender scent cutting through the earthy aroma of the pond. Reya ran the smooth bar over her skin, the lather rich and silky against her fingertips. She scrubbed away the grit and grime of the last few days, the sensation both cleansing and invigorating. The lavender lingered, a calming balm to her senses. When her skin glowed pink and her hair made a satisfying squeak between her fingers, she passed the soap back to Lily with a grateful smile and waded toward the shore.

The cool air nipped at her damp skin as she emerged, sending a shiver down her spine. Lily had only brought a single towel, its fabric soft and ready for use. Reya squeezed the water from her hair, the strands heavy and dripping, before patting her skin dry. She pulled on a clean outfit—a blue broomstick skirt that swished softly against her legs and a comfortable cream top that clung to her still-warm skin. She offered the towel to Lily and slid her slippers on.

As she combed the knots from her hair with her fingers, the strands tugged. She stepped to Ashur's side. The clean aroma of lavender still clung to her, mingling with the crispness of the air. "I'm afraid the towel we brought may be wet." Her voice was light but apologetic. "But you are welcome to use it when you finish cleaning up."

Ashur appraised her, his gaze steady yet unreadable, and Reya's pulse quickened. When color rose in his cheeks, it was as if the warmth of his embarrassment reached out to her, brushing against her own skin. "I do not have a change of clothing. But I will take the opportunity to clean my shirt," he said.

"I have the extra set of clothing that Tristan gave me for you." She pointed to the pile perched on a rock—the damp towel, the sliver of soap, and the neatly folded garments.

Ashur's eyebrows rose, a flicker of surprise softening his otherwise stoic expression. "Thank you. I will still wash my clothing, so I have a clean outfit for the next time we bathe."

Lily stepped beside her, her presence pulling Reya out of the moment. "The water is all yours," Lily said.

Ashur handed his sword to Reya, the mass of it solid and cool in her hands, and unclasped his weapons' belt with practiced ease. The clink of his buckle seemed louder than it should have, cutting through the steady hum of the falls. He dropped the belt by the clothing and began to undress.

Lily turned her back, her movements brisk and purposeful, but Reya found herself rooted in place. She wasn't as considerate as her lady-in-waiting. Her gaze lingered, drawn by the slow, deliberate way Ashur peeled off his dirty shirt. The fabric clung to him before sliding free, revealing a back corded with muscle, each line and curve etched with strength.

He pulled the leather tie from his hair, and the strands fell in a gentle wave, gleaming like silver under the muted light. It was as if the dirt and grime dared not mar the pristine glow of his presence. Reya's breath caught, her chest tightening with an unfamiliar ache.

When he stripped his pants, her gaze betrayed her, sweeping over the taut muscles of his form. The air charged with something she couldn't name. He emptied his pockets with methodical precision, gathering the soap and his clothing before stepping into the water.

Reya watched as he focused on cleaning his shirt and pants, his movements efficient yet unhurried. The water rippled around him, steam rising in soft tendrils that blurred the edges of his figure. When he turned to lay his clothing on the rocks to dry, his gaze caught hers.

Heat surged to her cheeks, a flush that burned and spread, but she didn't look away. His eyes held hers, and for a moment, the world seemed to still, the roar of the falls fading into the background. Reya's heart thudded in her chest, each beat echoing the electricity between them. He was the one who broke eye contact first, his gaze slipping away like a thread pulled taut and then released. Reya's breath hitched as he turned, the muscles in his back shifting beneath his skin with each deliberate step. Instead of wading into the pond, he moved toward the thunder of the falls, the mist curling around him like a veil. The roar of the cascading water seemed to swallow him whole, the sound vibrating through Reya's chest as she watched his retreating figure.

"Reya, you shouldn't be watching him. He's just a gardener," Lily hissed, her voice sharp and close, cutting through the haze of Reya's thoughts.

The words stung like a nettle brushing against bare skin. Reya forced her gaze away from Ashur's magnificent form. Her face burned as heat filled her cheeks. She turned to glare at Lily, her jaw tightening.

"He is more than just a gardener now." Her voice was low but firm, the words carrying a weight she hadn't fully realized until they left her lips.

Lily's eyes widened, her shock palpable, just as a corded arm clamped around Reya's throat.

The pressure cut off her breath and forced her against a chest as solid as stone. The scent of sweat and whiskey filled her nostrils, mingling with the damp air of the glen. Her pulse thundered in her ears, matching the roar of the falls behind her.

Another man stepped out from the trees, his movements predatory and deliberate. He carried a strange weapon, its metallic surface gleaming ominously in the muted light. The man raised it, aiming toward Ashur, who stood under the falls, his figure blurred by the mist.

"Kill the man, and we'll bring these two whores with us," the man holding her captive snarled, his voice a jagged edge that cut through the chaos.

Reya's instincts surged. Her grip tightened on the sword. She slashed, the blade connecting with the weapon and knocking it aside. A deafening crack split the air, the sound reverberating through her chest. Lily's gasp was sharp and raw, and Reya's gaze snapped to her. A red stain bloomed on Lily's shirt right over her heart, spreading like a cruel flower before she dropped to the ground.

The man holding Reya dragged her backward, his arm a vise around her throat as he wrestled with the sword in her grip. The rough fabric of his sleeve scraped against her skin. She twisted her wrist, her muscles burning with the effort, and heaved the sword into the man who was retraining his deadly weapon on Ashur.

The thundering sound of the falls seemed to amplify the chaos, each crash echoing Reya's pounding heartbeat. She glimpsed Ashur diving into the pond, his movements swift and desperate. The man with the odd weapon crumpled to the ground, his body lifeless.

Reya's grip on the sword slipped, and desperation took hold. She clamped her teeth into the arm of the man choking her, the skin breaking under her assault. Coppery blood filled her mouth, bitter and vile. He screamed, the sound raw and guttural, and she dug her teeth deeper, swallowing the foul liquid that flowed from his wound. Heat seared a path from her mouth to her stomach.

A blade appeared in her peripheral vision, its edge gleaming with deadly intent. "Let go or I will slice your throat open," he growled in her ear, his breath hot and rancid against her skin.

Reya's magic flared, a surge of power that burned through her veins. The knife flew from his hand, spinning through the air before landing with a dull thud. The stench of singed flesh filled the glen, pungent and suffocating. He yanked his arm away, his movements frantic, as the smell of burning skin lingered.

Reya spun to face him, her fist clenched tight as she summoned her magic. The vile thought took shape, crushing his insides with an invisible force. He sputtered, his body convulsing before dropping to his knees. His gaze met hers, wide and filled with terror.

"What are you?" he whispered, his voice barely audible before he collapsed face down.

The splashing of water pulled her attention, and her gaze darted to the pond. Ashur plowed toward her, his movements labored. His face was a mask of pain, his features taut as blood cascaded down his arm, staining the water around him.

She lunged for Lily, her hands trembling as they gripped her lady-in-waiting's shoulders. The damp fabric of Lily's shirt clung to Reya's fingers as she turned her over, her heart pounding so loudly it drowned out the roar of the falls. Lily's lifeless eyes stared at the sky, their once vibrant spark masked in the stillness of death. The sight hit Reya like a physical blow, stealing the breath from her lungs.

"No!" The cry tore from her throat, raw and broken, echoing through the glen.

Wet hands grasped her shoulders, their grip firm but not harsh. She twisted instinctively, her body coiled to strike, but the sight of Ashur's face stopped her. His steady gaze tempered the storm raging within her. He pulled her to her feet, his touch solid and reassuring, though the awareness of his bare chest sent a jolt through her, momentarily cutting through her panic.

"Your magic is back." His words carried a weight that made her stomach churn.

Her eyes dropped to the hole in his arm, the blood dripping in slow, crimson rivulets that stained the ground beneath them. The sight made her chest tighten, and she called upon her mending magic. It flared to life. A warm golden light surged through her fingertips. She ran her finger over the wound, and it stitched closed, the torn flesh knitting together seamlessly. She licked her lips, and the tang of copper slid over her tongue. It made her stomach twist, a sickening reminder of what she had done.

"Was it the water?" she asked, her voice scarcely above a whisper.

Ashur closed his eyes, his brow furrowing in thought. The crease between his brows deepened as he shook his head.

Her gaze shifted to the dead men sprawled across the ground, their bodies twisted and lifeless. The sight made her skin crawl, and she wiped her lips with the back of her hand. When she pulled it away, streaks of blood smeared her skin, vivid and accusing. A sick thought bloomed in her mind, dark and unwelcome, making her stomach clench painfully.

"Drink his blood." Her voice trembled with the order. She pointed at the dead man near Lily, her hand shaking.

"What?" Ashur's voice was sharp with disbelief.

"That's the only thing I did differently from you. I swallowed a mouthful of that bastard's blood." Each word dragged her deeper into the horror of the moment. She pointed again, her finger trembling.

Ashur balked, his expression a mixture of revulsion and hesitation.

"Do it." Her tone hardened as she forced herself to meet his gaze.

Ashur bent down, his movements slow and reluctant. He pulled the sword from the dead man's side, the blade slick with blood, and cupped his hand over the dripping wound. The red liquid pooled in his palm, thick and viscous, before he tilted it into his mouth. His throat bobbed with a loud swallow, the sound cutting through the tense silence. His face twisted in a grimace, his features contorting with disgust.

He blinked, his body stiffening for a brief, heart-stopping instant. Then, as if the earth itself responded to him, a barrage of growth sprang from the surrounding ground, vibrant and wild. Reya's breath caught, her chest tightening as she stared at the transformation.

If the magic pulsing in my blood resulted from a mouthful...

Reya shook her head, trying to banish the thought, but it clung to her like a shadow. Her stomach churned as Ashur seemed to reach the same conclusion. He leaned down, his movements deliberate, and covered the wound with his mouth. The wet, sucking sound that followed made her skin crawl, and she averted her gaze, but not before catching the way his throat worked as he swallowed.

When he stood, the glow of magic rippling across his skin was undeniable. It shimmered like sunlight on water, a living energy that seemed to settle into him. He waved for her to follow, his expression unreadable but his urgency clear. Reya hesitated, her heart pounding in her chest. The thought of what she was about to do made her stomach twist, but the sight of the magic coursing through Ashur's body spurred her into action.

She kneeled by the body, the iron-laced bite of blood already thick in the air. Her hands trembled as she leaned down, her breath catching in her throat. The first mouthful was warm and viscous, coating her tongue with a flavor so foul it made her gag. She forced herself to swallow, the coppery bitterness sliding down her throat like poison. Another mouthful followed, and then another, each one more revolting than the last. Her body rebelled, her stomach heaving, but she pushed through, desperate for the same power she had seen in Ashur.

When she finally pulled away, her hands flew to her face, scrubbing at her lips as if she could erase the memory of the taste. She stumbled to the pond, the cool water a welcome relief as she splashed it over her face. The ripples distorted her reflection, but she glimpsed her own wide eyes, the horror still etched in them. The hum of magic stirred in her veins, a sensation both foreign and familiar, and she shivered despite the warmth of the air.

"What if there are more of them?" Ashur's voice was low but tense as he handed her the towel. The fabric was rough against Reya's damp hands, and she barely registered its texture before he turned away, pulling on the clean shirt. The whisper of cloth in motion and the scrape of his boots against the rocky ground filled the heavy silence as he laced up his shoes and gathered the scattered items.

Reya crouched by one of the bodies, her fingers brushing against the cold, lifeless hand as she pried the metal weapon free. Its surface was slick with blood, the metallic tang sharp in the air. She turned it over in her hands, the weight unfamiliar and unsettling, before wiping it on a clean patch of the rebel's shirt. She dumped it into the pile of clothing Ashur carried. Her stomach churned as she moved to the next body, her hands trembling as she searched the pockets.

The leather items she pulled out were worn and creased, their surfaces smooth under her fingertips. Inside, she found pictures—faces frozen in time, smiling and unaware—and folded papers that crinkled softly as she tucked them into the bundle of dirty clothing. The knot she tied was tight, the fabric straining under the bulk of their grim spoils.

"What if there are more?" Ashur repeated, his voice cutting through her thoughts as he picked up her father's sword.

The sight of it in his hands sent a pang through her chest. Reya froze, her gaze darting around the glen. The air was thick with the lingering stench of blood and singed flesh, but no new sounds broke the oppressive quiet. The weapons these men had fired were loud—loud enough to echo through the trees and reach the camp. Yet no one had come. Her heart pounded, each beat a drum of dread as the realization settled over her.

Her breath hitched, and without a word, she took off, her feet pounding against the uneven ground. The sharp edges of rocks bit into her soles through her slippers, but she didn't slow. Ashur was at her side, his presence a steadying force as they sprinted toward the camp. The trees blurred around them, the cool air whipping against her face and stinging her eyes. Her chest burned with each ragged breath, but she pushed forward, her mind racing with prayers.

Losing Lily was already a wound that cut too deep. The thought of more casualties, of more lifeless bodies waiting for them, made her stomach twist painfully. The camp came into view, and her heart clenched, the echo of her fears pressing down on her like a suffocating shroud.

CHAPTER 15

ASHUR'S GRIP TIGHTENED ON Reya's arm as he yanked her behind the rough bark of a tree. The tremor in her muscles beneath his hand betrayed her tension, and his pulse mirrored her dread. His eyes scanned the camp ahead, where men moved with precision, strange weapons cradled in their arms and angry sneers on their faces. Their weapons gleamed with a cold, steely menace under the filtered sunlight that broke through the canopy.

Onc of their own lay sprawled on the ground, his limbs twisted unnaturally, eyes staring blankly skyward. Blood pooled darkly beneath his body, seeping into the dirt like ink bleeding across aged parchment—thick, slow, and inevitable. A few rebels were strewn nearby in similar lifeless poses, their clothing scorched and limbs marked with the telltale burns of arcane backlash. The air above the camp shimmered with the residue of magic, its sweet tang mingling with the scent of scorched cloth and iron. Stray embers still drifted through the haze, rising lazily from a smoldering coat caught on a broken sword. It was clear the clash had been short-lived, brutal—a desperate burst of power flaring out before the spellcasters had exhausted their strength and fallen.

Reya turned to him, her breath quick and shallow. "Do you think we can disarm them?" she whispered, the edge of fear threading her voice.

Ashur's jaw clenched as he glanced over her shoulder. The subtle stench of blood still lingered in the air. His magic thrummed beneath his skin, its intensity almost overwhelming, like a furnace stoked too hot. The blood of their enemies seemed to have ignited something primal within him, an amplification of power that was as exhilarating as it was unnerving. He forced the sensation into submission, his focus narrowing on the enemy ahead.

"I counted at least twenty men," he said, his voice low and deliberate.

"Can we disarm them before another one of those things goes off?" Reya asked, her words quick and desperate.

Her blue eyes locked with his, wide and blazing with fear, and the gravity of her question settled in his chest like a stone. He couldn't blame her—those weapons were unlike anything they had faced before, more advanced and dangerous than the fae's finest swords or arrows. The hum of tension in the air was palpable, each second stretching unbearably as the enemy shifted in their positions.

Ashur sucked in a breath, the scent of damp earth and gunpowder filling his lungs. His mind worked swiftly, assessing the possibilities. He met her gaze again, his resolve hardening. "Those weapons are metal, correct?" he asked, his voice a quiet rumble.

"Yes," Reya replied, the word clipped but steady.

"Heat the metal and the minute they drop the weapons, I'll bind the rebels." His power coiled like a predator ready to strike. The determination in her eyes answered his challenge, and for a moment, the fear in the air seemed to shift, replaced by a shared sense of malice.

Ashur crouched low, his palms flat against the cool, damp earth. The gritty texture clung to his skin as he concentrated, his breath steady but shallow. The dim fragrance of soil—rich and loamy—flooded his nostrils as he sent his will deep into the ground. Beneath his fingertips, warmth pulsed, the latent energy of nature waiting to be stirred. Thorny vines answered his call, restless beneath the surface, their sharp barbs itching to erupt.

He glanced up at Reya. The shimmer of her magic distorted the air in ripples, as if the camp were on the edge of a heat haze. Her knuckles whitened, her fists trembling as energy gathered like an impending storm. The hum of her magic danced in the air, electric and sharp. Ashur couldn't tear his gaze from her closed eyes, nor from the way her brow furrowed in fierce concentration. When her eyes shot open and her hands flung wide, the air crackled like a whip.

Ashur snapped his head toward the camp. His heightened senses caught everything—the sharp gasp of surprise, the clatter of steel hitting the dirt, the startled shouts that quickly became cries of panic. The vines answered instantly. They burst from the earth in a riot of green, their jagged edges gleaming like teeth as they coiled around ankles, arms, and throats with relentless intent. The satisfying sound of flesh hitting the ground was like music to Ashur's ears, and the rush of magic burned hot through his veins, fueling him like a wildfire. He stood, his smile tugging up, fierce and unrelenting, as his gaze met Reya's. A silent exchange passed between them—an acknowledgment of power shared.

Their boots scraped against the uneven earth as they moved toward the camp. The crunch of scattered debris underfoot blended with the symphony of chaos they'd orchestrated. Ashur's heart pounded with exhilaration. The bramble barrier was no match for their momentum, its thorns bending obediently under his command.

Opal's wide eyes darted between them and the still-wrangling intruders. "How?" she demanded, breathless.

Ashur smirked but didn't pause, his confidence sharp like the scent of the air after a thunderstorm. "Blood of our enemies, Opal," he said with a wicked undertone threading his voice.

"Lily died at their hands," Reya added without looking back, her voice calm but lethal.

Together, they plunged deeper into the camp, past tangled bodies and the echoes of fear-stricken cries. The world was alive with adrenaline, and Ashur's magic thrummed louder with each step, like a second heartbeat. But this wasn't over yet. Their foes were down, but Ashur's senses prickled with foreboding—a warning that something, or someone, still lurked beyond their reach, waiting to strike. Reya's eyes flicked to him, and he knew she experienced it too.

Ashur's fingers twitched, ready to summon another wave of destruction at the first sign of resistance. His magic was still coiled within him, waiting—dangerous, unspent.

CHAPTER 16

REYA'S HEART PLUNDERED AGAINST her ribs, each beat a painful reminder of Lily's loss and the surrounding chaos. The scent of trampled earth and burned flesh filled her nose, mingling with the coppery tang of blood that lingered in the air. Her boots crunched over broken twigs and scattered debris as she moved, her gaze sweeping over the bound vandals and the wreckage they had wrought. The sight of their destruction clawed at her chest, a visceral ache that only deepened as her eyes fell on Tristan.

He lay cradled in Cypress's arms, his face pale and slack as quiet sobs shook her frame. The sound was soft but relentless, like a knife scraping against stone, and it ignited a fury in

Reya that burned hot. Her blood roared in her ears, drowning out the distant croons of her people as she clenched her fists at her sides.

"Who is the leader of these criminals?" Her voice cut through the air, sharp and commanding, carrying the pitch of her anger. The question hung heavy, unanswered, as her gaze swept over her people. Their faces were etched with exhaustion and fear, but none dared to look away.

When Tristan's mate raised a trembling hand to point at a man among the captives, Reya's focus sharpened. Her steps were deliberate, each one sinking into the soft forest floor with a muted thud. The man's defiance faltered under her glare, his bravado crumbling like dry leaves underfoot. She crouched before him, the fabric of her skirt brushing against the damp earth, and a bare waft of moss and decay rose to meet her. The forest seemed to hold its breath, the air thick with tension as Reya's eyes locked onto his.

Her voice, low and steady, carried the promise of retribution. "You will answer for this senseless attack." The words were a quiet storm, and the forest seemed to echo them back, amplifying their weight. Reya's fury simmered just beneath the surface, a force as unrelenting as the earth beneath her.

Reya turned her gaze up to Ashur, her neck stiff from her tension. His steel eyes reflected a flicker of understanding, the sharp contrast of his calm control against the wild churn of emotions thrumming through her chest.

"Search them all and bring what you find to my tent." The bite of exhaustion threaded through her voice. The scent of damp soil and crushed pine needles lingered in the air, heavy with the evening's upheaval.

Her gaze shifted past him to the mess strewn across the camp—the chaotic scattering of belongings, weapons, and supplies that spoke of their struggle. The fractured remains of their order lay bare, glinting in the muted light like small wounds upon the earth. The rustle of the surrounding forest was almost mocking, too serene for the turmoil etched into every corner of the camp.

"Clean up your things," she added, her voice tightening as her eyes lingered on a broken strap dangling from a pack. She exhaled slowly, the stress of leadership pressing against her ribcage. "And then we will discuss these rebels' fate." The words hung in the thick air, a promise heavy with deliberation and the brewing storm of her judgment.

"If we are not back by midnight, they will send more men," the leader snarled, his voice a rough edge cutting through the still air.

Reya's gaze locked onto his dark brown eyes, pools of simmering contempt framed by dirt-smeared cheeks. Sweat and blood clung to him, sharp and invasive, stirring an anger deep within her. She let her smile stretch slowly, a silent taunt that defied the bitterness lurking in his stare.

"Let them come." Her words curled through the breath of space between them like smoke—dangerous and calm.

Turning on her heel, the cool press of the forest floor beneath her boots rocked unevenly and riddled with roots. The scents of earth and wood surrounded her, calming yet charged with the tension of everything that had transpired. Her skirt swayed lightly with each step, brushing against her calves as she strode toward her tent. Ashur followed close behind, his footsteps steady but soft, a quiet contrast to the storm rolling through her thoughts.

The moment the tent flap closed, muffling the camp outside, Ashur spoke, his tone measured but heavy. "We should make them show us how their weapons work." His movements were careful as he set the satchel of freshly laundered clothes on the ground.

The delicate aroma of soap and water wafted up before his hands worked the fabric knot loose. Reya's eyes traced his motions as he pulled the weapon free—the same one that had killed Lily.

Her breath hitched. The sight before her—unexpected, cruel—coiled something tight in her chest. The cold sheen of the weapon mocked her, glinting dully beneath the muted light of the tent. It sat like a ghost on the floor, a silent reminder of failure. The air thickened, heavy with the mingled scents of damp canvas and the crisp tang of Ashur's magic—a citrusy undercurrent that teased at clarity, even amid chaos. Rage curled at the base of her spine, tempered only by the sorrow of grief pressing against her ribs.

Reya closed her eyes for a heartbeat, drawing in a long, bracing breath. She gathered herself not from peace, but from the promise of what was yet to come—of justice, vengeance, and the fragile hope they might yet forge from this ruin.

She stepped through the opening of the tent, boots crunching against the gritty earth outside, where the camp smoldered in the aftermath of their too-brief clash.

"Where were you when all this was happening?" Quinn's voice cut through the noise like a dagger, sharp and damning. Heads turned. His tone carried fury wrapped in disbelief, threaded through with the sting of buried grief.

Tensions snapped taut, charged and brittle.

Reya spun on her heel, her wet hair slapping across her shoulder like a battle flag unfurling. "Getting accosted by more men," she snapped, every word clipped with fury honed from exhaustion.

Quinn stalked forward, boots grinding into the dirt, fire burning in his eyes. "How convenient," he sneered. "You vanish while our people bleed and burn."

She didn't look away. For a moment, her face was carved from stone—etched with choices no one had the right to make, her eyes dark with a coming storm.

Then she stepped into his path, close enough that her breath stirred the fabric on his collar.

"Do you think I *wanted* this?" Her voice was low and dangerous, coiled with steel. "I didn't vanish, Quinn. You knew exactly where we were. And when we broke free, we came back and crushed the bastards who dared touch our people." She gestured toward the rebels still twitching beneath Ashur's thorn-bound spells, their whimpers barely audible over the wind.

Quinn's lip curled. "Oh, well done, then. While you were off playing soldier in a riverbed, we were draining the last of our power to stay alive. And yet—you and your guard return brimming with magic. Did you *siphon* ours to refill your well?"

Reya's hands twitched at her sides. Magic surged at her fingertips, pulsing with heat and fury—but she strangled it down, spine straight and jaw clenched. Not here. Not now. Not him.

Ashur stepped into the tension like a shadow with teeth, placing himself at Reya's side. His glare fixed on Quinn with simmering menace. "Do not take that tone with your queen," he growled, voice like distant thunder. It rattled through the camp and made a few flinch.

Reya's eyes never left Quinn. "The House of Dawn does not siphon magic," she said with a hard-edge. "We never have. And throwing around false accusations to poison my rule is reckless at best." Her gaze narrowed. "Unless, of course, you intend to challenge me for the crown."

Quinn went pale. His mouth worked soundlessly for a second before he clenched his jaw and turned away, the accusation dying between his teeth. Silence settled like fog across the camp.

Then the wind stirred, and with it, the world resumed its broken rhythm.

Reya turned away from him without ceremony. Her voice rose, commanding, cool and unwavering: "Who among us has the power to manipulate stone and earth?"

The man who had forged the trough in the desert stepped forward, his mate close behind. Reya's gaze flicked to Ashur, his presence like a storm barely contained, before settling on the pair.

"What are your names?" she asked, her tone steady but edged with urgency.

"Nelly and Rob Flickerthorn," Rob replied, his voice tinged with frustration. "But we no longer seem to have access to our magic." His hands rubbed against his thighs, the coarse fabric rasping against his skin as his eyes dropped to the ground.

Reya's lips curved into a smile. "What if I could give it back to you tenfold?" Her words vibrated in the air, heavy with promise and foreboding.

Rob's eyebrows shot up, his gaze darting to his partner. Nelly nodded, her expression encouraging despite the tension in her jaw.

Reya inhaled deeply, the scent of earth and power filling her lungs. "It may mean that you do something that seems utterly disgusting."

Rob hesitated, his eyes flickering to Ashur, whose aura seemed to pulse with raw energy. "If it provides the same power that he is radiating, I would not be opposed to doing what is necessary."

Reya turned to Ashur, and her voice cut through the charged atmosphere. "Can you create a large bowl?"

Ashur crouched, his fingers pressing into the soil. The ground trembled beneath Reya's feet as a clay pot emerged, its surface smooth and cool to the touch. He lifted it and offered it to Reya as he stood.

Reya grasped the bowl and unsheathed the dagger from her belt. The blade gleamed in the dim light, a cold promise of what was to come.

The air thickened, and the camp silenced as Reya crossed to the leader of the band of thugs. She placed the bowl on the ground, the sound of its contact sharp against the silence. Her fingers tangled in the man's greasy hair, the strands coarse. With his head tilted back, the strain of his muscles resisted against her knife before her blade sliced cleanly through his throat.

The blood flowed in a hot, crimson stream, pooling into the bowl. Every face in the camp scrunched with a mix of horror and morbid fascination. When the last drop fell, Reya released the lifeless body, the thud of its collapse echoing in the stillness.

The warmth of the nearly full bowl seeped into her palms. Reya turned to Rob and Nelly. Her voice was steady, almost gentle, as she extended the vessel toward them. "Drink."

Nelly and Rob balked, their faces pale in the last rays of light. The other fae shifted uneasily, their movements stirring the dry, brittle grass beneath their feet. Reya's gaze swept over them, her expression unreadable, before she tipped the bowl to her lips. The warm sting of oxidized metal and salt hit her tongue, sharp and bitter, and she forced herself to swallow. The warmth of the liquid slid down her throat, thick and viscous, leaving a coppery aftertaste that lingered.

As the blood reached her stomach, a surge of power erupted within her, like lightning striking every nerve. Her muscles tensed, her skin prickling as if charged with static. She exhaled slowly, her breath visible in the cool evening air, and opened her eyes to find Ashur stepping forward. His movements were deliberate, his presence commanding as he took the bowl from her hands.

Ashur drank without hesitation, his throat working as he swallowed. The sound of his gulping seemed amplified in the tense silence. He lowered the bowl, his eyes glowing with renewed energy.

"You want to restore your power? This is the way." His voice was steady, resonating with authority as he extended the bowl to Rob.

Rob scowled, his jaw tightening as he reached for the roughly textured bowl. He closed his eyes, his breath hitching before he took a gulp. His Adam's apple bobbed with the effort to force the liquid down. His eyes flew open, wide and bright, as power radiated from him in waves. He stared at the remaining blood, his fingers trembling as he took another, larger sip.

Rob turned to Nelly, his expression softening as he offered her the bowl. She shook her head, her hands clenched at her sides.

"Just take a sip," he urged, his voice low but insistent.

Nelly reached out, her fingers brushing the bowl's rim before she grasped it. Her grip faltered, and the bowl tilted precariously, but Ashur's hand shot out to steady it. She nodded in gratitude, her lips pressing into a thin line as she took a tentative sip. She shuddered, her face contorting briefly before she handed the bowl back.

Ashur brought the remaining blood to Reya, his movements fluid and purposeful. "The rest is yours," he said, his voice softer now.

Reya tipped the bowl to her lips, the heaviness sinking into her bones as she chugged down half the contents. The blood coursed through her, its warmth spreading like wildfire. She offered the bowl to Ashur, her gaze locking with his. "I'll need you at your strongest," she said.

Ashur drained the bowl, his movements precise, and then set it aside.

Reya wiped her lips on her sleeve, the fabric rough against her skin. She turned her attention to the mountain looming behind them, its shadow stretching across the ground. Ignoring the disgusted stares of their prisoners, she strode toward the edge of the campground, her boots crunching against the gravel. "I want a fortress stronger than that of our home," she said to Ashur, her voice carrying over the stillness. "And I want it to encompass the falls and pond we bathed in."

Tilting her head back, she reached for the thrumming power inside her and willed the earth to shift, to form what her mind's eye crafted.

CHAPTER 17

ASHUR STOOD AT THE edge of their camp, the lingering scent of damp earth and moss rising from the forest floor as he gazed at the rock wall taking shape before him. His sharp eyes studied its surface, smooth as polished marble and shimmering in the dying light filtering through the tree canopy. Unlike the jagged, climbable walls of their fortress in the fae realm, this barrier was seamless, an unbreachable shield against whatever waited in the shadows.

A deep sense of satisfaction warmed his chest, and his lips curled into a quiet smile. The wall bore the strength of home—their sanctuary in the fae realm—forged by necessity and survival. He crouched, the movement stirring the cool air against his skin, and placed his palms flat against the ground. The dampness seeped into his calloused hands as he closed his eyes, focusing on the raw energy thrumming beneath his fingertips.

Reya's power was already there, a shimmering golden thread woven through the earth like sunlight itself. Ashur's own energy, darker and heavier, intertwined with hers. A connection crackled, like lightning crawling through his veins, as the earth quivered and responded to their combined will. The ground shifted under him with a deep, resonant rumble, as if the land itself recognized their determination.

Shapes rose, the rocks pulling together and melding in perfect harmony. The rhythmic sound of the stone forming—like muted thunder—echoed through the clearing. Ashur opened his eyes, his breath coming in slow, controlled draws. The wall grew taller, steadier. It had the same commanding presence as the fortress back home, but now it bore the imprints of their struggle, their resilience.

A shuffling of footsteps broke his concentration. He glanced over his shoulder to see Nelly and Rob approaching, their faces lit with determination. Nelly's auburn hair caught the sunlight as she kneeled beside Reya, her quick fingers already weaving her magic into the process. Rob, silent but focused, joined on the other side, his sturdy frame radiating strength.

Ashur's gaze flicked toward the rest of the camp, scattered behind them. A ripple of awe passed through the rest of the fae, their mumbles low but charged with wonder. Some stood frozen, their hands resting lightly on packs and tools; others edged closer, eyes wide as they took in the collaborative display of magic and creation.

Ashur pulled his focus back to the task at hand. The air hummed with power and purpose, with the shared belief that this wall would protect them—a tangible promise of safety and hope. His pulse quickened as the earth yielded to their combined will.

Since their arrival in this blighted land, Ashur hadn't allowed himself to believe in the possibility of holding onto what mattered most. It had been just the raw need to survive until this moment. Now, the true spark of hope bloomed in his blood.

Behind him, the forest trembled as if exhaling its ancient breath. The trees groaned and shuddered, their sturdy trunks splitting apart with a deafening crack. Splinters filled the air, sharp and fleeting, carrying the sharp scent of raw wood and sap. Ashur turned, his sharp gaze catching the extraordinary transformation as the fractured trees reassembled, reshaping into quaint cottages and homes. Their walls seemed to sigh into place, lining the hillside like jewels scattered on green velvet.

The air buzzed with the hum of magic, a prickling sensation that danced across Ashur's skin. He could almost taste its syrupy tang on his tongue, sharp and electric, mingling with the richness of the mountain breeze. The cottages climbed higher and higher, their neat chimneys puffing wisps of smoke as if they had always been there, nestled snugly into the hillside.

And then his breath caught as his eyes were drawn upward. From the mountain's rugged face, stone emerged, seamless and deliberate. The castle rose with a commanding grace, its walls glowing as they drank in the last of the light. Each stone seemed to hold a pulse of life, shimmering with an otherworldly radiance that illuminated the clearing below. The structure stood proud but not ostentatious—a haven rather than a throne.

Ashur's gaze followed the obsidian barrier as it surged from the mountain's shadow, its glossy surface reflecting the golden glow of the castle. It coiled down like a protective serpent. As the dark barricade reached the valley floor, it melded with the smooth, impenetrable wall he and the others had forged. The connection sent a low vibration through the earth, a deep, resonant hum that Ashur felt in his bones.

For a moment, all was still. The world seemed to hold its breath as the camp took in the sight. Ashur let himself linger on the scene, the mingling of creation and protection stirring something deep within him. The castle and cottages, the wall and the barrier—all of it sang of their will to endure. And though the heavy scent of earth and stone drifted on the air, a thread of hope weaved through Ashur, lifting the intensity of the moment just enough for him to breathe again.

CHAPTER 18

REYA STEPPED FORWARD TO the wall, its surface dark and rippling like oil in the evening light. The tang of ancient magic hung in the air, prickling her senses. She took a steadying breath and sliced her palm, the sting sharp and immediate as warm blood welled up and trickled down her wrist. Pressing her hand to the icy stone, she muttered the incantation under her breath. The spell carried a honeyed flavor that lingered on her tongue.

The wall resisted at first, pulsing against her palm, before groaning with a deep, resonant sound that sent vibrations up her arm. Cracks spider-webbed across its surface, releasing a gust of cold, stagnant air redolent of damp earth and stone. Slowly, the massive slabs swung open with a grinding noise, revealing the expanse beyond.

Reya turned to the fae gathered behind her, their expressions a mix of awe and ambivalence. "Come forward," she commanded, her voice sharper than intended, as exhaustion clawed at her edges.

Ashur stepped forward without hesitation. Reya reached for his hand, and the calloused warmth of his palm steadied her nerves. She swiftly drew her blade across his skin. A crimson bead formed, stark against the pale tone of his hand.

"Place it on the wall so it will recognize you as fae and open or close at your command." Her voice carried a rasp of weariness.

Ashur obeyed, pressing his bloodied palm to the stone. The wall groaned as it shifted closed, the sound heavy and final. One by one, the other fae followed, each ritual marked by the tang of blood in the air and the rustle of boots against stone.

When the last of them had completed the rite, Reya closed the great doors by putting her hand on the wall and whispering an ancient fae command to close the door. The outer world vanished behind the wall, leaving them enclosed in the eerie quiet of their new sanctuary.

Fatigue settled over Reya like a weighted cloak. Her muscles cramped with the strain, and the well of magic within her drained, its once-bright ember now a flickering spark. She glanced at Ashur, noticing the dark smudges beneath his eyes, mirrored in the hollowed expressions of Nelly and Rob.

"I need to restore my reserves," she admitted, her voice softer now. Her gaze drifted to the prisoners, their wide eyes reflecting their fear. A grimace twisted her lips. Vulnerability was a luxury they couldn't afford—not even behind the towering wall of their carved-out haven.

Ashur let out a breath, the sound soft but heavy, as his gaze swept over the bound men alongside Nelly and Rob. The quiet flutter of leaves and the creak of thorny vines tightening around the prisoners filled the tense silence.

"They aren't much different from us," Rob said, his voice low and uncertain.

Reya's gaze sharpened, her eyes narrowing like blades. "No. But they are the key for us to keep our magic strong." Her words carried the mark of resolve, though a flicker of agitation stirred deep within her. With her back erect, she marched into the camp, the crunch of dirt beneath her boots sharpening her focus. She picked up the bowl, its cold, smooth surface pressing against her palms, and headed toward the nearest prisoner.

The man's eyes widened, the whites stark against his flushed face. His head shook frantically, and the thorny vines binding him rustled as he struggled. "Please, no," he pleaded, his voice trembling and raw, each word scraping against the air.

Reya set the bowl down with a deliberate clink against the ground. The metallic scent of blood already lingered in the air, mingling with the sharp tang of fear. She grabbed a handful of his hair, the strands coarse and damp with sweat, and yanked him into place over the bowl. His cries turned to choked gasps as she drew her blade across his throat. Warm blood gushed forth, splattering her hands and filling the basin with a steady stream. The coppery tang of it filled her senses, sharp and overwhelming. When only drips remained, she tossed the lifeless body aside, her movements brisk and unflinching.

She lifted the container, tipping it to her lips; the liquid, thick and warm, flowed down her throat. Power surged through her veins, a fiery rush that made her muscles hum with renewed strength. She stopped before the sensation overwhelmed her, handing the bowl to Ashur. His fingers brushed hers briefly, cold and trembling, before he followed her lead.

The bowl moved from Ashur to Nelly, then to Rob—their hands trembling, faces pale but determined. As each brought it to their lips, a shimmer lit their eyes, the flicker of returning vitality sparking behind fatigue. Rob handed the vessel to the next fae without a word. One by one, they drank in silence. Their motions were slow, ritualistic, as if compelled by something older than fear. Grimaces tugged at their mouths as the liquid burned its way down, sculpting their expressions into solemn masks of resolve.

The ritual didn't just feed their strength—it wove them together, linking breath, blood, and purpose.

When the bowl finally returned to Reya, she raised it without hesitation and drained the last of its contents. A final rush of power surged through her, settling low and heavy within her core. She exhaled through parted lips, then wiped her mouth with the back of her hand. A smear of blood remained across her skin—proof of the price paid, and the pact sealed.

Her gaze landed on the half-dozen men still tied up, their faces etched with terror. Fear radiated from them in waves, palpable and suffocating. Reya turned away, her jaw tightening. Vulnerability was not an option.

"Can you get rid of the rebel's bodies?" she asked Ashur, her voice steady but hollow. "And then we will bury Tristan and Lily in the pine grove beyond the falls."

The vines shifted, their movements slow and deliberate, as they pulled the dead into the soil. The ground swallowed them whole, leaving behind only disturbed dirt and a trace of decay.

"Thank you." Reya turned her attention back to the camp. The reality of what they had done settled over her, but she pushed it aside. Survival demanded sacrifice.

But what would this sacrifice cost?

CHAPTER 19

A SHUR'S BODY BUZZED WITH renewed energy, as though lightning coursed beneath his skin, alive and thrumming. The air felt heavier now—charged, almost electric. He met Reya's gaze, her steady eyes hinting at the consequences of decisions yet to come.

"What do we do with the rest of them?" His voice crackled in the quiet tension, his nod directing her attention to the bound men scattered throughout the camp, their faces etched with rage and resignation.

"Can you create a cell for them over there?" She pointed toward the slick, gleaming face of the newly raised wall, its surface damp and reflective in the subdued light. The subtle bouquet of earth and rain lingered, mingling with the sweat and grime of the prisoners.

He chewed his lip, tasting the copper tang of blood as his teeth pressed too hard. He glanced down at the ground, the rough blades of grass tickling his fingers as he lowered his gaze. He didn't want to question her authority, but the misgiving twisted in his stomach like coiled vines.

"Do you think having them in one cell is wise?" The words escaped in a muted whisper, his chest tightening as he dared to look back at her.

She rubbed her chin thoughtfully, her finger rasping against skin. "You're right. They could gang up on us if they are together. Do you have enough power to do separate cells with space between, so there is no chance of being attacked?"

"Yes, Your Highness." He bowed deeply, the gesture mechanical yet steeped in respect.

Crouching down, the cool earth pressed against his knees as he spread his fingers. They tangled in the grass at his feet, dry and fragrant from the last remnants of daylight. His thoughts sharpened into clarity, picturing thorned cages rising from the ground—impenetrable and unyielding. The rumble began, deep and resonant, vibrating through his bones. Walls of jagged rock surged upward, their edges raw and sharp, like ancient wounds torn open. Gaps of space separated each cell, suffused with the dark, sweet aroma of freshly churned soil.

The prisoners, bound in writhing vines, shouted in protest as they were dragged toward the open maws of the cells. Their voices were swallowed by the sound of growth—a cacophony of cracking earth and creaking wood. Thorns curled across the openings, their glossy surfaces glinting like cruel knives. The pull of Ashur's magic sang through his muscles as it tethered to his command, surging forward with precision. He allowed the binding vines to retreat once the cells were secure, sinking back into the ground like obedient sentinels.

He stood, his hands shaking as he flexed his fingers. The cool air brushed against his flushed skin. With a slow, deliberate breath, he closed his eyes and assessed his reserves. Energy pulsed steadily within him, calm yet potent, mirroring his natural state in the fae realm. Relief flickered through him—twenty vessels remained at his disposal, though he did not wish to rely on them again until another day had passed.

"Who will carry Tristan?" Reya's voice rose above the stillness. Not a command, but a call to honor.

Several of the remaining men stepped forward without hesitation. Their faces were tight with grief, but their strides were steady as they lifted Tristan's body in a practiced, almost reverent motion. Ashur stood silently at Reya's side, the hush of silence pressing in from all sides as they moved toward the falls.

The air was thick with mourning, laced with the scent of churned earth, torn roots, and the bittersweet perfume that clung to Lily's hair. He turned toward her still form and bent down. Her limbs were soft and pliant, but heavy in that unnatural way only the dead carried. He slung her body gently over his shoulder, careful not to let her head loll. Her weight pressed into his frame—cold and final.

The procession moved through the trees toward the edge of the forest, their footsteps muffled by damp leaves and soft soil. The wind whispered through the branches overhead, rustling like spirits offering their eulogy. Ashur's arms strained with each step, but he bore it silently, jaw tight, eyes fixed on the space between Reya's shoulders. The king's sword rested in her hands now, its presence solemn, like a piece of a world they were already beginning to lose.

When they emerged from the trees, the field yawned open before them—golden grass waving gently in the breath of the falls beyond. Reya shaped it into a sanctuary. A short wall of stone ringed the space, sculpted from the earth itself, pale and smooth, like a cradle for the dead.

Rob was already kneeling, his hands dark with soil as his magic dug through the loam with quiet purpose. Two graves opened side by side, earthy mouths ready to receive what they were not meant to.

Tristan's body was lowered first. A ribbon of moonlight crossed his brow like a blessing, casting soft halos in his blond hair. Then Ashur stepped forward and, with the gentlest motion he could summon, laid Lily into the ground.

A hush fell, the kind that swallows breath and time alike.

Ashur straightened, stepping back as the first shovelful of soil hit Tristan's chest with a dull thud. The noise struck him like a blow. One after another followed until the scent of fresh-turned earth eclipsed everything else.

He didn't speak. He couldn't. Grief weighed heavier than any sword.

Reya lifted the king's blade and held it skyward for a long, still moment before plunging it into the soil between the graves—a silent vow.

They would not be forgotten.

One by one, the others drifted away from the gravesite, their footsteps hushed against the softened earth. Some lingered a moment longer, heads bowed, before turning toward the cottages that now offered a fragile sense of shelter. Soon, only Ashur and Reya remained, the silence between them heavy, but not strained—an understanding bound by loss and duty.

Reya exhaled, the sound quiet but laden with weariness. When she looked at him, her eyes held the weight of a thousand unseen decisions. "I know it's a lot to ask." She brushed a damp strand of hair from her face as the breeze tangled it again, "but can you make sure the tents are packed? Stow them in the castle armory, along with the weapons."

Ashur studied her for a brief moment—not the queen, not the warrior—but the woman carved raw by the day. He gave a small, respectful nod. "Yes, Your Highness."

Together, they turned from the graves and began the walk back to the encampment. Around them, the fae were already gathering their things, movements slow but steady. The world hadn't paused for grief, and neither could they.

He waited until the crew finished packing their items before he started dismantling the half-dozen tents dotting the ground. His calloused fingers tightened around the edge of their tent canvas as he stripped it away from the skeleton poles. The fabric stank of damp earth and smoke from the campfires, mingled with the lingering tang of blood that haunted his senses no matter how many times he closed his eyes and forced himself to focus.

One by one, the others peeled away, muttering in low voices as they carried their belongings to the cottages scattered across the hillside. Ashur's eyes followed them for a moment, a pang of something unnamable twisted in his chest as each pair disappeared behind weathered doors and shutters. The cottages stood like sentinels against the deep green mountain forest, their stone faces tinged in shadows in the rising moonlight.

He dropped his gaze and shook out the stiff folds of the tent before rolling it with practiced efficiency. His hands worked on autopilot, the roughness of the canvas biting against the scars on his palms. By the time he lashed the last tent and piled it with the rest of the camping gear, the encampment had been dismantled, leaving behind only patches of trampled grass and the lingering scent of charred wood. The silence pressed against him like an unseen weight.

Ashur straightened, his back aching from the strain, and cast a weary glance toward the cottages. Each bore the telltale signs of occupation—smoke curling from chimneys, warm candlelight flickering against the windows. All of them taken. He let out a sigh, the breath escaping in a cloud that hung momentarily in the chilly air before dissipating. The ache in his chest deepened, though he shoved it aside, unwilling to let it fester.

With the bag of confiscated weapons readjusted on his shoulder, Ashur looked at the castle perched higher on the hill. Its graceful silhouette threw ominous shadows against the face of the mountain, as if warning Ashur of darker trails still ahead.

He trudged forward, his boots crunching against the gravel path; the rhythmic clink of steel echoed from the bag at his side. The air grew colder the closer he got, and a shiver of granite steeped in silence seemed to seep from the castle's very walls.

Reya had long since disappeared, her silhouette engulfed by the castle's vast shadow. Ashur swallowed hard, his thoughts briefly straying to her confident stride and the resolute set of her jaw. She had made the uphill journey look effortless, her figure light against the burdens she carried. He pushed the thought away and adjusted his grip on the sword at his hip, the leather-wrapped hilt solid and reassuring beneath his fingers.

As he reached the ornate door that separated the royal from the non-royal, the world seemed to quiet further. The rustle of the breeze through the trees faded, leaving only the whisper of his own breath and the weighty stillness of the castle watching over him.

Ashur's fingers brushed against the pommel of the King's sword at his belt; its gold-plated engravings glimmered in the waning light. He sighed. The presence behind the blade dragged at him in more ways than one. For all its majesty, the weapon reminded him of what he was not—and would never be. Wearing the sword of a royal might intimidate others, but for him, it chafed against the undeniable truth that he did not belong. Residency in the castle seemed like a lie he had no choice but to live.

With a sense of resignation curling in his chest, Ashur pressed his palm to the heavy oak door, its surface cool and ridged with age. A subtle creak echoed through the air as he pushed it open, revealing the interior Reya had designed—her vision come to life in unsettling perfection. Polished marble mingled with beeswax candles, their warm glow reflecting off the ivory-white walls with an almost unnerving precision. It was as if someone had plucked a miniature version of the fae realm's castle and brought it here, sterile and pristine, untouched by the chaos they'd just survived.

Ashur hesitated at the threshold, the stillness inside pressing against his skin like a cold mist. His boots scuffed softly against the marble floor as he stepped inside, each sound too loud in the oppressive quiet. The building's grandeur should have reassured him, yet it seemed alien—a hollow echo of the castle in the fae realm, but stripped of life and vibrancy. Shadows lingered in the corners where candlelight couldn't reach, their flickering forms whispering of something unseen.

To shake off the growing unease that gnawed at him, Ashur turned his attention to the layout. The armory was to the left, the living quarters to the right—if he remembered Reya's instructions correctly. His feet carried him forward, and the expanse of the great hall opened before him like a gaping maw. The vaulted ceiling loomed overhead, adorned with chandeliers that sparkled as if holding court over the emptiness. He thought of balls and banquets held in spaces like this, the clinking of goblets and laughter that should fill the air—but there was none of that here. Just silence, deep and foreboding.

He turned left, his movements stiff as tension pulled at his shoulders. Three doors lined the hallway, the middle one bearing the mark of an armory. Ashur exhaled and shoved the bag of confiscated weapons onto the ground, the metal within clanking against the marble with a harsh finality. The sound reverberated, and for a moment, he thought he heard something deeper echo back—but the castle remained still. His nerves hummed with the sense of being watched, though he saw no one.

Carefully, he began emptying the bag, hanging knives and firearms on the wall hooks. The weight eased from his arms, but not from his chest. He stepped back and eyed the bare sack and the threadbare outfit he had carried with him— everything he owned reduced to a single set of clothes and the weapon at his side.

They'd need seamstresses soon; otherwise, they'd have nothing left to wear. He thought of the piles of finery they had left behind—the silks, the embroidery, the tokens of their lives before. He sighed, his breath catching as a whiff of iron crept into his nose, sharp and lingering like bloodstains that refused to wash away. He turned toward the door, his fingers brushing against the leather-wrapped hilt of his sword. The sting of their losses seemed to press against the walls themselves. This castle was meant to be their haven—but it already felt like a cage.

CHAPTER 20

REYA LEANED AGAINST THE smooth, cool stone of the window frame at the front of her room, the chill seeping through her sleeves. The sun dipped below the jagged edge of the horizon, painting the sky in deepening strokes of amber and violet. Shadows stretched long over the hillside, cloaking the cottages below in a gentle dusk. From this vantage point, she could see the stone wall that encircled their new home, its pristine surface catching the last glimmers of light. The wall rose sharply where it carved into the mountain behind the castle, its sheer height an imposing barrier to any who might approach from that direction.

She shifted her gaze to the southern windows, where the view opened to a winding mountain river, its silvery surface glinting like a ribbon of light as it tumbled down into the lake below. The sound of rushing water reached her ears, faint but constant, a soothing hum amidst the growing silence of the evening. The river's path cut cleanly through the stone wall, creating a natural sieve for intruders while allowing fish and wildlife to move freely. Her lips pressed together as she considered the practicality of it—how soon they would need to hunt, to plant, to grow.

Ashur came to mind, and the thought settled like an ember in her chest. She would task him with establishing vegetable gardens for their people. There would be time for that in the morning. For now, her eyes caught on a lone figure moving up the hill toward the castle—Ashur, his broad shoulders hunched under the burden of the weapons bag she'd instructed him to retrieve. The clink of steel accompanied his every step, a sound that carried farther than it should in the stillness of the settling night.

He was a sight to behold, even in the limited light. The motion of his muscles beneath his worn tunic, the deliberate determination of his stride— it stirred something she had no business feeling. Her heart fluttered, unbidden, as she pictured his rough hands offering her a bowl of vegetables from the garden they would one day build. Hands that bore the marks of toil, strength, and silent resilience.

Reya shook her head, banishing the thought like brushing away a curl of smoke. He wasn't of royal blood—she reminded herself firmly, her fingers curling against the cool stone of the ledge. Only one survivor bore a true claim to lineage, and that was Quinn—a self-important thorn she had no interest in aligning with. Her gaze drifted back to the cottages below, their windows aglow with the amber light of evening. What, in the name of all that was sacred, had her parents been thinking when they sent *him* among the last of their people?

Her chest tightened as the realization twisted through her. She would rather share her bed with one of the heathen rebels than submit to Quinn. She huffed, pushing away the gnawing frustration and the tendrils of guilt that accompanied it. Turning abruptly from the window, she let the heavy curtains fall, their folds muffling the view, and the emotions tangled with it.

Tomorrow, there would be tasks to focus on, and surely that would be enough to silence the questions that lingered on the edge of her thoughts.

A soft knock at her door echoed through the quiet room, sharp against the backdrop of the evening's muted whispers of nature coming from her open windows. The sound sent her teeth on edge, like the scrape of a blade against stone. Reya rubbed her clammy palms against the fabric of her skirt. The absence of Lily's dependable presence weighed heavily on her. The air in the room held the lingering warmth of the day, but still held the oppressive weight of her parent's expectations.

The knocking sounded again, reminding her that tonight, she had no choice but to answer her own door—a task Lily usually performed with unfaltering grace.

She crossed the room, her bare feet brushing against the cool marble floor. The door creaked open on its hinges, revealing Ashur standing there, bathed in the soft glow of candles lining the hallway. His white hair hung in disarray, like freshly fallen snow disrupted by a gust of wind. He brushed it away from his face with an almost impatient flick of his hand, giving her a clear view of his crystal blue eyes—eyes that glinted like shards of ice catching the pale light.

Her chest tightened as her heart fluttered uncontrollably. Warmth spread through her like a match struck in a frigid room. A mist of pine and cedar clung to him, mingling with the night. "What can I do for you?" she asked.

"There are no more cottages left." His weight shifted from one foot to the other, boots scuffing against the stone doorstep. "Is there a room available in the castle?"

Her lips stretched into a smile, pulling at the tension in her face like the first bloom of spring. She motioned toward the room next door, the knot of hesitation in her stomach uncoiling. "That's where the personal guard to the royals would typically stay, and since you were given that role before we came here, that was created for you."

Blush bloomed across his cheeks, subtle yet unmistakable in the dim light of the corridor. His gaze flicked toward the room next to hers, and for a moment, his shoulders seemed to sag under the flurry of thought.

"I never fancied living in a castle," he said, the words so quiet they blended with the rustle of leaves outside, as though spoken for the night itself.

When he lifted his eyes back to hers, worry swirled in their crystalline depths, like storm clouds churning over an ocean. The thick silence between them pressed against her chest.

"Thank you." He inclined his head with a grace that seemed at odds with the hesitation in his movements. The soft scuff of his boots against the floor as he stepped toward the adjoining room reverberated in the quiet, each sound nudging at her like a call unanswered.

"Have you eaten?" Reya blurted before she could second-guess herself, her voice sharp against the stillness. The words hung awkwardly in the air, surprising even her.

His eyebrows arched in mild surprise, his expression softening just enough to send a twinge of self-consciousness through her. "You have food?" he asked, a thread of hope weaving through his tone.

Her gaze darted away from his, landing on the flickering shadows cast by the oil lamp on the wall. "Well, no," she admitted, her voice faltering. Her finger rose almost instinctively, pointing toward the sound of water tumbling over rocks in the distance. "But I'm sure there is game out near where we bathed." The image of the falls came unbidden to her mind—the cool mist against her skin, the earthy scent of moss and water, and the image of Ashur's perfectly formed backside. "And we have a bow and a fully stocked quiver," she added, lifting her chin to regain a semblance of composure.

"And what of the men our prisoners said were sure to come?" Ashur asked, his voice steady but laced with a quiet intensity that sent a ripple of doubt through her. As he tilted his head, strands of disheveled white hair fell forward, catching the light like threads of spun silver. His crystalline blue eyes locked onto hers—not harshly, but with a piercing clarity that made her chest tighten.

"We should not leave the rest to fend for themselves again," he added.

The impact of his words settled heavily around her, like the lingering smoke of an extinguished fire. Reya's breath hitched, and she glanced away, her fingers curling against the fabric of her sleeves. The hum of the wind outside brushed against the shutters, mingling with the distant cries of nightbirds, yet the world seemed stiflingly silent—waiting for her response.

The memory of losing Lily flashed before her, stirring a pang of guilt that twisted in her chest like a dagger. She swallowed hard. Apprehension's sour tang lingered on her tongue. A deep well of determination bubbled up within her, though it wrestled fiercely with her uncertainty. She nodded slowly, her lips parting to speak, but no words came, only the exhalation of her breath.

As if answering for her, a rumble cascaded in from outside, vibrating through the walls of the castle like a distant growl of thunder. Reya's stomach tightened. The sound prickled at her nerves. She traded a confused glance with Ashur, his furrowed brow mirroring the restlessness taking root in her chest.

She crossed to the window, her fingers brushing against the stone of the frame. The scent of dust and dry earth wafted in, mingling with the tang of oily smoke carried on the breeze. Ashur followed silently, his presence steady, but the shadow of his movement unsettling in her peripheral vision.

Together, they gawked at the sight that met them—a line of giant metal insects gliding across the endless stretch of dirt. Their bodies gleamed as the full light of the moon caught on their polished surfaces, casting fragmented beams of eerie light across the barren expanse. They moved with a thunderous growl that reverberated in Reya's chest. The sound swelled and ebbed like the rhythm of crashing waves. Trails of dust billowed up behind them, twisting into the air like ghostly serpents coiling toward the dark sky.

Each machine balanced improbably upright, its two wheels spinning so quickly they blurred into circular shadows. The sight sent a ripple of disquiet through her—*how could such creatures exist in this world?*

The riders perched atop them were cloaked in protective shells and helmets, their silhouettes sharp against the gray horizon. To Reya, they resembled knights from a realm she had never dreamed of, charging through an otherworldly battlefield on monstrous steeds.

"What in the world?" Ashur said, his voice breaking the spell of silence. But his words did nothing to ease the dread pooling in Reya's belly.

Cheers erupted from the prisoners down at the wall, their voices cutting through the layered rumble of the machines. The sound sent a jolt of fear through her, sharp as the snap of a whip. She clenched her jaw, her mind swirling with unrest. First the deadly weapons, now these mechanical beasts—this world was terrifyingly foreign, a defiant shift from the ethereal safety of the fae realm. The bitter truth settled deep within her. There was no escaping how different this place was, and the unknown seemed boundless, like the horizon stretching endlessly before her.

CHAPTER 21

ASHUR'S GAZE FLICKED BETWEEN the spectacle outside and his queen, his heart pounding with a measured but insistent rhythm. The clatter of boots and the jangle of reins from beyond the walls set his teeth on edge. The riders were too many, their presence a smothering weight on his already fraught calculations. From this distance, he could hardly distinguish their faces, let alone trust his power to immobilize them all.

"They can't get in." Reya's blue with lavender speckled eyes scanned his face. Yet the quiver in her tone betrayed her uncertainty, curling in the air like the thin wisps of smoke from the incense that lingered in the room.

"The walls are solid," Ashur replied, straightening his posture. His fingers brushed the stone of the window ledge; its cool surface grounded him momentarily. "I don't think their weapons can carve through rock. And I'm not certain I can neutralize the threat from this distance." He kept his tone even though his words carried a bitter tang of doubt.

The clamor outside waned as the posse halted, their collective rumbling replaced by an unnerving silence that pressed against Ashur's ears. The mountains amplified the quiet, as though the peaks themselves held their breath. From this vantage, he watched the riders dismount, their booted feet sinking into the churned earth. They removed their helmets, revealing faces etched with grim determination, eyes narrowing as they scrutinized the impassable barrier before them. Low murmurs rippled through the group, the words indistinct but charged with tension.

One man raised his hand abruptly, cutting off the scattered discourse. "John?" he called, his voice slicing through the heavy atmosphere like a blade.

The prisoners beyond the walls erupted in cries, their voices hoarse yet fervent, overlapping in desperate pleas for salvation. Their words stabbed at Ashur's concentration, stirring an undercurrent of guilt he refused to acknowledge.

Reya turned to him again, her expression unreadable but her intent clear. "Can you bind them now that they are closer and off their machines?"

"Yes," Ashur said, the word tight, clipped. He pivoted toward the door, his movements stiff but purposeful. "But I'm not sure I can move them inside or create new cells for them." He left without waiting for her response, his boots echoing sharply on the polished stone floors as he descended to the grand hall.

Outside, the sharp bite of the wind stung Ashur's face, carrying with it the acrid scent of damp earth and the copper tang of blood. The prisoners' frantic yells reached a fevered pitch, their voices splintering as they shouted warnings to their comrades.

Ashur crouched low, his fingers splaying against the ground as he reached into the earth with his will. The dirt beneath his palms was gritty and cold, alive with latent energy. "Heed me," he whispered, his voice audible over the trembling in the air. The ground obeyed. It bucked and churned, roots and vines tearing through the soil with feral urgency. The echoes of startled cries rose, the men's fear spilling over like a dam breaking. Screeches rang out as the vines coiled around ankles and wrists, dragging them down with an unrelenting grip.

Sweat beaded on Ashur's brow, mingling with the crimson smear on his temple—a grim reminder of his earlier struggles. The magic siphoned his strength, leaving a hollowness in his chest that gnawed at him. He knew, deep down, that when this was done, it wouldn't just be blood he'd need to recover. It would be time—time he might not have.

CHAPTER 22

REYA WAITED UNTIL EVERY man outside the wall was pinned with thorny vines, the haunting symphony of their groans and the snap of straining foliage finally silenced. Only then did she step through the towering doors of the castle, her boots striking against the flagstones with muted precision. Outside, the air carried the sharp tang of crushed greenery, mingling with a hint of sweat and damp earth.

Ashur sat slumped on the ground, his breathing ragged and uneven. The tremor in his shoulders betrayed the toll his magic had taken on him. Dirt streaked his hands, smeared across his palms like remnants of a battle fought silently and without respite. His face was shadowed, but his jaw remained set with grim determination. The glow of his magic now flickered within his exhausted frame.

Reya kneeled beside him, her fingers tracing across his brow, brushing aside strands of hair damp with sweat. His skin was clammy, but beneath the weariness, there was still that resolute spark she'd come to rely on. She smiled gently, her lips curving to offer him reassurance, though the toll of the moment hung heavily between them. The sickly scent of blood lingered in the air, pungent and undeniable—a reminder that their survival depended on its abundance.

She rose and made her way past the cottages that lined the village path. The others stood in the doorways of their homes, their faces pale and drawn. Eyes followed her progress, wide and wary, as though she were a ghost passing through their lives rather than their queen. Their fear splashed over her like an oppressive wave, thick and suffocating, as it mingled with the cold bite of the mountain air.

Quinn was the only one who met her stride with a contemptuous glare, arms crossed as if his disdain were armor. As she marched past, she felt the sting of his gaze, sharp and deliberate, like the scrape of a blade just shy of drawing blood. It wasn't just arrogance in his eyes—it was a challenge, bitter and unspoken, as if he were searching her face for any crack in her resolve. Reya didn't spare him more than a glance, but the heat of his judgment clung to her like ash in the wind. He always looked at her like that—as though he'd been born with a crown and she'd stolen it from his grasp.

But she kept her spine straight, her expression unreadable. Let him stare. Let him stew. The path forward didn't wait for the approval of men like Quinn.

Behind her, footsteps broke the stillness. She glanced over her shoulder, catching Ashur's gaze. His eyes burned with a brightness that seemed almost unnatural, cutting through the gloom like stars in a midnight sky. She nodded to him, a silent acknowledgment of her gratitude that he'd found the strength to follow her, despite his exhaustion. The steady rhythm of his steps reassured her, even as it echoed in the chilled air.

As she reached the wall, its smooth surface caught the light, glinting like obsidian gold. Reya pressed her palm against it, the texture cool beneath her hand. The wall rumbled deeply, its grinding noise reverberating through her bones as the stones shifted. Beyond the wall, the tangled mess of vines rose like serpents coiled around their prey. At least two dozen men lay pinned, their leather scraped where the thorns had bitten, their faces twisted in varying shades of defiance and fear.

Reya's voice cut through the air like a whip, sharp and commanding. "Who is the leader of this group?" Her gaze swept over the men sprawled on the ground, their bodies tangled in vines that pulsed with Ashur's magic. The rustle of leaves and the occasional groan from the prisoners filled the silence, but Reya's focus remained solid, her presence towering over them like the shadow of the mountain itself.

One man raised his head, his glare slicing through the tension like steel. "Who the fuck are you?" he spat, his voice rough and jagged, carrying an accent that grated against her ears. It was foreign, unfamiliar, yet the meaning was clear enough. Her parents' insistence on mastering the languages of the realms had prepared her for moments like this, though the venom in his tone still struck a nerve.

Reya's lips curled into a calculated expression that masked the simmering anger beneath. "I am Reya Dawn, queen of the fae," she declared, her voice steady and deliberate, each word laced with authority. The title hung in the air, heavy and undeniable, as though the very earth acknowledged her claim. She stepped forward, her boots crunching against the gravel. The man's glare didn't falter, even though a flicker of uncertainty shone in his eyes—a crack in the armor of his defiance.

The wind tugged at her hair, sending strands dancing across her face. With a practiced motion, she flipped it over her shoulder, the gesture as much a display of control as it was practical. Her frigid stare locked onto the man like the frost that clung to the mountain peaks. The air hummed with tension, a taut string ready to snap.

The man's laughter grated against Reya's ears, sharp and mocking, like the screech of metal on stone.

"Queen of the fae, my ass," he sneered, his voice dripping with derision. His dark eyes roved over her, slow and deliberate, the storm behind his gaze crawling across her skin like an unwelcome touch. When his stare returned to her face, it was laced with a smugness that made her fingers twitch with the urge to summon her magic.

"Fae don't exist," he continued, his tone dismissive, as though his words could erase her very being. "So, you can just take those pointy prosthetics off your damned ears and tell me who the hell you are and what sort of hallucinogenic did you use on us?" His breath carried the stench of stale tobacco.

Reya's jaw tightened, but she refused to let his words pierce her composure. Instead, she turned her head; her gaze finding Ashur. The glow of his magic still clung to him, a subtle shimmer that seemed to pulse in time with the tension in the air. "Strip them of their weapons." Her voice cut through the man's bravado like a blade.

"Yes, your majesty," Ashur replied, his tone steady despite the weariness etched into his features. He moved with purpose, his hands deftly tugging metal weapons from their holders. The clink of steel hitting the ground echoed sharply, each thunk a reminder of the threat these men had posed. Ashur's fingers worked methodically, patting each man down with a precision that left no room for error. Knives, daggers, and other concealed devices piled up inside the gate, their gleaming surfaces catching the light.

When Ashur crouched to remove their boots, the men shifted uncomfortably, their protests muted by the vines that bound them. Another half-dozen weapons emerged, hidden in the folds of leather and fabric. Reya's lips pressed together until they nearly disappeared, her eyes narrowing at the sheer audacity of their defiance.

When Ashur finished, he rose and stepped behind her, his presence a steadying force at her right shoulder. An echo of cedar and pine clung to him, calming her racing heart. Reya's gaze returned to the man who had spoken. Her authority pressed down like a storm about to break.

"What is your name?" Reya's voice sliced through the air.

The man before her tightened his lips, his jaw locking into a defiant edge. A ripple of tension seemed to emanate from him, as though the resolve in his stance might harden into steel. Reya's gaze drifted over him, taking in the tight leather encasing his body and his grime-smeared hands.

Her attention shifted to the machines— monstrous, clattering beasts of iron and smoke, their metal carcasses glinting with streaks of soot and oil under the dim light. The tang of gasoline settled in the air, mixing with the earthy smell of disturbed soil. She raised her hand, her focus settling on the closest vehicle, its structure screaming violence and dominance.

The moment she willed it, heat erupted with a furious roar, consuming the mechanical beast. Flames crackled and snapped, their color an angry orange tinged with white-hot intensity. The choking stench of burning fuel and scorched metal clawed at her senses, and the vibrations from the blast reverberated up her legs through the ground.

The bound men scrambled desperately, their muffled cries laced with panic. Their sweat-drenched faces contorted in terror, their eyes brimming with unshed pleas. Their fear hung in the air, thick and suffocating, amplifying the raw energy coursing through her.

"Let my men go before that thing explodes!" the leader's voice shattered the rising chaos, a mix of fury and desperation.

Reya shifted her stance, her fingers dancing in the air as she summoned another force. The ground quivered underfoot, and then a torrent of water surged upward, enveloping the inferno. The blaze hissed in defiance, steam spiraling upward in ghostly plumes, and soon the glowing wreckage cooled to a shimmering black husk.

Silence fell heavy, broken only by the sharp exhale of men catching their breath. The leader's face paled in a mask of disbelief as he stared at the twisted remains of the machine. Damp ash lingered, clinging to the air like a memory refusing to fade.

"I'm Dominic." His voice wavered, rough and uneven, as though it scraped its way up from his throat. His eyes, wide and dark like storm clouds about to break, flicked back to Reya. They lingered on her, filled with a raw mixture of dread and wonder. His gaze darted past her, toward the high stone wall, the spires of the distant castle catching a gleam of moonlight. Finally, his attention returned to her, a flicker of realization dawning.

"Fae?" he whispered, the word carrying the shadows of a thousand whispered legends.

"Yes. We came through the veil because goblins destroyed our world." Reya's voice, low and razor-edged, cut through the tension like a blade. She scowled at the man before her. "And then your people attacked us." She bit back the words that would expose their secret—the twisted blessing that human blood had become to their dwindling magic.

"You are in my domain. I own everything east of the Hudson River." The man jutted his chin forward, the veins in his neck pulsating with defiance. His eyes, sharp but unblinking, held her gaze. The dim torchlight danced off his gaunt face, the shadows playing tricks that made him appear even more skeletal.

Reya unsheathed the knife from her belt with a whisper, the hilt cool and familiar in her grip. She glanced at Ashur, who stood just behind her. His grimace betrayed his weariness, and she could see the pale tinge to his lips—he needed to feed.

"Do you need to refuel?" she asked softly, though the words held no warmth.

Ashur gave a reluctant nod, his jaw tightening.

Without hesitation, Reya flicked her wrist, conjuring a bowl at the man's feet with a burst of heat that made the air shimmer. The magical residue prickled her fingertips as she stepped forward, her boots crunching softly against the grit-strewn ground. The sour tang of fear permeated the air as the man finally faltered. A single bead of sweat traced a path down his temple.

Reya grabbed a fistful of his hair, the follicles greasy between her fingers, and yanked him forward. His gasp was wet and guttural as she forced his neck over the container, stretching it taut. The world seemed to slow as she angled the blade to the pulse beneath his skin. "Now I own everything east of the Hudson," she said, her voice devoid of emotion.

The knife cut clean, the sudden spray of warm blood hitting her hands like a scalding tide. She tightened her grip on his body as he convulsed, holding him firm as the crimson torrent poured into the bowl below. The stench filled her nostrils, thick and cloying, as she watched his life drain away in jerking spasms. Her own heartbeat remained steady, a cold counterpoint to the chaos in front of her.

When the last drop of blood spilled, Reya tossed the lifeless body aside. Its weight hit the ground with a dull thud, like discarded refuse. The silence that followed was suffocating, pressing down on her like a heavy fog. Yet, the air was saturated with the scent of blood and the sharper, almost electric tang of fear radiating from the bound prisoners. Their wide eyes darted between her and Ashur, their terror palpable, a living thing that clawed at her senses.

She turned to Ashur. "Take what you need to create cells and move these prisoners inside them." Her gaze lingered on him for a moment, noting the tremor in his hands and the hollowness in his cheeks. He needed strength, and the prisoners' fear would only fuel his resolve.

CHAPTER 23

ASHUR STARED AT THE bowl, its surface shimmering with the dark, viscous liquid. The acrid, rust-tinged scent reached his nose, sharp and nauseating, but he forced himself to move toward it. His throat tightened as he tipped the edge to his lips, the warmth of the liquid spreading across his tongue like molten iron. *It's just a warm cocktail,* he told himself, trying to suppress the shudder that rippled through him. He relaxed his muscles and swallowed, the vile taste coating his throat and leaving a bitter aftertaste.

As the blood coursed down, a surge of magic flared within him, sharp and electric, like lightning striking his core. His veins burned with the sudden influx, the sensation both invigorating and overwhelming. He handed the bowl to Reya, his fingers trembling from the rush.

"You need more," she said.

"I know," he replied, his voice hoarse. "But I have enough to create the cells. I'll get some more after that is finished." He crouched, the cool dirt centering him as he pressed his palms flat against it. The earth beneath his hands pulsed in response to his touch. Closing his eyes, he envisioned the cells—rows of confinement carved from the very ground, enough to house the two dozen men. The unrest in their stares bore into him, a silent pressure urging him to finish quickly.

The magic within him drained, seeping out like water through a sieve as he channeled it into the earth. Vines and rock twisted and contorted under his influence, the ground groaning in protest as another twenty-four cells erupted from the walls of their oasis. Each cell took a piece of him, the effort leaving his limbs heavy and his breath shallow. By the time the last cell formed, his magic felt like a flickering candle, dangerously close to extinguishing.

He stood, unsteady but determined, and took the bowl from Reya once more. The blood slid down his throat in thick gulps; the warmth spreading through him like a fire reigniting. The magic surged again, filling the void left by his earlier efforts. This time, he directed the vines with precision. They snaked their way toward the cells, dragging the bound prisoners into their new confines.

When the last door slammed shut, he took the bowl for a third time, the strain of exhaustion pressing on him like a leaden cloak. He drank deeply, nearly draining it, the magic flooding his system in a final, desperate rush. He left just enough for Reya, knowing she might need it after her own expenditure. The bowl felt heavier in his hands as he passed it back to her, his body humming with the renewed but fleeting energy.

Before they stepped inside the gate, Ashur's gaze lingered on the towering structure. The rock glimmered in the darkness, calling to him like a beacon on the dark waves of night. Rust and damp earth created an unpleasant tang that clung to his senses. Reya moved with purpose, her boots crunching softly against the gravel as she crossed to one of the machines. The hum of its dormant power reached his ears, a low, almost imperceptible vibration that set his teeth on edge.

"Do you think these would be of use to us?" Reya's voice cut through the stillness, steady and sharp.

Ashur took a deep breath, the cool air filling his lungs. He let it out slowly, his breath visible in the chill. "Like the weapons, we would need one of them to show us how to use them." His voice was calm, but his mind churned with doubt. He met Reya's gaze, her eyes reflecting the glow of the machine's control panel. The thought of their prisoners— broken, terrified—flashed through his mind. They wouldn't be of much help, not after witnessing the brutal end of their leader.

His jaw tightened as a surge of protectiveness flared within him. If someone ever dared to do that to Reya in front of him, he wouldn't hesitate.

He could almost feel the phantom sensation of his fist driving through flesh, the sickening crunch of bone as he imagined ripping the heart from their chest with his bare hands. The thought was visceral, raw, and it burned in his veins like a promise.

CHAPTER 24

SUNLIGHT BURST THROUGH THE bedroom, harsh and unrelenting, making Reya squint and roll away from the window. The golden rays illuminated the room, catching on the dust motes that floated lazily in the air. Her body ached, every muscle protesting from the strain of pushing half a dozen machines inside the gate. The memory of their weight lingered in her arms, a dull throb that refused to fade. Outside the massive walls, only ash and soot remained. The scent of charred metal and burned earth still clung to her senses.

The muffled noise of the prisoners reached her ears, a low, incessant hum that grated against her already frayed nerves. Reya groaned, the sound rasping in her dry throat, and swung her legs over the edge of the bed. The cool floor sent a shiver up her spine as her bare feet touched it. She had drained the bowl last night, the bitter tang of blood still a phantom taste on her tongue, replenishing her magic. But the question gnawed at her—how many more men would have to die to keep their magic alive in this desolate, unforgiving place?

Her chest tightened as a wave of homesickness washed over her. She missed her realm. The vibrant colors of the fruit and flowers that grew in abundance, their sweet, heady fragrance a stark contrast to the sterile, oppressive air here. She missed her parents, their laughter and warmth, the way her mother's hands always smelled faintly of jasmine. Her stomach growled, the hollow ache a reminder of how far she was from the lush feasts of her home.

The stiffness in her muscles was a dull reminder of the endless demands on her. The chill of the stone floor seeped through her bare feet as she shuffled toward the bathroom, her steps heavy with exhaustion. She glanced at the tub, its smooth porcelain surface standing in stark contrast to the rough-hewn walls of her magically created castle. Her chest tightened as a flicker of doubt gnawed at her—had she remembered to include working pipes in her rushed creation? The thought of yet another failure made her throat constrict.

Holding her breath, Reya reached out and turned the handle. The silence that followed was suffocating, each heartbeat a loud drum in her ears—until water burst forth. The cascade of crystal-clear liquid hit the basin with a powerful rush, the sound echoing like a symphony of relief. Her shoulders sagged as the tension drained from her, replaced by the fleeting comfort of one small success.

But the reprieve was short-lived. The moment her fingers dipped into the warm water, her mind erupted with a barrage of unfinished tasks. They had protections now, yes, but the gardens still needed to be created—a daunting effort in this barren realm. Food needed to be hunted. The constant gnawing presence in her stomach needed to be addressed. A prisoner would need to be coerced into explaining the weapons and machines they had confiscated. The imprint of these responsibilities pressed down on her, suffusing the steamy air with an almost oppressive heaviness.

Reya scrubbed her body with methodical precision, but her thoughts remained chaotic, spiraling with everything that demanded her attention. The floral scent of the soap did little to soothe her nerves. Her magic, though replenished from the blood, felt stretched thin, a frayed cord holding her together. She dressed quickly, the coarse fabric of her clothes rubbing against her skin, a sharp contrast to the silken garments of her lost home.

As she faced the doorway to the next grueling day, a lump formed in her throat. This godforsaken realm seemed to devour every ounce of energy and resolve she summoned, leaving her with a hollow ache that no amount of blood or magic could fill.

The moment Reya opened the door, an intoxicating wave of aromas rolled over her like a warm embrace. Smoky roasted meats mingled with the buttery richness of sizzling eggs, and beneath it all was the sweet tang of seared vegetables caramelizing in their juices. Her mouth watered instantly, her tongue pressing against the roof of her mouth as though tasting the air itself. Her stomach clenched with a hunger that no queenly restraint could dismiss, urging her feet to move with a swiftness unbecoming royalty. Her silk slippers whispered against the stone floor as she all but raced toward the source of the tantalizing smells.

Skidding to a halt at the kitchen doorway, she paused, her fingers curling tightly around the doorframe as her eyes darted over the organized chaos before her. The kitchen was alive with movement and sound: the rhythmic chop of knives against wooden boards, the hiss and spit of oil on a hot pan, and the occasional thud of heavy bowls being set onto the counters. Indigo, Opal, and Cypress stood over a robust iron stove, the heat causing a shimmer in the air above it as they expertly tended to crackling strips of meat and golden-edged eggs. The sharp scent of spices tickled her nose, making her nostrils flare.

To the left, Nelly and Rob worked with quiet precision, slicing through ripe oranges and glossy red apples, the fresh, crisp fragrance of the fruits cutting through the heavier smells of the meal. Ivy and Smokey tackled a cascade of greens, their hands slick with moisture as they tossed leaves into a bowl, the scent of basil and mint swirling in the background. The abundance of colors—the deep red of roasted peppers, the lush green of herbs, the sunny yellows of beaten eggs—was nearly as overwhelming as the tantalizing promise of flavors.

Her stomach growled fiercely, a traitorous bellow that reverberated in the room and caught Ashur's attention. He turned to her, his lips curling into an endearing smile that held both mirth and warmth. For a fleeting moment, all she could see was that smile—his shining eyes crinkling at the corners, as if the sight of her alone was enough to brighten his day. A delightful flutter stirred in her abdomen, her earlier hunger momentarily competing with a swarm of butterflies. She drew in a breath, the mingled scents of the kitchen flooding her senses once more as her heart thudded in a rhythm that had little to do with hunger and everything to do with Ashur.

He left his station, the scuff of his boots barely audible over the lively symphony of cooking sounds that filled the kitchen. The room was alive with energy, and Reya noticed the warmth emanating from the stove as Ashur approached. A teasing curl of spices in the air brought to mind faraway feasts and family gatherings.

"It seems the others had the same thoughts as we did about growing food and calling wildlife into our domain here," Ashur said as he crossed the floor, his voice carrying an undercurrent of pride. He glanced over his shoulder, his gaze lingering on the bustling scene behind him. "They may need some blood later, though." The words hung heavy, like the sharp copper tang she imagined would accompany the act, and his smile faded with the tide of the thought. When he turned back to her, his sigh was soft, almost absorbed by the hum of the busy kitchen.

Reya followed his gaze, her own landing on the growing platters of food. The sight was almost overwhelming: piles of roasted meats glistening under golden oil, platters of vibrant fruits, their juices pooling like gems on the porcelain surfaces, and pitchers of deep amber juice that exuded the scent of freshly squeezed citrus.

"Is there enough for the prisoners as well?" Her stomach tightened with a blend of gratitude and awe.

"Yes. Plus, there is clean water and freshly squeezed juice. The others are setting up tables in the grand hall," he added.

Reya's eyes flickered over the scene once more, taking in the sheer magnitude of her people's efforts. She felt humbled, her chest swelling with admiration. Her people had created abundance out of scarcity, each effort a testament to their resilience and innovation.

"Thank you." Her voice was quieter now, tinged with reverence. "Is there anything I can do?"

Ashur offered a small, reassuring smile. "No, Your Highness. Go sit and the food should be out shortly."

For a moment, she hesitated, her fingertips brushing against the wooden frame of the doorway. The energy of the kitchen was intoxicating, the sights, sounds, and smells calling to her senses in a way that was uplifting. With a nod, she turned away, the echoes of their labor following her as she made her way toward the grand hall.

CHAPTER 25

ASHUR STARED AFTER REYA, his gaze lingering on the sway of her hair as she disappeared into the hall. The smile that had briefly graced his lips vanished, replaced by a weight that pressed down on his chest. A cloying tang lingered in the air—a reminder of the blood magic they'd used to survive thus far, and the toll it had already taken. The low hum of voices and the clatter of utensils faded into the background as his mind churned.

They couldn't continue down this path. The lives they'd claimed had been necessary to establish their foothold, but the thought of taking more—even with the justification of survival—left an icy pit in his stomach. It would destroy any chance of peace with the humans, and it would destroy Reya, bit by bit. He could see the shadows creeping into her eyes, and it terrified him more than any enemy lurking in this hostile world.

Ashur forced himself to breathe deeply, drawing in the mingled scents of charred meat, fresh herbs, and citrus. The savory and vibrant smells were almost oppressive now, reminders of the bounty they'd summoned into being—a fragile abundance balanced precariously on blood and magic. His fingers twitched as he rubbed his palms against his pants, trying to dispel the restless energy coiling in his muscles. He needed to talk to Reya, to make her see that there had to be another way. But not now—now, their people needed to eat, and he couldn't bring his burdens into the fragile moment of victory.

"You will never be worthy of a queen."

The words rang out like a blade drawn across stone—grating, deliberate. Ashur's head snapped up, his gaze locking onto the far side of the hall. Quinn leaned against the stone wall, arms crossed, one boot braced with theatrical ease. That ever-present sneer twisted his mouth, as if the very air offended his aristocratic sensibilities. His tone had been light, almost bored, but the venom beneath it coiled like a serpent waiting to strike.

Ashur's jaw tensed so hard it ached. Words pressed against the back of his throat—sharp, scathing things that would have tasted like blood if he had let them loose. But he didn't. Because he was Reya's guard. And guards did not bite, not unless commanded to.

He inhaled slowly through his nose, eyes narrowing. Reya bore herself with strength and command even in exhaustion. Ashur had watched her hold the line while others faltered, speak when silence would have been easier, bleed so that others didn't have to. And while Quinn might cling to some faded idea of pedigree, Ashur had seen firsthand the difference between *title* and *worth.*

He stepped forward just enough to let Quinn see him watching. A warning passed in silence: measured, quiet, unmistakable.

Let the snake slither. So long as it didn't strike, he could live.

But if it did? Ashur would be ready to cut off its head.

Quinn pushed off the wall with casual indifference, his steps unhurried as he sauntered into the hall, not sparing Ashur so much as a glance.

Not worthy. The words clung to the edges of Ashur's mind, echoing through the hollow spaces left behind by duty and silence. He'd tried to shake them, bury them beneath the force of command, the rhythms of routine—but they smoldered there, relentless.

He'd overheard the whispers in the kitchen. The soft murmur of speculation passed like contraband between serving women. They spoke with wide eyes and knowing looks of a possible union—Quinn and Reya. A strategic match, they said. Bloodline to bloodline. Royal to royal. He'd paused outside the archway, unseen, the scent of baked roots and citrus peel heavy in the air, and listened.

He had said nothing. What could he say?

But the thought had struck like a spark in dry kindling. It spread through him, slow at first, then blistering. The image of Quinn standing at Reya's side—handsome, smirking, entitled—gnawed at something raw inside him. He could imagine the crown on Quinn's brow, the smug curve of his lips as he drank in the power that came with it. And Reya... how would she look beside him? Distant? Diminished?

Ashur clenched his jaw, the muscles ticking beneath his skin. He wasn't a man who let emotion cloud his thoughts, but this—this was different. It wasn't jealousy, he told himself. It was protection. It was loyalty. It was knowing that Quinn wasn't the kind of man who'd bleed for the people the way Reya already had.

Still, the fire in his chest burned hotter than he'd ever admit. And in its heat, he wondered: what made someone truly worthy of a queen?

He shook the thoughts from his head and turned back to the bustling kitchen. The clang of metal against stone rang out sharply as Rob handed him a heavy platter laden with roasted meats glistening under a sheen of oil. Ashur's muscles strained as he adjusted his grip, the warmth of the food seeping through the plate and into his hands. Steam wafted up toward his face, carrying the sharp aroma of pepper and the sweetness of caramelized onions. The chaos of the kitchen pressed in around him, with voices calling out instructions and plates sliding across counters. He navigated through the frenzy, dodging Ivy as she darted past with a bowl of greens and Nelly, who was lugging a pitcher of juice almost too heavy for her.

Ashur stepped into the grand hall, his boots scuffing against the polished stone floor. The tables were being arranged with almost reverent care; long wooden slabs adorned with simple cloths were coming to life under the hands of the workers. Bowls of fruit added pops of color, their glossy skins gleaming under the glow of the enchanted lights that hung above. The grand hall felt different now—not hollow and forbidding, but warm, almost welcoming. The echo of footsteps as workers moved to and fro was softened by the steady hum of preparation.

Placing the platter carefully on the center table, Ashur looked around and caught sight of Reya across the hall. She stood near the far wall, her back to him, gazing at the stained-glass window that refracted shards of color across her figure. Her posture seemed relaxed, but he noted the subtle tension in the way her fingers curled into her palms.

Ashur made his way toward her, his footsteps heavy against the floor.

"Stop following her around like a lost puppy."

Ashur stiffened at the jab, his spine locking into place as Quinn brushed past him with all the subtlety of a dagger slipping between ribs. The words struck harder than they should have—soft in tone, but barbed with intention. Ashur didn't turn, didn't bite, though his fists curled at his sides. Quinn's voice carried that easy, taunting lilt he used when he knew the blade would land just beneath the armor. And it had.

The hall smelled of citrus and warm bread—comforting, familiar—but even that was soured now by the bitterness rising in Ashur's throat. He stared at the space where Quinn had been, jaw clenched against a dozen things he wanted to say and couldn't.

He told himself it didn't matter. That Reya's judgment was her own, that his loyalty wasn't defined by who noticed it. But it gnawed at him, that the man with the sharp tongue and royal blood could stand at her side, untested and unworthy, while he—who had shed blood for her, with her—was left in the shadow of decorum.

Still, he didn't move. He wouldn't give Quinn the satisfaction.

Ashur inhaled slowly, forcing the noise in his mind to settle. There would be time to speak to Reya—privately, honestly. To show her that a crown didn't have to demand sacrifice without purpose. That leadership could be forged not just in power, but in compassion.

But as he watched Quinn saunter toward her, all arrogant stride and polished ease, Ashur's pulse ticked faster, like the warning beat of war drums in his chest.

This wouldn't be a conversation.

It would be a reckoning.

CHAPTER 26

REYA FINISHED HER MEAL and leaned back in her chair, her fingertips idly tracing the smooth curve of the armrest as she surveyed the grand hall. The candlelight glinted off the polished stone walls, casting flickering shadows that danced like silent sentries. Yet her skin still crawled, a prickling anxiety blooming just beneath the surface where Quinn's presence had brushed too close. He'd delivered word that the meal was served with that same oily smile he always wore around her—less courtesy, more challenge.

Throughout the feast, she'd felt the pierce of his gaze, heavy and insolent, like fingers brushing where they had no right. His leer hadn't left her face, even as he bowed with exaggerated deference. He'd lingered behind her chair longer than necessary, close enough for her to catch the scent of his breath—wine-laced and sour. She'd kept her posture still and composed, forcing herself to ignore the way her instincts recoiled.

The rest of her people were winding down now, their laughter and low conversation weaving a warm blanket over the hall. But Reya heard the edge beneath it—the exhaustion, the cautious hope stitched into every chuckle. Plates and goblets sat half-empty on the long tables, the remains of fruits and glistening meats forming a vibrant collage that belied how close they'd come to losing it all. The tang of basil and citrus still lingered in the air, tangled with the comforting weight of smoke and roast.

Her gaze drifted down the table, taking stock of her people's full bellies and relaxed shoulders, and a quiet satisfaction settled in her chest. At least they had enough—this time.

Her thoughts turned almost reluctantly to the prisoners. Mercy, she knew, should not feel like surrender. There was enough food left to offer them some. But the act, though necessary, would be seen as softness. And softness, Quinn had once told her in that low, condescending tone, would break a leader faster than steel.

Her jaw tensed.

She would offer the food. Not because Quinn doubted her strength—but because she knew exactly where her strength lay. It wasn't in spectacle or sharpness of tongue. It was in the quiet, deliberate choices that forced others to question their convictions. And this would be one of them.

"Your Majesty, what should we do with the men outside?" Opal's voice, gentle as a harp string, cut cleanly through the din of clinking silver and fading laughter.

Reya turned her gaze to the fae across from her, watching as Opal delicately dabbed at her lips with a linen napkin, composure wrapped tightly around her like silk. The question hung in the air, sticky with implications. Reya could already feel Quinn's eyes on her from the side— the sharp twitch in his jaw, the slight shift of his boot on the stone floor.

She straightened. "Perhaps we should bring them in here to eat and then have peace discussions."

The room stilled. Surprise crackled in the silence—Ashur's brows shooting up, a fork clattering against a pewter plate, mouths parted mid-chew. Even the hearth fire seemed to hesitate.

And then, predictably, Quinn spoke.

"They are prisoners," he said, his voice low but edged like a blade poorly sheathed. "Feeding them here—at *this* table—will be seen as appeasement. Weakness."

Reya didn't look at him. "It will be seen as strategy."

"They will take advantage of your mercy."

"They may," she allowed, her tone deceptively calm. "But if peace is even a distant possibility, I will not let pride starve it at the door."

Quinn stepped forward, just enough to breach the invisible border she'd set with her silence. "You risk too much."

Reya turned her eyes to him then, cool and unflinching. "No, Quinn. You fear too much."

He held her gaze a moment longer than was proper. Long enough for the others to notice. Long enough to register the pull of history between them. But in the end, he inclined his head—just enough to count as a concession, and just hollow enough to burn.

"Reset the table." Reya's voice rang with finality. "And I will return with whoever is the new leader."

As she rose, the legs of her chair whispered against stone, and the mumbles that followed weren't just of surprise—they were of uncertainty. Of tension. Of a fragile balance shifting.

And Reya welcomed it.

As she stepped out of the grand hall, the echo of her boots on the stone floor seemed louder than before. The air beyond the warmth of the feast carried a distant chill that wrapped around her arms like a whisper. She glanced over her shoulder at the sound of measured footfalls behind her. Ashur approached, his figure tall and steadfast against the dimly lit corridor.

"I will accompany you." His tone left no room for protest.

Reya raised an eyebrow, her steps deliberate as she faced forward again. "No need," she replied, her voice calm but sharp enough to convey authority.

"It is my job to protect you, Your Highness," Ashur insisted, his hand falling to the hilt of the sword at his side. The clink of metal resonated softly, an audible promise of his duty.

Reya exhaled quietly, her pace steady as they continued down the corridor and out the castle gate. The morning dew glistened under the bright sunshine as they passed the cottages, heading toward the cells lining the stone walls. Long shadows stretched and curled as though mimicking the uncertainties in her mind. The air grew heavier as they neared the cells, carrying a hint of dampness that tugged at her senses.

Ashur walked at her side, his presence a shadow, and Reya couldn't help but notice the way his footsteps fell in perfect rhythm with hers—steady, determined, unshakable.

The prisoners stirred at her approach, their weary faces barely illuminated in the darkness of their small, cavernous cells. Reya paused and clasped her hands behind her back as she let her gaze sweep the dimly lit prisons.

"Who among you is the new leader?" she asked, her tone carrying an authority that demanded respect despite its measured softness. She waited as the silence stretched, punctuated only by the quiet breaths of the prisoners, until finally, a man halfway down the line of cells claimed leadership. Reya's gaze narrowed, and she moved in front of the man who had spoken.

The prisoner before her was striking in a way that demanded attention, even in the dim light of the cells. His dark hair, tousled with dirt and grit, framed sharp features that seemed hewn from stone. Her gaze lingered on the curve of his jaw, the smudges of grime accentuating the strength in its lines. The leather jacket hanging loosely from his shoulders bore the marks of wear—scratches and creases that hinted at battles fought and survived. Beneath it, his tight shirt clung to every defined muscle; the fabric strained as he crossed his arms. The stench of earth and sweat mingled with the stale air around him. His eyes—vivid as a green kaleidoscope—held an unsettling depth, their cautious flicker capturing every movement as she studied him.

"Your name?" Reya's voice cut through the silence.

"Malek," he replied, his tone smooth yet guarded. "And yours?"

"Reya," she answered, inclining her head in acknowledgment before shifting her gaze to Ashur. The rustle of fabric accompanied her turn, and her fingers brushed against the rough texture of her clothing.

"Open his cell," she commanded. Her words, though calm, carried the echo of inevitability.

Beside her, Ashur's jaw tightened visibly, the muscle pulsing under his skin. The soft ring of metal followed as he unsheathed his sword, its polished edge catching the torchlight. The air thickened, charged with tension, as Ashur waved his hand. The thorny vines that curled around the cell dissipated, their sharp, menacing edges wilting into nothingness.

Malek remained motionless, his posture rigid with defiance. "I rather like my neck in one piece," he muttered, his voice tinged with dry humor as his wary gaze flicked to Ashur's blade.

"We are not here to kill you. Come." Reya's words were clipped, dismissive, as she pivoted on her heel. The hem of her dress whispered against the ground as she strode toward the castle without waiting to see if either man followed.

The echo of Ashur's boots against the earth reached her ears. She glanced over her shoulder to see him moving steadily behind their prisoner.

"You attempt to harm my queen, and I will relieve you of your head," Ashur warned, his voice low and laced with menace.

Reya didn't bother to look back, her tone cool but unwavering as she replied. "He won't harm me." Her confidence rang through the air, leaving no room for doubt.

The delicious scent of baked bread and herbs wafted toward her as they approached the grand hall, the warmth of it curling under her nose and tugging at buried memories of simpler seasons. It mingled with the richer aromas of roasted meat and spiced fruits—the perfume of survival and abundance layered in the air. Reya pushed open the great doors, the echo of iron hinges creaking as if in an announcement. Her gaze swept across the hall.

The once-disordered chamber now buzzed with quiet purpose—her people moved briskly between the tables, arms laden with platters and polished goblets, the clatter of crockery underscored by hushed voices. There was a kind of reverence to it. A need to obey her command, yes, but also a fragile hope clinging to the act.

She scanned the room once, twice.

Quinn was nowhere to be found.

The knot in her shoulders loosened, not fully, but enough to breathe without feeling his scrutiny pressing into her spine. Without him lurking at the edge of her vision, the hall felt lighter—her will unshadowed. Her jaw unclenched before she even noticed it had been tight.

The air, though rich with spice and smoke, felt a little clearer.

She strode forward and reclaimed her seat, the carved wood smooth against her palms. Turning her attention to the prisoner, she nodded toward the chair opposite her, its seat surrounded by the bounty of food. Malek hesitated, his eyes widening as they swept over the platters of succulent meats, colorful fruits, and freshly poured drinks. He moved cautiously, sinking into the chair as though testing its solidity, his gaze darting to Ashur, who loomed behind him like a silent sentinel, sword still firmly in hand.

"Eat." A thread of impatience tugged at the edge of her words.

Malek arched a brow, the corner of his mouth lifting into a sardonic half-smile. "How do I know it's not poisoned?" he asked, his tone a careful balance of suspicion and swagger, as if daring her to confirm his worst fears.

Reya exhaled slowly and pinched the bridge of her nose. The rich scent of roasted meat and citrus clung to the air, but it did little to dull the throb forming behind her eyes. She didn't have the patience for this—posturing and bravado, as if they weren't both wading through the ash of broken trust.

"If I wanted you dead," she said, her tone flat and unflinching, "I would've done it in front of the others."

Her words cut through the hum of the grand hall like a blade drawn too fast. The sound of movement ceased. With one look from her and the remaining fae quietly filed out, their silence as deliberate as their retreat. It left her alone in the grand hall with Ashur and Malek. The negotiations ahead laid bare—no witnesses, no distractions.

Just truth. However bloody it needed to be.

The growl of his stomach reached her ears, a sound that seemed almost louder in the quiet pause that had settled over the room.

"I can hear your stomach growling. Eat." She dropped her hand, the cool air brushing against her skin as she fixed her gaze on the man across from her.

Her eyes narrowed as she studied him, noting the way his green, kaleidoscope-like eyes flickered with a mix of wariness and curiosity. He scanned the food, his gaze darting over the platters piled high with roasted meats, vibrant fruits that seemed to glow under the enchanted lights, and golden-edged eggs that exuded a buttery aroma. The clink of his plate against the table broke the silence as he reached forward, his movements cautious at first, then growing more urgent as he loaded his plate with an assortment of food.

He picked up his glass, the shimmer of the juice catching the light. He sniffed it tentatively, his nostrils flaring as he tested the scent—a blend of sweet oranges and tart lemons. The tension in his shoulders seemed to ease as he took a sip, his lips pressing against the rim of the glass. His eyes closed briefly, the lines of his face softening as if savoring the taste. For a moment, the guarded edge in his demeanor faded, replaced by something almost vulnerable.

"Where did all this come from?" he asked, and his eyes slowly opened.

Reya did not answer his question, her silence deliberate as she leaned back in her chair. Her gaze remained steady, unwavering, as she observed him—waiting, calculating, and silently asserting her control over the moment.

"I don't remember this castle or the wall being here." Malek waved his fork in a lazy circle, the metal catching the flicker of torchlight as it cut through the air. His movements were casual, almost dismissive, as he stabbed another piece of meat and shoved it into his mouth.

"That's because we created it after we were attacked by your men." Reya's tone was calm, yet an edge lingered beneath it, a coolness that matched the chill in her veins as she recalled the brutality of the attack.

Malek's eyelids fluttered briefly as his gaze fell to the table laden with food. The glossy sheen of roasted meats, the vivid hues of fresh fruits, and the warm golden crusts of bread seemed to captivate him, his expression shifting from indifference to something resembling hunger—or envy. "If you had all this, I understand why our men attacked." He gestured with his fork toward the bounty spread before him.

Reya's lips tightened, her chest constricting as she recalled the struggle it had taken to summon such abundance. "We did not have that either," she countered, her voice steady but laced with subtle frustration.

Malek's movements slowed, the scrape of his silverware against the plate halting as he set them down. His fingers rested lightly against the table, and his gaze sharpened. "What exactly are you?"

"Fae," Reya replied simply.

Malek's brows furrowed, his green kaleidoscope-like eyes narrowing as he studied her face. "Fae can create things out of nothing?" His voice cracked, the question sinking into the static that bristled between them.

Reya let out a wry smile. She raised her gaze to Ashur, who stood unwavering behind Malek. Then she met Malek's searching eyes.

"No," she explained, her words carrying a quiet pride. "We call on different factions of nature to bend to our will. We don't create from nothing."

"Oh," Malek muttered, his voice just an octave above a whisper. Slowly, his hand moved, his fingers curling around the knife on the table. He glanced down at it, his thumb brushing the edge of the blade as if testing its sharpness. The torchlight overhead cast shadows across his face, darkening the intensity in his narrowed gaze.

Reya's eyes remained fixed on him, her senses prickling with suspicion as she caught the subtle shift in his posture—the way his shoulders tensed and his grip firmed on the knife.

Without warning, Malek flicked his wrist. The knife shot toward her, spinning through the air with lethal precision. Reya turned instinctively, her heart jolting at the sight of the gleaming blade, but the sharp metal sunk into the flesh of her arm before she could fully evade it. Pain flared, searing and immediate, as her breath caught in her throat.

She hissed, the sound escaping her lips involuntarily, but her hand shot up, stopping Ashur from springing into action. His blade had already been raised, his expression twisted in fury, his eyes blazing with the promise of retribution.

"No," Reya commanded firmly, her voice cutting through the charged air. Her fingers pressed against her arm. Warm blood trickled over her skin and stained the fabric of her sleeve. She met Malek's narrowed gaze, her own steady despite the sting of pain.

The room vibrated with animosity. Every breath, every shadow held the tension of the moment. Reya did not waver. Instead, she held Malek's gaze. Her eyes dared him to speak, dared him to act again.

Reya gripped the knife, her fingers curling tightly around the hilt. The sting of pain radiated from her arm, hot and pulsing, as she yanked the blade free. She swallowed the pain without letting so much as a wince show on her face as she kept her gaze trained on Malek. She set the knife on the table with a deliberate clink. The sound cut through the tense silence like a blade itself. Her gaze locked onto Malek, her eyes unwavering and sharp as steel.

"Try that again," she said, her voice low and edged with menace, "and I will not stop Ashur from cutting your head off."

Malek swallowed hard, the movement of his throat visible as he lowered his gaze to the table. The defiance in his posture seemed to crumble, replaced by a flicker of nervousness that Reya didn't miss.

She pressed a napkin against her wound. The fabric soaked up the warm blood seeping from the gash. The sting was sharp, but she ignored it, her focus entirely on the man before her.

"We have a problem," she continued, her tone steady but carrying the pulse of truth. "We need human blood to sustain our magic. And from the way you devoured the food on your plate, you seem to need what we can provide."

Her words hung in the air as she adjusted the napkin against her arm. The rustle of fabric was drowned out by the tension that thrummed between them.

"While we have the power to just take what we need, that puts us at odds. And as you have seen, that could mean the slaughter of your kind right out of existence."

Malek's gaze shot up to hers, his green eyes narrowing as his jaw clenched. The muscles in his face tightened, his expression hardening into something unreadable. Reya held his gaze, her own steady and unflinching, as her words settled over them both like a storm cloud.

"You slaughtered my men like pigs." His words fell from between clenched teeth, each syllable sharp and cutting.

"Your men drew first blood. We were entitled to defend ourselves." Reya's voice was cold steel, slicing through the room. The heat of her anger simmered beneath her skin, a wildfire barely contained. "And I made an example out of those who led the charge. War is messy, and loss is inevitable." The hematic flavor of blood seemed to linger in her memory, a phantom taste that made her jaw tighten.

"You know nothing of loss." His sneer was a dagger aimed at her pride, his anger radiating off him like a furnace.

Reya rose from her chair. The scrape of its legs against the stone floor echoed through the hall. Fury flamed in her chest, a searing heat that made her vision sharpen. She waved at the table, and it slid across the room with a deafening crash, the sound of splintering wood echoing like a war drum. Plates clattered, food smeared against the wall, the scent of roasted meat mingling with the tang of spilled wine.

She stalked across the distance, her boots striking the floor with a rhythm that matched the pounding of her heart. Grabbing his shirt, she yanked him to his feet, the fabric rough against her fingers. "You know nothing about me." Her tone was a deadly whisper, a storm gathering strength. She saw the flicker of fear in Malek's widened eyes, a crack in his defiance.

"You are not old enough to know what war is." He growled in her face, his breath hot and sour. His hand wrapped around her throat, the pressure a fleeting threat before he hissed and yanked it away. His fingers reddened as if scorched. A drift of singed flesh hung in the air.

"I know more about slaughter and near extinction than you'll ever understand." Her voice was a low growl, vibrating with her stormy memories. "And if you think fae are bad, you have not seen the worst of what lies beyond this realm." She shoved him back, her palms tingling with the force of the push. He collapsed into the chair, the wood creaking under his weight.

Reya stood over him, her shadow casting him in darkness. Her glare was a blade poised to strike. "If you insist on being insolent, I will slaughter you and everyone else who takes the same stance until I find someone wise enough to negotiate with me." Her words hung in the air like the final toll of a bell.

"More of our forces will come." His growling voice carried every drop of defiance he held in his stance.

Reya smiled, a sharp, cold curve of her lips. Her gaze flicked to Ashur, standing tall and silent behind this rebel scum, his hand resting lightly on the hilt of his sword. The glint of steel caught the light, a quiet promise of violence.

"Let them," she hissed, her voice dripping with venom as she stepped back. Her anger unfurled inside her, a coiled serpent ready to strike. It burned hot and wild, threatening to consume her. "And since you don't seem willing to have a civil conversation, none of your men will get to eat in this civilized setting." The words tasted bitter on her tongue, but she relished the way they made the rebel's jaw tighten.

Her eyes moved to Ashur, who met her gaze with a slight nod. "Take him back to the cell."

"Yes, Your Highness," Ashur replied, his tone steady and respectful, though his eyes flickered with a hint of disenchantment.

Reya turned on her heel, the hem of her dress sweeping the floor as she stormed out of the grand hall. The heavy doors groaned in protest as they swung shut behind her, the sound echoing like a final judgment. Her boots struck the stone floor with a sharp rhythm, each step a release of the fury that threatened to overwhelm her.

The air in the corridor was cool, but it did little to soothe the fire raging within her. Her chest tightened, as if her grief and anger were pressing down on her ribs, threatening to crack them open. She had not had a moment to grieve—for her family, for the life they had all left behind. The pressure inside her was building, a storm gathering strength, and she knew she was nearing the flash point.

CHAPTER 27

ASHUR PRESSED THE TIP of his sword to Malek's back, feeling the slight give of muscle beneath the rebel's leather jacket. "Get up," he snarled, his voice low and guttural, vibrating with controlled menace.

Malek shifted, trying to arch away from the blade, but Ashur followed his movement, pressing the steel harder into his flesh. The resistance of the leather gave way, and Ashur smiled as he heard the sharp intake of breath and the hiss of pain when the blade bit into skin, just enough to draw blood. The scent of iron filled the air—a reminder of Ashur's promise of violence.

"I will gladly run you through with this sword if you attempt to try anything." His deliberate words were laced with venom. "And I'll bring your fucking head to my queen as a gift. Understand?" The heat of his anger coiled tightly in his gut, fueling his resolve as Malek grunted in response. Ashur noted the flicker of resentment in the rebel's gaze but dismissed it as inconsequential. Malek was prey in this hunt.

"Now move," he ordered, his tone sharp enough to cut through any lingering defiance.

As he marched Malek back to his cell, Ashur kept a deliberate pace, his boots crunching against the dirt path. The cottages lining the way seemed eerily silent, their occupants watching from behind shuttered windows. He recreated the thorny bars over the cell, the magic sparking in his palm and leaving a fleeting tingle on his skin as the prison reformed. The rebel scum glared at him, but Ashur met his gaze with an icy stare, one that promised unrelenting punishment for any misstep.

Ashur ascended the path toward the castle. The scent of smoke mingled with the morning dew. He stopped in the great hall, where the remnants of Reya's fury lingered. The fae who had hidden in the kitchen now emerged, cleaning up the debris with quick, efficient movements. The air smelled of spilled wine and charred skin, the tension still palpable.

"Bring the food to the prisoners. But no silverware or anything that can be used as a weapon against us." Ashur's authoritative voice was edged with exhaustion. He received nods in response, the rustle of cloth and clinking of plates echoing in the cavernous space.

He ducked out of the hall, his focus shifting to Reya. His responsibilities pressed against his shoulders as he headed toward her room. Her wound troubled him; the image of the blood streaking her arm surfaced in his mind, unshakable. He didn't know if she could heal herself the way she had healed his gunshot wound. Magic could be fickle that way, and since they did not have a true healer in their midst, it was a valid concern that had him moving faster through the hallways.

The air grew colder as he approached. The castle stone whispered its ancient chill.

Drops of blood marred the floor, each crimson smear stark against the cold gray surface. Ashur's boots echoed softly as he moved through the castle, the rhythmic sound doing little to drown out the pounding of his heart. Her door wasn't shut all the way, the gap revealing a sliver of her quarters. His pulse quickened, and a sharp jolt in his chest that left him breathless for a moment.

He didn't bother knocking. The urgency clawing at him demanded action, not decorum. Stepping into her room, the air shifted—warmer, tinged with the scent of lavender and the lingering tang of blood. Reya lay face down on her bed, her figure trembling so violently that the bed itself shuddered beneath her.

"Your Highness?" His voice was steady, but inside, alarms screamed, a cacophony of fear and concern that made his throat tighten. He closed the distance between them, his boots shuffling on stone with each cautious step.

Her body stiffened at his words, the tension radiating from her like a taut bowstring ready to snap. She didn't look up, but her muffled voice reached him, shaky and raw. "Go away."

Ashur hesitated. Her grief pressed against him like a physical force. He crouched, his movements deliberate and slow, as if she might bolt at any moment. "I need to check your cut," he said softly, his tone gentle, almost coaxing. Her trembling form made his chest ache with a sharp pang of helplessness that he rarely allowed himself to feel.

She finally turned her head toward him, the movement slow and hesitant, like she carried the constant challenges of this world in her neck. Her cheeks glistened, streaked with the trails of her tears, catching the flickering light from the candles in the room. When her shining eyes met his, a sharp twist sunk into Ashur's chest, as though her grief had pierced the armor he had so carefully constructed. Another tear escaped, sliding down her face and landing on the bedspread—a dark stain marking the fabric.

"They're all gone," she whispered, her voice breaking like glass underfoot. "My parents, my cousins, my friends." She sniffled, the sound raw and jagged, scraping at the silence between them.

Ashur swallowed hard, the gesture audible in the room's stillness. "Mine, too," he admitted, his tone subdued, restrained. He hadn't allowed himself to grieve—not for his parents, nor the brothers he had trained with, nor the friends who had drunk with him at the local pub. That grief was locked away behind the walls he had built inside his mind. But now those walls trembled, the sorrow knocking relentlessly against them, a slow but insistent force that threatened to break through.

The pressure in his chest was unbearable, a weight that pressed against his ribs and made each breath labored. He clenched his fists, the skin over his knuckles stretching white as his fingers tightened. The room carried Reya's lavender scent, a soothing trace that had no power here—not against the storm brewing just beneath his calm exterior. Ashur's gaze flickered back to Reya, her trembling form a mirror to his own buried anguish.

He took another breath to hold the pain back just a little longer. At some point, he knew it would catch up with him. When it did, it would be a torrent—a flood that would drown him, just as it was drowning Reya. But for now, he had to stay strong. He had to keep those walls standing, even as the cracks formed and widened with every shared whisper of loss.

Ashur forced his gaze away from her tear-streaked face and onto her arm, his stomach twisting at the sight. Blood soaked her sleeve, the fabric saturated with deep crimson, the scent thick in the air. His pulse quickened, a sharp, instinctive rush of alarm crawling up his throat like bile. He didn't waste time on gentleness—there was no room for hesitation.

He sat heavily on the edge of the bed. The mattress dipped under his weight as he seized her arm. The fabric resisted for half a second before tearing under his grip; the sleeve coming away in a jagged shred. "Damn it, Reya," he muttered, the frustration in his voice masking his underlying fear.

Her skin was sticky with blood, the wound an angry gash that wept fresh rivulets down to her wrist. Ashur cursed under his breath, yanking off his shirt, the material damp with sweat and warmth from his own body. He gripped the hem, fingers stiff with tension, and tore a strip off the bottom. The sound of ripping fabric was sharp in the quiet space, a harsh contrast to the softness of her trembling form.

Ashur kept his eyes on the torn skin rather than her face, wrapping the crude bandage just above the gash. He pulled it tight, hands moving with the muscle memory of someone who'd done this too many times—even so, a tremor betrayed him. The tension knotted deep in his forearms, like something coiled and waiting. He tied it off, firm and efficient, but the blood—her blood—seeping through the cloth made his jaw tighten. Too much, too fast.

"Can you heal it?" he asked, finally daring to meet her eyes.

She shook her head. "Not without more blood, and I'm not killing another human unless I have to."

His voice held steady. "Do you have a needle and thread?"

When he looked up again, her eyes locked with his. Wide. Glassy. No longer wet with tears, but emptied—as if the sheer momentum of what they'd endured had driven the grief underground, where it waited, quiet and burning.

She just stared at him, mouth slightly parted, as though words had abandoned her entirely.

"Did Lily have a sewing kit?" he asked again, his voice quieter this time. He held her gaze, watching as she blinked sluggishly, processing his words. A beat of silence stretched between them, thick with implicit weight.

Slowly, Reya lifted her hand and pointed toward a small bag in the corner.

CHAPTER 28

R EYA STUDIED ASHUR AS he crossed the dimly lit room, his silhouette shifting against the firelight's flickering dance. The warmth of the flames cast golden edges along his frame, sharpening the lines of his shoulders, the taut muscles flexing beneath his tattered shirt as he bent over Lily's bag. The soft rustle of fabric and the muted clink of metal against glass filled the silence, each sound punctuated by the steady cadence of his breath.

She shouldn't have been watching him like this. But there was something about the quiet confidence in his movements, the fluid precision of his hands as he rifled through the supplies, that pinned her attention in place. Even the sensual scent of him—cedar and pine mixed with a fresh ocean breeze, along with something darker, something uniquely his—mingled with the charred air and stirred a heat beneath her ribs.

Her arm throbbed, a reminder of why he was searching in the first place. Blood trickled sluggishly down her skin, warm and insistent, the iron tang thickening in her throat. She exhaled slowly, but the motion did little to steady her pulse.

Ashur straightened, a vial of salve and a needle in hand, and turned toward her. His gaze locked onto hers, unreadable, but something in his expression sent heat curling low in her stomach.

"We shouldn't have given that bandit a weapon," he said, his voice a low rasp against the hush of the room.

She didn't argue. She didn't trust herself to.

And when he kneeled before her and took her arm into his calloused grip, warmth spread from his touch like wildfire—deliberate, inescapable

The lingering scent of dried herbs and cooked meat clung to Ashur's skin as he leaned closer, threading the needle with practiced fingers. Reya's breath hitched—not from the sting of the thread piercing her torn flesh, but from the way his calloused fingertips brushed her arm, careful, precise. She clenched her jaw, forcing herself to stare at the flickering lantern on the table, rather than the storm in his eyes.

The needle bit into her skin, sharp and sudden. A tremor jolted up her spine, but she swallowed it, refusing to let the pain steal her control. The world blurred at its edges—heat from the fire stoked the room, thick with warmth, mixing with the iron tang of her blood. A drop slid down her forearm, slow and deliberate, as if savoring its own escape.

"Hold still," Ashur said, his voice like velvet over stone.

Her pulse quickened at his nearness, at the steady rhythm of his breath brushing against her cheek, almost like a secret meant only for her. The low timbre of his voice curled around her like smoke, filling the breathless pause aching to be crossed between them.

He tied the last stitch with a deft flick, fingers lingering longer than necessary. Silence weighed between them, heavy as an unshed truth.

She should have moved. Should have pulled away.

Instead, she leaned in.

A mistake. One she didn't care to correct.

The scrape of his knuckles against her jaw sent sparks skittering down her spine. His gaze darkened, flickering to her lips, hesitation warring against a command they both refused to acknowledge. Then, before reason could tear them apart, he was kissing her—firm, restrained, yet unraveling all the same.

And gods help her. She kissed him back.

CHAPTER 29

ASHUR PULLED AWAY, HIS breath shallow, pulse hammering against his ribs like a caged animal. The warmth of Reya's lips still lingered—phantom fire against his own, burning, demanding. He blinked his eyes open, but the world felt unsteady, as though gravity itself had shifted beneath his feet.

Heat surged up his neck, flooding his cheeks with something dangerously close to vulnerability. He tore his gaze from hers, but the sight of her—lips parted, breath uneven, eyes searching his face with something he dared not name—held him like a vice.

"I'm sorry," he said, voice rough as stone. He forced himself upright, his muscles stiff with the shimmer of undeclared words.

"Why are you sorry?"

Her voice was quiet, but it curled around him, pulling at the edges of his resolve. He swallowed hard.

"You're a queen, and I'm just a gardener."

The words tasted bitter. He had spoken them before, hadn't he? Used them like a shield, a reminder of the chasm between them. But after that kiss—after the way she had pressed into him, after the way he had let himself fall into her—those words felt more hollow than ever.

Reya's brow rose, and something flickered in her expression—something fierce, something unwavering.

"You are my protector."

The certainty in her voice struck like an arrow to the chest. He scoffed, but the sound lacked its usual bite.

"I did a piss-poor job of that in the grand hall."

The memory scraped against his mind—one instant their prisoner was eating and the next a knife sailed at his queen, the moment he had failed to anticipate before the blade had torn through her skin. His grip tightened at his sides, fingers curling as if he could still feel the blood slipping between them.

And yet, as he looked at her now—alive, defiant, too close and still too far—he knew the wound that truly unsettled him wasn't the one on her arm.

It was the one carved into him, with the way she had kissed him back.

Ashur's breath was shallow, his pulse loud in his ears—a steady drumbeat against the quiet tension between them. He lowered his gaze to the stone floor, but the rough texture did little to anchor him, did nothing to quell the fire still burning beneath his skin. His lips tingled, haunted by the memory of hers against his.

"Still. I should not have taken the liberty." His voice was gravel, scraping against the heavy air.

Reya stood with arms crossed, the set of her shoulders immovable, like stone carved by will alone. "Do you see any other available men, Ashur?"

The question landed like a strike, sharper than he expected. Ashur made himself meet her gaze. Those eyes—azure and blazing with challenge—dared him to flinch. But he didn't. Not outwardly. Inwardly, he felt the slow churn of heat in his chest, equal parts frustration and something dangerously close to yearning.

"Anyone who perhaps is fit to stand beside a queen?"

She wasn't asking a question. She was testing.

His jaw twitched as the words escaped, more reflex than thought. "Quinn is available."

The bitterness in his voice surprised even him. It curled around his name like poison.

Reya threw her head back and laughed—a rich, cutting sound that echoed louder than it should've. "Quinn is not fit to rule over anyone."

Ashur didn't laugh. He couldn't. He watched her—the way she burned so fiercely she didn't seem to notice she'd scorched him in the process. She wanted a partner who could stand beside a queen. What she didn't see—what he wasn't sure he could say—was that he already had been, in every silent way that counted.

She waved toward the prisoners; the torchlight casting restless shadows across the cold stone walls. "Am I to choose one of those men to meet my needs?"

The word *needs* pressed against something deep in him—something dangerous.

Her voice softened, yet held steady. "You are strong and handsome, and I do not know what to do with these butterflies in my stomach that flutter when you are around me."

His brow rose, his mouth parting, words failing him. The breath of space between them was thick—charged, alive.

"I'm sure you've felt them before, My Queen."

She cut him off without hesitation. "No. This buzzing energy is new and just as foreign as this land."

Ashur swallowed, watching as she wiped her face with her clean hand, frustration flickering across her features.

"I noticed you on the grounds back home," she continued, voice quieter now, more raw. "But I never approached because my parents had other designs for my future. If I had, these butterflies would have bloomed and doomed us both."

Ashur remained still. He had noticed her, of course—more than once. The way she carried herself, the way her presence shifted the very atmosphere around her. But noticing her had been a dangerous thing, and so he had pretended he hadn't.

"There were others who were supposed to come through the portal with us. Including the one my father attempted to arrange my future with. But they never made it to the castle."

The thought of her being bound to another struck like flint against stone, sparking something hot and unwelcome in his chest. His jaw tightened.

"So, I'm a consolation prize?" The words were sharp, edged with something closer to pain than he would admit.

Reya didn't hesitate. She stepped forward, and the distance between them—already too thin—became suffocating.

"No." Her voice was steady, sure. "You're what my heart desires."

Ashur inhaled sharply, her words unraveling something carefully locked away. She wasn't supposed to say things like that. She wasn't supposed to look at him like that.

Her fingers hovered near his, barely a breath apart. And he knew—if she reached for him, he would not pull away.

Would not stop himself this time.

Would not let reason win.

And maybe, for once, he wouldn't want it to.

CHAPTER 30

THE RUMBLING STORM THEY had encountered the night before drifted through the window, but this was no mere whisper of passing winds. The growl of engines rolled in low and steady, a warning more than an arrival. The vibration hummed beneath her boots, threading through the stone, shaking loose the moment still hanging between her and Ashur.

Reya swallowed hard, the bitter taste of unfinished words settling against her tongue. The warmth of their previous exchange—dangerous, delicate—had already faded, replaced by the cold bite of reality. His guarded look lingered, but she tore her gaze from him, refusing to drown in what could not be answered now.

Crossing to the window, she pressed her fingertips against the jagged frame, the stone cool beneath her touch. Riders approached. Their shadows stretched long beneath the pale, unforgiving sky. The chill in the air did little to mute the acrid scent of fuel and sweat carried by the wind.

Dread crawled up her spine, prickling like icy needles beneath her skin. She inhaled deeply, tasting the dampness of the coming storm—not rain, but blood.

"We will need another sacrifice," she said, her voice steadier than she felt.

The number had doubled. Twice as many men. Twice the threat. Some rode on two-wheel cycles, but others arrived in hulking vehicles—metal beasts, armored and faceless, their covered frames concealing whatever horrors lay inside.

Her fingers curled against the windowsill.

Behind her, Ashur shifted, his presence as solid as the surrounding walls, yet somehow farther away than before.

The words they had spoken minutes ago still hovered, unresolved. The flicker of something dangerous, something she had never dared to name before, had cracked open between them. But now, with the rumble of approaching enemies and the sharp edge of duty slicing through whatever had bloomed, the possibility of continuing that conversation slipped through her grasp.

She clenched her jaw.

Later. If there were a later.

Outside, the engines roared, closing in.

Reya wiped her eyes, the dampness of her skin cooling too quickly against the chill in the air. She marched out of the room, each step sharp and precise, her pulse drumming beneath the surface like an unrelenting war cry. Ashur's presence ghosted behind her—silent, steady—but even his quiet strength did little to quell the tightening in her chest.

The fae emerged from the castle's shadow, their movements as silent and swift as breath. They fell into formation behind her—not by command, but by instinct. Their presence pressed against her back like a mantle of windless power: quiet, expectant, poised for action. She could feel their loyalty humming just beneath the surface, waiting for a single word.

"Kill every one of these pests," Quinn snarled, his voice slicing through the charged air as his gaze swept over the prisoners like a blade.

Reya didn't turn. She didn't need to. A single glare, sharp as steel, cut him off before more poison could spill from his mouth. The silence that followed rang louder than any shout.

But even as she held the moment, her sharp gaze flicked across the gathering. A few of the fae had gravitated toward Quinn—subtle, but undeniable. Most had aligned behind Ashur, as though an invisible line had been drawn between them. A fracture forming. Or perhaps already there.

The division was veiled, but Reya felt it in her bones. And it tightened something in her chest—not fear, exactly. Awareness.

The prisoners had finished the food they had been given, and now they sat in stiff, uneasy silence. Some shifted, their eyes dashing between her and the growing numbers around them, the fear in their expressions sharpening with every breath. The scent of stale bread and damp stone lingered, blending with the distinct bite of blood still soaked into the ground from previous sacrifices.

Reya picked up the bowl, its rough clay edges biting into her palm. The uneven weight of it sent a familiar sensation coursing through her—duty, necessity, inevitability. She strode toward the row of prisoners, the earth beneath her boots firm.

"Don't do this!" Malek's voice ripped through the thick air, the raw edge of desperation threading through every syllable.

She barely flinched.

Stopping before the last cell nearest the entry, she turned, fixing her gaze on the prisoner trembling in the corner, his breath coming in uneven gasps. The scent of fear rolled off him in waves—sweat, grime, and the unmistakable sting of impending death.

"Pull him out, Ashur."

Her command cracked across the stone like a blade, sharp and unarguable.

The prisoner began blubbering, his words garbled pleas, his hands clawing at the walls as if he could force himself into the stone, escape the fate already closing around him.

Ashur crouched, pressing his hands to the ground. The gnarled spikes melted away, retreating like living things responding to his will. Vines slithered forward, coiling around the prisoner, dragging him from his futile refuge, pulling him to his knees over the bowl Reya placed on the ground.

His whimpers turned to choked sobs.

Then, one swift slice.

Blood splattered into the clay pot, thick and vivid, pooling in dark ribbons as the vines held the man's spasming body still. His sputtering turned to gurgling, then to nothing at all, his lifeblood spilling out in a slow, steady rhythm until the final drop fell.

The vines moved again, curling like serpents as they dragged the lifeless body into the soil, swallowing him whole, erasing the last trace of his existence.

Silence settled over the assembled men, heavier than the humid air, thick with the scent of sacrifice.

And beneath it all, the rumbling approached, deep and unrelenting.

The thick, iron-laced sludge burned against her tongue as she forced the first swallow down, its warmth curling through her insides like fire clawing through dry wood. The taste was bitter, earthy, heavy with power that coiled deep in her gut, threatening to empty her breakfast in retaliation. She suppressed a shudder, forcing herself to drink, to let the strength embed itself into her bones. The blood was thick, viscous, sticking to the roof of her mouth like an offering she couldn't refuse.

When she gave the bowl to Ashur, her fingers trembled—but not from fear. The energy surged through her veins, thrumming like a second heartbeat, pushing against the limits of her flesh. She exhaled slowly, steadying herself, though the intensity of her people's gazes pressed against her skin like judgment given form.

Their frowns were brief, flickers of distaste beneath their obedience. Even so, each of them drank. Their expressions shifted—uncertainty replaced by resolve, disgust overshadowed by necessity. When the bowl returned to her, she drained nearly all of it, the warmth pooling in her belly, thickening, settling into something dark and undeniable.

She met Ashur's eyes as she handed him the last mouthful. He knew as well as she did that hesitation had no place here.

Reya pressed her palms flat against the surface of the wall, the cold stone biting into her flesh as she willed the barrier to turn translucent. Not open. Not this time. The last thing she would do was invite death inside. The forces beyond the wall had bullets, and she would not spill more of her people's blood than necessary.

The hum of magic answered her call, pulsing beneath her fingertips, rippling outward. The wall shimmered, revealing the shifting mass of bodies beyond—the approaching horde, their weapons gleaming beneath the gray light.

She pulled her knife, the bulk of it familiar in her grip, cold but steady.

"Bring me Malek."

The vines responded before Ashur did, writhing, twisting, the earth itself shifting as the ground vibrated—not just from the engines creeping closer, but from something deeper, something more primal.

Malek's sharp cry cut through the air as Ashur seized his arm, dragging him forward with little ceremony. The rebel leader's boots scraped against the dirt, his breath ragged, frantic, but Ashur's vines were faster—coiling, binding, forcing him onto his knees before his people.

The moment hung heavy, thick with expectation. Reya stepped behind him, pressing the blade to his throat.

The horde slowed.

Their leader kneeled before them, powerless, contained.

For the first time since the storm had begun, silence reigned

CHAPTER 31

REYA SCANNED THE GROUP as they shut off their machines, the hum of power fading into an eerie silence. The sharp scent of oil and metal hung in the air, merging with the sweat of too many bodies packed into too small a space. Shadows flickered against the wall as they gathered on the other side, the sheer number of people sending a sharp pulse of intimidation through her—an instinctual recognition of how easily they could overwhelm her if they somehow got through their walls. Yet, beneath that trepidation, another truth settled: their sheer numbers meant an immense well of power lay at her people's disposal.

Malek trembled in her grip, the frantic rise and fall of his chest, each breath shallow and quick, jerking on her hold of his hair. He was afraid, but he wasn't dead—at least, not yet. His life was hers to spare or to take, depending on the next move of the people outside.

A man, just as tall and built as Malek, stepped forward, his jaw clenched tight, muscles rippling beneath his jacket. His mouth moved, but only muffled sound reached her, drowned beneath the fortification of the wall as heavy stillness pressed against her ears.

Reya glanced over her shoulder, the gravity of the moment thrumming against her skin, and zeroed in on one woman.

"Jamie, you have air magic. Can you amplify the sound?"

"Yes, Your Highness." Jamie closed her eyes, and the atmosphere shifted—like the air itself had taken a breath, coiling and expanding. A sudden gust swept across Reya's face, cool and sharp, carrying the distant scent of damp earth.

"What did you say?" Reya asked, and her voice spilled outward, layered with magic, twisting through the air like a tangible force.

"Where's Dominic?" the man repeated, his gaze locking onto Malek with something feral.

"Dead," Malek answered, his voice rough, torn with exhaustion.

The man wiped his face with a slow, deliberate hand, leaving behind streaks of dirt and sweat. Then his eyes lifted, burning with fury as they settled on Reya.

"Let my men go," he growled, low and venomous. "And I will allow you to serve as my personal slave."

"For fuck's sake, Vander," Malek snarled, the curse dripping with disbelief.

"What?" Vander snapped, his head whipping toward Malek on his knees. His arm jerked upward—a single motion, sharp and commanding.

A metallic click echoed as every person in the crowd outside drew their weapons, the sound striking like a blade against stone.

Reya tasted the tension in the air—thick, electric, like the charged atmosphere before a storm.

"Put your guns away," Malek ordered, his voice tight, strained. "I am in command, not Vander."

"It looks like you're compromised, my friend." Vander smiled as if he had aspirations of ascending into the leader spot.

Reya let a slow, calculated smile touch her lips, tilting her head. "I suggest you surrender," she said, the words curling around the space like a whispered promise. "Because the more magic we use, the more blood will be spilled."

The sunlight caught on the sharp angles of Vander's face, making the sweat on his brow glisten like oil. His grip on power wavered—she could feel it in the way he hesitated, his stance no longer firm but subtly uncertain. The air was thick with the stench of machine grease, mingling with the bite of blood. Beneath it all, something more primal lingered—the unmistakable stench of fear.

Tension pressed against her skin, humming beneath the surface like the gathering of a storm. Every breath she took tasted of iron and heat, her lungs tightening as if drawing in the fire of impending violence. Magic pooled in her veins, restless, aching to be unleashed.

Vander's sneer faltered for just a fraction of a second, but it was enough. A crack in his confidence. A weakness.

"Magic isn't real," he muttered, though there was no strength in the claim.

Malek laughed, the sound dark and curling with amusement. "Yeah. About that."

Jamie shifted beside Reya, the movement slight but charged with power. The air vibrated, subtle at first, then growing—a sharp, unseen force that pressed outward. A low gust curled past Reya's cheek, lifting strands of her hair and pulling at the hem of her dress. The wind carried whispers—stray murmurs of breath, drawn from the atmosphere itself.

"Would you like a demonstration?" Reya asked, the words soaked in venom.

Jamie raised a hand, fingers trembling, and the change came fast. The still air twisted, forming a pulse—a ripple of power that shuddered through the space, reaching Vander's men first. Their coats billowed, boots skidding over the dust-covered earth.

One man cursed, stumbling back as if he had felt something invisible shove at his chest.

"Tricks," Vander hissed, forcing himself to remain unmoved.

Reya exhaled, slow and deliberate. She let the magic curl through her fingers, invisible yet undeniable, a whisper of energy skimming along her skin. The moment held, taut and seething.

"You're going to want to lower your weapons," she advised, her voice cold and sure. "Because we haven't even begun."

Vander swallowed, his jaw clenching. The hesitation was stronger now, creeping into his posture, into his fingers that twitched near his gun. He glanced around, eyes darting from Malek to Jamie, to the crowd behind him.

Something deeper rumbled beneath them—a shift in the ground, faint but threatening. A warning. Reya didn't have to look to know the earth magic users were preparing their own retaliation.

"You think you can intimidate me?" Vander spat, but his voice lacked its earlier edge.

Reya merely tilted her head. "No," she said, her smile curling at the edges. "I think I can end this before you even blink."

The sun sliced through the sky, glinting off metal in sharp, blinding flashes. A deafening boom shattered the silence—a rupture of sound so violent it seemed to fracture the air itself. A split second later, a rush of displaced wind howled past her ears, carrying the scent of burning fuel and scorched dust. The projectile tore through space, its trajectory precise, merciless, speeding straight toward Reya.

Instinct gripped her, coiling like a steel wire along her spine. She braced, feet planted firm, the air vibrating with tension as Ashur, Rob, and Ivy dropped to their knees, their hands pressing hard against the earth. The ground pulsed beneath her, an almost sentient force responding to their magic.

Malek's bellow ripped through the chaos, raw and desperate.

The missile struck the wall. The explosion was instant—a detonation that split the air apart. Heat punched through her, a burning wave that should have obliterated stone, flesh, and bone. But instead, Raye screamed as she and others fortified the walls. Her body absorbed the energy like a conduit, taking it in, drinking its force. It seared through her bloodstream, igniting something primal, something unstoppable. The magic threaded itself into her muscles, rattling her bones with its violent charge.

Her gaze snapped to the crowd beyond the gate, their wide-eyed expressions reflecting the flickering light from the dying flames still licking the untouched wall. Open-mouthed and rigid, they stood frozen. Fear pressed down on them like a suffocating force. Their uncertainty thickened the air, palpable as the scent of sweat and scorched metal curled into her lungs.

Fury surged within her, molten, relentless—a living thing clawing to be unleashed.

Without hesitation, she nicked the side of Malek's throat. The blade whispered against his skin, slicing a thin, deliberate line—not deep enough to kill, but precise enough to remind him that control was hers alone. A crimson bead welled at the wound before spilling down the curve of his neck, trailing hot against his skin. The scent of fresh blood bloomed, filling her senses with something primal.

She leaned in, her breath mingling with his, the pulse beneath his skin fluttering like a trapped bird. With a slow, deliberate movement, she pressed her tongue to the streak of red, the copper tang sharp against her taste buds. Magic rushed in, cool at first, then feverish, streaking through her veins, replenishing what had been drained. Strength coiled tighter, wrapping around her muscles, sharpening her vision. The hunger remained—insatiable, unrelenting—but for now, she had enough.

She shoved Malek away, unconcerned that his hands were bound behind him. He tumbled face first onto the ground with a grunt. She ignored him, her focus shifting to the battlefield beyond.

The heat of magic still churned beneath her skin, eager, restless. She crouched, pressing both palms to the ground, fingers splaying wide against the dirt and fractured stone. Fire rose within her, coiling through her arms, licking at her fingertips before she sent it outward—a pulse of blistering energy.

Beyond the walls, metal groaned. The earth trembled beneath her hands, alive with change. Metal buckled, weapons sagged, barrels twisted, all melting into liquid ruin. Molten steel seeped into the ground, absorbed into the hungry soil, leaving nothing but the pungent scent of burning iron.

The crowd gasped—a symphony of horror and disbelief.

Reya rose to her full height, rolling her shoulders back as she surveyed their faces. Their fear fed her. Their shock empowered her.

She cocked her head, her voice steady, unrushed. "I offered Malek a deal at breakfast this morning," she announced, letting the words stretch, letting them sink in. "But he attacked me instead of choosing peace."

Silence followed, thick and suffocating.

Let them understand, she thought. *Let them see what happens when they defy me.*

Reya threw her hands into the air, fingers splayed wide, the motion sharp and commanding. A tremor pulsed through her veins, her dwindling magic grasping for one last surge of strength. The ground rumbled beneath her feet—deep, guttural, as if the earth itself was groaning under the weight of her command.

The molten metal buried in the soil shivered, then convulsed upward in jagged streams. Liquid fire twisted and stretched, dragging itself free from the earth, its glow pulsing a sickly gold before hardening into a shimmering wall. The scent of scorched iron thickened the air, acrid and suffocating, burning the inside of her throat as she gasped for breath.

Heat rolled off the barrier, waves of energy licking at her exposed skin. Sparks cracked and hissed along its surface, lightning-like veins spreading through the cooling metal as it solidified, forming an impenetrable blockade surrounding the rebels. Malek's men and women reeled back, some stumbling, hands flying up as if the sheer force of the magic could scorch them without touch.

A sharp pain lanced through Reya's skull, white-hot and blinding. Her body recoiled, muscles locking in protest, magic clawing at the fringe of her consciousness. Exhaustion slammed into her—heavy, merciless, tearing into her limbs like stone shackles. Her knees nearly buckled, her vision swimming, black creeping in at the edges.

The last of her magic burned out, leaving her hollow, spent, and the world tilted.

CHAPTER 32

ASHUR STEPPED FORWARD, THE earth beneath his boots uneven, still trembling from the remnants of Reya's magic. She swayed, her body betraying the depletion of energy, her skin too pale, her breathing too shallow. The raw edges of exhaustion clung to her like a second skin.

"Get me the bowl," he ordered Jamie, his voice sharp, commanding.

"Not Malek," Reya whispered, the words barely a thread of sound. "We need him to broker peace."

He nodded once, then called upon his magic. The air thickened, humming with unseen force as the ground obeyed. Vines writhed, twisting up from the earth like grasping fingers. They lashed forward, coiling around another prisoner—a man whose breaths came in short, panicked bursts. His limbs spasmed against their grip, futile, desperate, the scent of fear rolling off him in waves.

Jamie handed him the bowl, the ceramic cool in his palms, slick with condensation from the humid air. Without hesitation, Ashur unsheathed his blade. The steel gleamed under the bright sunlight, a cruel, uncompromising edge.

He didn't pause.

The knife sliced cleanly. The sound dampened beneath the rush of blood that poured into the waiting bowl. The prisoner's body sagged, the last of his strength unraveling as his life drained away. Warmth spread across Ashur's hands, sticky, thick, coating his fingers as the scent of copper flooded his senses.

The vines obeyed his second command, dragging the lifeless body into the earth. The soil parted, swallowing flesh and bone in one seamless motion, leaving nothing behind but an indentation in the dirt.

Ashur turned back to Reya, lifting the bowl toward her. The blood shimmered darkly, the surface still rippling.

"Drink what you need." Exhaustion tightened his throat. "We'll share what's left."

He gestured toward Rob and Jamie, knowing they were just as drained—just as battered—as he felt. The magic had taken its toll, leaving behind an ache deep in his core, a weariness that clung to his limbs like iron chains.

But there was no time for weakness.

Not in front of their prisoners.

Reya took the bowl from Ashur's hands, her fingers steady despite the tremor still lingering in her muscles. The blood glistened darkly, thick and warm, pooling at the edges as she raised it to her lips. The moment stretched—silent, weighted—until she drank.

Magic responded instantly, latching onto the life within the blood, threading through her veins like liquid fire. She inhaled sharply, her pupils dilating, her shoulders rolling back as strength coiled through her limbs, restoring the energy that had nearly abandoned her. The exhaustion didn't vanish, but it loosened its grip, allowing her to straighten fully.

Ashur exhaled, the tension in his chest easing. He reached for the bowl next, fingers curling around the slick surface. The scent of iron was heavy, clinging to his skin, sharp against his senses. He ignored the discomfort, tilting the glass to his lips. The warmth settled in his throat before unraveling through his body—slow, creeping, like roots winding deep into the earth.

Jamie and Rob took their turns, both drained but steady. Ashur watched as the blood worked through them, reviving their depleted magic, restoring the energy they'd burned in the fight. The tension in the air shifted—not gone, but different. Calculated.

Outside the barrier, Malek's people watched in stunned silence, still caged behind melted, reformed metal.

Ashur wiped his mouth, dropping the empty bowl to the ground. His gaze flicked to Reya. She looked stronger now, but he knew how close she had been to collapsing. The cost of power was always steep.

"What now?" Jamie asked, her voice quiet, hesitant.

Ashur glanced at Malek, still lying on his side on the ground, staring at them with menace in his gaze, blood drying on his skin.

Reya met Ashur's gaze, her smile slow and deliberate, the kind that held an edge of quiet triumph. The sunlight caught on the sharp lines of her face, making her eyes gleam like embers beneath a dying flame. Her voice was low, controlled. "Now," she said, stepping forward, "we decide how much peace is worth."

The stench of smoldering metal lingered in the air, curling into Ashur's lungs like a ghost of the explosion that never was. The ground beneath his boots still quaked, a reminder of the chaos that Reya had effortlessly snuffed out.

"Bring him back to the castle and keep him bound this time." Her words were clipped, final, already distancing herself from the nullified threat outside. She turned, the swirl of wind tugging at the hem of her dress as she strode toward the castle.

Ashur exhaled slowly, tightening his grip on Malek's collar before yanking him upright. The man carried tension in his limbs, announcing his defiance. Ashur felt it like a coiled wire, resisting him with every step. He hauled Malek forward, his footsteps heavy against the uneven stone, the rhythmic crunch filling the silence Reya had left in her wake.

"She stopped that explosion," Malek said, as if Ashur were interested in conversing with him. His voice carried a rough edge, hoarse from whatever fight he had put up before witnessing his forces captured so easily.

Ashur's silence was deliberate, a shield against the fatigue settling deep in his bones. His grip on Malek remained firm, fingers digging into the fabric of the rebel's coat, rough and worn with the dirt of battle. He barely glanced at the man beside him, his gaze locked on the silhouette of the castle ahead—its jagged edges carving into the light like a gash torn through the sky. A whisper of wind carried the scent of charred wood and blood, remnants of the earlier destruction lingering in the crisp air.

"How?" Malek's voice grated, raw from shouting, defiance still woven into the cracks of his tone.

Ashur didn't waste breath on unnecessary words. "Magic." His voice was a quiet thing, steady, unshaken. "We fortified the wall with it."

He reached out, pressing his palm against the heavy wooden door, feeling the cool grain beneath his fingers as he shoved it open. The hinges groaned, protesting his force, and the sharp scent of fire and ash hit him full on. Inside, the grand hall loomed with its vaulted ceilings and flickering shadows. Reya stood still in the center, her attention drawn to the fireplace, where embers pulsed like dying stars in a sea of darkness.

She turned, slow and deliberate, her gaze sweeping over Malek with the precision of a blade. "Are you willing to strike a peace treaty with us?" Her arms folded, a measured pose that belied the venom in her eyes.

Malek shifted beside him, licking his lips as if words might slip easier that way. His nod was hesitant, reluctant.

Reya pursed her lips.

"Say the words," Ashur commanded, his grip tightening, pushing against muscle and bone until Malek sucked in a sharp breath.

"I agree to your terms," Malek growled, his pride fraying at the edges.

Reya laughed, the sound curling in the air like smoke. Ashur nearly smiled himself—there was a fire in her eyes that set something sparking in him, something that made the corners of his mouth twitch. She was shrewder than he had given her credit for.

The conversation took a darker turn as Reya stepped closer and the tempest of survival settled between them. Ashur felt the heat of Malek's resistance in the way his muscles tensed beneath his grip. The rebel leader flinched when Ashur's fingers dug in again, a subtle reminder of who held control here.

It was a moment suspended in tension, the air thick with the scent of burned wood, sweat, and iron. The hall's quiet swallowed every breath, leaving only the flicker of embers and the quiet crackle of decisions being made—some that would shape the fate of them all.

"And in exchange for not slaughtering you like the pigs you are, I require three blood slaves per fae."

The tension in the room thickened, pressing against Ashur's skin like damp heat before a storm. Reya's words carved through the air with merciless precision, each syllable landing like the sharp edge of a blade. The scent of charred wood lingered, mingling with the sour tang of blood—a reminder that the battlefield was never far, even within these walls.

Malek's reaction was immediate. His eyes narrowed, the dark irises hard as stone beneath the flickering torchlight. His lips thinned, pressed into a tight line as if sealing away the venom he was desperate to spit. Ashur felt the slight shift of his muscles, the barely restrained tension coiling under his skin. It was a familiar thing—the instinct to lash out, to resist, even when the ground beneath him had already given way.

Ashur let amusement curl at the edges of his mouth, his gaze flicking between Malek and Reya like a spectator enjoying a brutal match. The rebel leader's defiance, though admirable in its own foolish way, was pointless. The terms had been laid before him, and no amount of indignation would change them.

The unrest living in the moment pressed into Ashur's chest, not with disquiet, but something darker—something that made the edges of his smile sharpen. The air was thick with power. The reality settled in Malek's bones as well. No matter how much he struggled, the game had already been decided.

"Three blood slaves per fae at all times. They will live within the walls and serve their masters at will. We will require blood and in exchange, we will provide housing and food to those here."

"And what of my people outside your walls?"

"You may rotate the three blood slaves every full moon, but the moment you come up short, we will slaughter you."

Ashur could not suppress his grin any longer and had to turn away so Malek would not see the admiration painted on his face.

Malek balked.

"I am willing to set up trade negotiations for exchanges of goods, but that will only come once we have the people inside our walls."

"You are one crazy lady," Malek snarled.

She narrowed her eyes. "And you will be my worker for a year."

Heat coiled through Ashur's veins, thick and smoldering, like embers fanned by the wind. The very thought of Malek in Reya's presence sent a bitter taste pooling at the back of his throat—a mix of iron and rage. His jaw tightened, muscles straining with the effort to hold his tongue, to resist the primal urge to bare his teeth in warning.

The dim torchlight sputtered against the stone walls, casting elongated shadows that danced like specters around them. The air was heavy with the raw aroma of stone kissed by moisture and the tang of dried blood. Ashur's fingers twitched at his sides, aching for the hilt of his weapon, for something solid to tether his fury before it burned too bright.

"Fuck you."

Malek's words echoed, sharp and biting, but Ashur barely heard them through the rush of his own pulse, loud as a war drum in his ears. His gaze cut to Reya, standing unwavering, her expression cool, unreadable. But Ashur saw past that—saw the coiled tension in the set of her shoulders, the unwavering command in her posture. She was fire in human form, and gods help anyone who thought they could extinguish her.

Was this what admiration felt like? To ache with devotion and simmer with rage all at once? Ashur forced a breath through his nostrils, slow, measured, but it did little to douse the inferno raging beneath his skin. Malek had no idea what he'd agreed to. And Ashur would make sure he never forgot it.

Reya looked directly at Ashur and said, "Kill them all and collect their blood."

Shock ricocheted through Ashur like a blade dragged across a raw nerve. His breath hitched, heartbeat hammering against his ribs as though demanding escape. He barely heard the words— only the sharp, authoritative edge in Reya's command. Her will pressed against him, tightening his muscles, guiding his limbs into motion before thought could catch up.

"Wait." Malek's sudden movement sent a ripple through the charged air, his boots scraping roughly against the stone as he backpedaled, eyes wide with desperate calculation.

The scent of sweat and iron filled Ashur's senses, a visceral reminder of how precarious this moment was. He halted, muscles coiled tight, instinct screaming to act, but years of discipline kept him still.

He turned to his queen, but the current between them crackled with something colder— something undeniable. Malek's words reached him through the thick tension, each syllable laced with stalling desperation, but Ashur had no pity to spare. Instead, he studied Reya, the unwavering fire in her eyes, the way she tilted her chin—a quiet mastery over the room, over the fate of everyone in it.

"If I'm not leading them, they may not follow through on the deal," Malek stalled.

"If you are not here to keep your people in line, there very well might be bloodshed inside the walls, too." Reya crossed her arms.

Malek snarled, frustration thick in his voice, and Ashur felt the reverberation in his own chest like a growl waiting to be loosed. The air pressed heavier, oppressive with the scent of leather, dust, and implied threats.

"If any of my people are harmed. I will consider the deal forfeited," Reya relentlessly continued.

When Malek's final "Fine" slipped past gritted teeth, Ashur exhaled, slow and steady, feeling the room shift with the decision.

Reya had him. Ashur had seen enough battles to know when the victor had already been crowned.

"And I will not accept children as blood donors," Reya added.

The air in the chamber felt heavier as Reya's words settled over them, the finality of her decree pressing down like the weight of a closing gate. Ashur had been coiled tight, every sinew strung taut beneath his clothing, but at her last condition, something inside him loosened. His pulse, once thundering, found a steadier rhythm.

Malek's expression shifted, the hard lines around his eyes softening as if Reya's words had chipped away at something brittle within him. His brows lifted, surprise flickering like a hesitant flame, and Ashur could almost feel the shift— could almost taste the quiet resignation in the air, as palpable as the iron tang of blood lingering in his throat.

Ashur exhaled through his nose, the scent of aged wood and candle smoke filling his lungs as he recalibrated. The terms were fair—calculated, yes, but fair. His fingers curled at his sides. The phantom sensation of a sword hilt pressing against his palm calmed him. While he had been prepared to carry out Reya's orders no matter how ruthless, the alternative had threatened to scrape away at something raw beneath his skin.

He studied Malek, the slow nod, the way his posture lost some of its rigid defiance. The man had felt it too—the inevitability; the surrender wrapped in uneasy acceptance. Ashur let the tension bleed from his muscles, but his gaze remained sharp, watching Malek with the same wariness a predator affords a wounded animal.

The game had changed. Reya had made her move. And now they would all have to play by her rules.

CHAPTER 33

REYA'S VOICE CUT THROUGH the charged air, firm and unwavering. "Release him," she said to Ashur.

Ashur's lips pressed together, tension coiling in his jaw as he inhaled through his nose, the scent of iron and damp earth mingling in the fracture held between them. His gaze flicked toward Malek, assessing, deciding. Then, with a measured wave of his hand, the bindings unraveled, the thorny restraints dissolved into nothing.

Reya's eyes tracked the movement, lingering on Malek's forearms, where angry red indentations marred his skin. The wounds glistened, beads of blood welling at the surface before slipping in slow rivulets toward his wrists. The scent curled into her lungs, dark and heady, igniting an ache in the pit of her stomach. She swallowed against it, steadying herself, forcing her focus back to the matter at hand.

She dragged her gaze up to his and inhaled, steadying the sudden need for blood before she waved at the door. "You should inform your people of the agreement."

Malek extended his arm, the motion deliberate, taunting. "Did you need a boost?" His voice dripped with sarcasm, the edges of his words curling like smoke around her.

Reya's stomach tightened, a slow knot of heat pooling low as she locked eyes with him. The mockery sharpened his gaze, daring, testing. The coppery scent of blood brushed against her senses, an invisible tether pulling her closer, fraying her control.

She narrowed her eyes, forcing the hunger back, willing steadiness into her limbs. "We will need to work out how we get your blood." Her voice was a blade honed smooth. "Slitting your throat doesn't seem like the best course of action. At least not if we intend the donor to live."

Her words hung between them, thick as the tension lacing the air.

Malek's jaw muscle ticked—a tight, rhythmic pulse beneath his skin—before he gave Reya a curt nod. His eyes were sharp, ice-bound, holding whatever storm churned beneath the surface at bay.

She gestured toward the door with a casual flick of her fingers. "After you."

The scent of scorched stone and damp earth clung to the castle walls as Malek stormed out, Ashur moving like a shadow at his side. Reya followed, her footsteps gliding over worn flagstones. The cool air rushed against her skin like a sigh of relief. As she passed through the cottages, she lifted her hand, the energy humming in her veins. Magic crackled at her fingertips, an almost imperceptible vibration in the air before new walls unfolded into existence— smooth wooden beams stretching and settling with a low creak. The freshly formed rooms exhaled a scent of warm cedar and untouched linen.

Gasps broke the quiet as the fae stared at their transformed homes. Their eyes widened with wonder. Their breathless awe tangible enough to give the air an edge. Reya let their astonishment brush against her, feeding into the undercurrent of tension that already rippled through the day.

Next, she turned to the cells. Another flick of her fingers, and the tangled vines evaporated in a whisper of dust. The prisoners blinked against the sudden openness, the daylight spilling in where only confinement had existed moments before. Yet none of them moved. They stood rigid, the scent of rain-soaked mineral air mixing with the sharp tang of fear, their gazes flickering to the edges of the enclosure, as if the walls themselves could snap shut at any moment.

The air thickened, waiting—for a choice, for defiance, for surrender

Malek cleared his throat, the rough scrape of it breaking the brittle silence. He glanced at Reya, his gaze heavy with unvoiced questions.

Reya turned to Jamie, catching the slight nod—a confirmation.

"Yes." Nerves curled in her stomach.

Malek stepped forward, his presence filling the space as he addressed those outside. His words carried through the charged air. "Citizens of Lincoln. We have been given an opportunity to join this encampment and have a chance to enjoy good food and warm beds." His voice rolled outward, beyond the confines of the enclosure, threading into the air like a lure.

He turned his gaze to Reya again, the sunshine catching the tense line of his jaw. "How many of you are there?" His words were hushed, keeping from Jamie's broadcast, but the question still cut through the stretch between them like a blade.

"Twenty-five," she answered, the number tasting stark in her mouth, a measurement of bodies, of survival.

Malek nodded, though the tightness in his posture didn't ease. "But that offer is only for seventy-five of us, and it rotates monthly."

A breath of silence stretched taut. Then—

"What's the catch?" Vander's voice lashed out, sharp against the cold metal of his enclosure. The iron bars hummed, absorbing his frustration, his mistrust.

"The catch is those who take this offer become blood donors to the fae." The words landed with a quiet finality, sinking into the gathered bodies. A ripple of sound followed—a low, uneasy rumbling through the ranks, voices rising like distant thunder.

Vander sneered, stepping closer to the gate, his fingers curling around the bars. "You saw how well that worked out for Stewart." His voice was laced with warning, with something dark, something irreparable.

Malek squared his shoulders, exhaling slow and deliberate before speaking again. His voice cut through the whispers. "This would be akin to donating blood to a blood bank prior to the war. I would not sign us up for slaughter."

The air held its breath for a moment, tense, waiting. It rippled through Reya's skin, charging the gravity of decision pressing down on every soul present.

"And what, you just get to waltz out of there while you subject your people to being their blood bags?" Vander's voice sliced through the air, sharp with accusation, thick with venom. The murmurs that followed churned like an unsettled current, rippling through the crowd.

Their suspicion pressed against Reya's skin, an invisible tide shifting with every breath. The dense air was flavored with damp earth and the lingering scent of rust, confinement, something bottled up yet suffocating. She could almost taste the tension in the back of her throat.

Malek exhaled. "No. I will remain here as an emissary to the queen and make sure our people are not mistreated." His voice carried with deliberate control, firm enough to hold back the rising wave of distrust. "Vander, you will lead the village until I return."

Silence settled over them, thick and suffocating, as if the very air had turned to stone. The prisoners stood unmoving, shadows cut against the flickering sunlight, their expressions unreadable in the wavering glow.

Then—finally—a voice broke through the stillness. Tentative, thin. "How long?"

Malek's reply came steady, unshaken. "I have agreed to remain here for a year."

A year. Her sentence for Malek to bear. The length lodged in Reya's chest like a foreboding of something cold and final. The mutters rose again, brushing against her like a restless wind, carrying the scent of uncertainty and muted fear. She flexed her fingers, feeling the familiar hum of magic just beneath her skin, a reminder of power, of choices yet to come.

CHAPTER 34

ASHUR HELD HIS BREATH. The crowd's indecision pressed against his ribs like a vise. The thick scent of blood still gripped the air, mingling with the sweat of men who had spent too long in confinement.

The freed men stood restless, their bare hands twitching—a dangerous energy simmered beneath their skin. They were unarmed, but Ashur knew desperation could sharpen bone and fist into lethal instruments. A murmur rippled through the masses, shifting like dry leaves caught in the wind, carrying unease in its wake.

Malek stood rigid, his presence a thin veil over the raw uncertainty in the men's eyes. Ashur could see it—the glances exchanged, the stifled doubt.

The air crackled with anticipation, thick enough to choke on. Ashur's pulse hammered beneath his skin, a warning, a countdown. Everything could shatter in an instant.

"And if we refuse?"

Ashur's breath thinned, barely enough to fill his lungs as he stood amid the shifting bodies, the mark of countless silent stares pressing down on him. The area swelled with tension.

Malek's voice rang out like a blade dragged across stone, sharp and cold. "Then you have sentenced us to slaughter."

The words cut through the noise, scattering the whispers like embers flicked into the wind. Ashur felt it then—the gravity of the choice settling deep into his chest. If they refused, there would be no undoing it. No reasoning, no reversal. He could already imagine it: the echo of steel meeting flesh, the smell of blood thick in the dirt, the screams sharp enough to carve through bone. It was a future he did not want to see—but it was one he might be forced to bear.

He clenched his jaw, eyes locking onto Malek and then at Malek's second in command outside the gates. That barrier—so deceptively fragile, yet unbreakable—felt like an omen. A reflection of the distance between them, of the gulf that separated leadership from mere survival. The man's expression was unreadable, but Ashur could sense the expectation buried beneath the surface.

The crowd waited. The freed men shifted, restless. The scrape of boots against stone, the breath of a man exhaled through clenched teeth as they waited for the final word dictating their fate.

If they refused, Malek's fate was sealed. As well as their own.

Ashur's thoughts churned like a tide against jagged rock, relentless and impossible to still. No choice was free of consequence—only varying degrees of suffering, only different shades of sacrifice. The strangers before him, exhausted and stripped of certainty, would bow to his queen's will, their futures molded by the decisions of those with power.

At least she had a heart. A tempered sense of mercy, however fragile. If it had been the goblin king dictating their fate, there would be no mercy, no bargains. The world itself would be forced to its knees, and even then, slaughter would be inevitable—without reason, without hesitation.

Vander's voice cut into the moment like the swipe of a dull blade. "Fine. I will go get the women and children, and they can serve."

The words landed heavy, like stones dropped into a still lake, sending ripples of distress through Ashur's chest. His pulse quickened—not with fear, but with a deep, slow-burning anger.

"No children." Malek's response was instant, solid as iron.

Vander stiffened. "You expect us to deplete capable hands?"

Ashur's gaze flickered between them, reading the tension in the set of their shoulders, in the way Malek's stance grounded itself with quiet authority.

"No one under the age of eighteen is to be offered for this role," Malek continued, crossing his arms, his expression dark with conviction. "You know as well as I do, children cannot safely give blood. I will not have you endanger our future in that manner."

Ashur exhaled, slow and measured, his fingers curling against his palms. There was still morality left in this—to some extent. A thin, wavering thread of principle, unraveling in the brutal tides of necessity.

Even so, their choices loomed over them all, inevitable as the coming storm.

Vander's frustration unraveled, the growl slipping from his throat like a wounded beast backed into a corner. The air around him grew heavier, charged with the simmering discontent of those confined within the metal enclosure. Their wariness was clear—the way their eyes darted between Vander and the others, assessing the cracks in his composure. He could feel it too, the tension rippling through the crowd like a slow-building storm.

Then came the voice—quiet but unwavering. A woman behind Vander lifted her hand, her gaze fixed on Reya. "I will serve," she declared, cutting through Vander's muttered protests like the snap of thunder.

Ashur shifted as the ripple of change spread across the imprisoned group. Vander's gaze darted toward the woman, then swept over the gathered bodies, registering the silent agreement in the subtle nods of their heads. Their acceptance was clear, though begrudging, like men submitting to the undertow of a current too strong to resist. And Vander—bristling, scowling—turned his glare on Malek, as if expecting the man to falter beneath the scald of it.

But Malek stood firm.

Reya stepped forward, her voice quiet but threaded with caution. "Are you sure you can trust him?"

Malek's stance shifted. The way the words settled seemed like a challenge he refused to entertain. His reply came sharp, tinged with cold inevitability. "No. But you are going to have to live with whatever is decided, since it was your mandate." His gaze flicked toward her, a sideways glare carrying the force of his resentment.

Ashur let out a slow breath, observing the dynamic unfolding like a carefully balanced game of strategy. Vander was losing ground, and he knew it. His next words came with the bitterness of reluctant submission. "You will need to let us go so we can go back to the village and gather volunteers."

Reya did not hesitate. Her voice cut through the pause that had settled, its force undeniable. "Why? There seems to be close to the number we need between the men already here and those in your confined area."

Ashur's lips twitched at the sheer audacity of it. He couldn't help the flicker of amusement—brief, restrained, but present nonetheless.

The moment had shifted yet again, a new thread of tension woven into the fragile arrangement of power and survival.

Ashur studied Malek, watching the strain tighten his expression, the flicker of conflict playing out in the rigid set of his jaw. The man's words came fast, sharp—an attempt to seize control before Vander could collect himself enough to retaliate.

"I cannot leave my village unprotected."

The weight behind the statement was undeniable, but Ashur could see the cracks lurking beneath the words. Malek was clinging to a duty already unraveling, a defense long compromised. And Reya saw it too.

"It seems you already have."

Her tone was precise, slicing through the moment like a blade against a taut fabric. Ashur caught the subtle shift in Malek's posture, the way his shoulders stiffened, his jaw muscle jumping as he held back whatever retort threatened to escape. He could feel the mounting frustration pulsing beneath Malek's skin, pressing against his control like a flood held at bay.

"At least offer them the option."

The words ground out from between Malek's clenched teeth, forced, reluctant. Ashur could hear the struggle buried within them—the quiet resignation masked beneath stubborn resolve. Malek wasn't ready to let go, not entirely. But even he knew there was no clean victory left to claim.

The tension in the space thickened, pressing against Ashur's ribs, threading through the air like smoke curling from a dying flame. He flicked his gaze between them, absorbing the moment, weighing the inevitable. It was a fragile battle of wills, teetering on the edge of collapse.

Reya inhaled, slicing a look at Malek that would have struck down a lesser man. "Go ahead."

Malek glanced at his men within the walls and those outside in the metal confines. "Who besides Bonnie would like to stay?"

Ashur stood still, feeling each raised hand like stones stacking on his chest—one by one, slow, hesitant at first, then gathering momentum. The decision had been made, in part. Half of them. Enough to spread across the homes, enough to fulfill the demand that had been looming over them like a specter since the moment this bargain was struck. But the tension remained, thick as the humid air pressing against his skin, settling in the spaces between shifting bodies.

"Janine?" Malek asked.

He tracked Malek's gaze to the woman Malek had called to. Even from where Ashur stood, he could see the way her expression tightened, the way the bright glow of the sun carved doubt into the delicate features of her face. Still, she nodded, accepting her role before it could be contested. A name, a purpose—one step further into permanence.

"She's not staying," Vander spat, his protest quick, instinctual, his possessiveness a blade sharpened not by logic, but by desperation.

Ashur didn't move, but his eyes flicked toward Malek, catching the subtle shift in his stance. Malek's control had never seemed fragile, but now—now there was a storm brewing beneath the surface, barely restrained. His growl cut across the courtyard like the snap of a whip. "You have the doctor to help the village. We need Jenine."

Reya's response came without hesitation. No wasted words. With a flick of her hand and the metal enclosure crumbled into nothingness, dissipating into the air like dust scattered into the wind. Ashur's breath steadied as she marched forward, her presence casting long shadows against the stone walls, radiating an authority no one dared challenge.

She pressed her palm against the rock. The gates responded to her touch with a slow, deliberate release, allowing the transfer to begin.

Ashur watched the shift—men moving past the threshold, exchanging places, the hesitant glances, the tension laced in their every movement.

"No weapons are allowed inside the gates," Reya commanded, her gaze locked on Vander, daring him to argue.

"There will be medical supplies," Malek countered, his voice still edged with the remnants of his earlier growl. "Needles to draw blood at the very minimum, sutures, and surgical items that would be needed for more serious ailments."

Ashur exhaled slowly, his arms crossing as he observed the unfolding exchange. This was happening. A decision made, a deal struck, consequences now moving into place, inevitable as the turn of the stars overhead.

Yet even as he stood in the eye of it all, a part of him couldn't shake the lingering chill—the knowledge that choices like these never settled cleanly.

CHAPTER 35

THE SCENT OF SCORCHED earth clung to the air as Reya stepped next to the gate, the iron-rich haze of blood lingering just beneath it. The ground under her boot was uneven, coated in dust and remnants of melted metal from the destroyed vehicles.

"You have until this time tomorrow to bring the rest of the people back," she said, voice smooth but edged like a sword dulled by repeated use.

Vander's lips thinned at her words, but before he could go on another tirade, Malek's sharp exhale cut through the brittle quiet like a blade grating against stone.

"A week. You destroyed their vehicles, so they will have to walk back to our village. And there are precious few working vehicles left." His words carried a rasp that scraped against her patience, like the wheezing breath of something too sick to die but too weak to fight.

Reya studied him, taking in the way tension had settled in his shoulders, how his fingers curled—whether in restraint or frustration, she couldn't tell. The hollowed-out fear behind his eyes was scarcely masked, a flicker of resistance that had yet to be fully broken. She gave a slow nod, the movement deliberate. She waited until the prisoners inside had been traded for their blood slaves, the scent of terror thickening the air like spoiled meat. Then Reya pressed her palm to the wall. The stone was cold beneath her touch, pulsing as the gate sealed with a low, rumbling thud.

"What happens if they don't show?" Malek asked, his voice tighter now, controlled—but the tremor didn't escape her notice.

Reya leveled a glare at him, letting it linger long enough that his throat bobbed in a hard swallow. Her mind moved to how ruthless these humans had been with Lily, and she wouldn't abide beings just as vile as the goblins living. "Then you get to watch your people die as we launch an attack on the remainder of the human race."

Malek swallowed again, the movement rigid, before nodding in tight compliance.

"You and the medic are to follow me." Reya's voice sliced through the tense air, low but edged with steel. The charged atmosphere held its breath, the gathered fae stiffening as her command settled over them like the pressure that precedes lightning. She turned deliberately, her dress whispering against the ground, and faced them—her people, once proud, now fractured and wary.

Her eyes scanned the crowd, lingering just long enough to remind them of her scrutiny. The humans stood nearby, confused and frightened, the scent of their fear mingling with the sweet tang of magic. Reya suppressed the twist of guilt in her gut. It was necessary. They were all caught in the same storm, whether or not they understood it.

"Choose your blood slave, but do not harm them. If they attack, subdue only. Understand?" Her words were ice—measured, controlled, but pointed. She saw the flicker of discontent ripple through the group, subtle but unmistakable.

Quinn's scowl darkened as he turned his gaze on the humans, revulsion flaring openly. "You expect me to have one of them in my house?"

Reya held his stare, unflinching. She let the silence stretch, the tension build, before answering.

"Yes." Each syllable articulated deliberately, each beat of the pause echoing her resolve. "And I expect you to treat them better than you treated the servants in our homelands."

His jaw clenched, but he didn't respond. Reya didn't need him to. She hadn't said it for Quinn's benefit—she'd said it for everyone listening. For the fae still clinging to old hierarchies, to old cruelty masked as tradition.

She turned away before the flicker of memory behind her own words could catch fire. There was no time for sentiment. Not now. Not with everything unraveling.

"Understand?" she repeated as she eyed each of the fae.

The group nodded.

"Once we work out how to obtain the blood without irreparable harm, then we will start that process." The air thrummed with a tense silence, the scent of desperation, sweat, and iron melding into something suffocating.

Reya glanced at Malek again, holding his gaze. The lowering sun cast jagged shadows over his face, sharpening the angles of his frustration. "No harm will come to your people unless they try to harm their masters, understand?"

"Yes," Malek agreed, but the taut set of his jaw, the slight twitch at the corner of his eye, gave away his resentment. It was enough for Reya to pause. His anger settled between them like a palpable heat.

"I am serious. I do not wish to start a war with you, but we will if it is a matter of surviving or perishing. We've already seen the destruction of our world at the hands of monsters. I do not wish to repeat that atrocity."

The words sat heavy in her throat, a bitterness she refused to let seep into her expression. She turned without waiting for Malek and Jeanine to follow, the soles of her boots scraping over the gravel path. She gave a nod to Ashur, who understood without needing further instruction—his movements crisp as he set about gathering their charges. Behind her, voices rose in debate, hushed and sharp, as the others squabbled over who would claim which slave.

Exhaustion wove its way into her muscles, stiffening her shoulders, dragging at her limbs like an unseen weight. A dull throb pulsed at the base of her skull, but she resisted the urge to rub the back of her neck in front of the others. Weakness, even in something as simple as fatigue, was not something she would display—not now.

The castle halls stretched before her, dimly lit by flickering sconces that cast uneven shadows across the stone walls. Reya moved with purpose, exhaustion dragging at her limbs as she strode toward her quarters, the intensity of the day settling over her like an iron mantle.

She stopped at one of the empty rooms, pressing her fingertips against the cool wood of the door before gesturing toward it. "Your quarters." She cut her gaze briefly to Malek and Janine.

Janine stepped inside with measured caution, eyes sweeping over the sparse furnishings—the single bed, the heavy wooden dresser pushed against the far wall, the thick curtains drawn over a window that let in only a sliver of sunlight. Malek, however, hesitated in the doorway, his presence an anchor of silent resistance.

"There's only one bed," he muttered, his voice edged with irritation.

Reya exhaled slowly, pinching the bridge of her nose as the tightness in her temples pulsed with renewed frustration. With a flick of her wrist, the air shimmered for the briefest moment before a second bed solidified next to the first. The scent of magic lingered—sharp and electric, a whisper of energy woven into the fabric of the space. "You have an attached washroom as well."

Malek grunted, stepping inside at last, his presence thick with reluctant acceptance.

Without another word, Reya placed her hand against the door and ran her palm down its grain. The wood shifted beneath her touch, reshaping itself until the knob remained only on the outside. A quiet finality settled in as the latch clicked into place, locking Malek and Janine within. The lingering warmth of the magic pulsed against her skin before fading, leaving behind only the solid certainty of her choice.

Ashur's steady steps approached, his expression calm but keen with observation.

"Is everyone settled?" she asked, turning to face him.

"Yes, your majesty."

"It's just Reya when we are alone," she corrected softly, letting herself lean back against the cool stone wall for the first time that day. The strain in her muscles stretched taut beneath her skin, an ache that settled deep in her bones. Closing her eyes for a breath, she let the exhaustion seep in, her voice just above a murmur. "I need a warm bath and a warm bed."

When she opened her eyes again, her gaze lingered on Ashur, drinking in the solidity of him—the sharp lines of his face, the unwavering steadiness in his stance.

"I need to look at your arm and then get you tucked in. You need sleep, Reya." His voice was gentler now, threaded with quiet insistence.

Her lips twitched into a ghost of a smile, something fleeting and edged with weariness. "I need more blood," she admitted, her voice almost drowned by the torches sputtering in their sconces. "But I have a feeling I would do more harm than good by trying to get some right now."

Ashur stepped closer, his presence warm despite the lingering chill in the stone corridor. The scent of cedar and ocean breezes clung to him as he offered his arm. Reya threaded her hand through his elbow, feeling the firm muscle beneath his sleeve, the quiet strength that had carried them through battle. His warmth seeped into her skin, steady and unwavering.

At the doorway, Reya paused. The coppery scent of dried blood hung in the air, sharp and out of place against the trace of lavender that Lily used to bring into the space. Her bedspread—marred by dark stains—stood as a cruel testament to all that had been lost. If Lily had lived, this room would have been cleaned, the linens fresh, the world just a little kinder. She exhaled, the ache in her chest deepening.

Ashur's brow creased. "Is everything okay?" His voice was low, a tether pulling her back.

"I miss Lily." Reya glanced up at him. The way the dim firelight flickered over his features made him seem softer, almost vulnerable.

"I would offer you my blanket if I had one." He removed her hand gently from his arm, lingering at the door.

Her gaze swiveled to him. "You don't have a blanket?" His soft smile melted her heart, something delicate threading through her ribs—an unfamiliar but not unwelcome warmth.

"I didn't have the luxury of packing for this trip." He lifted a shoulder, glancing at the ground, his quiet admission carrying the truth of his sacrifice.

On impulse, Reya lifted her hand to his cheek, fingertips grazing the stubble along his jawline. The contrast of roughness and warmth sent a shiver down her spine. Ashur leaned into her touch, his breath steady, his gaze locked on hers in silent understanding.

"I should be going." His voice held reluctance.

"Stay." The word left her lips in a hushed whisper, but in it, a plea—perhaps for comfort, perhaps for something more.

CHAPTER 36

ASHUR STARED INTO THE depths of her eyes, and for a fleeting second, the war raging inside him threatened to spill over. She was too fierce, too certain, too unshaken by the reality pressing in around them. And he wanted her—more than he should, more than was wise. His fingers curled at his sides as if he could physically restrain the impulse to reach for her.

"You know they will never accept me." His voice was carefully measured, an attempt to keep the rawness buried beneath layers of reason.

Reya cocked her head, her features hardening. "They don't have a choice in who I choose to stand as my king."

Ashur laughed, though there was little humor in it. He needed to remind her—needed to remind himself—that this wasn't some fantasy where will alone could bend the world to their desires. "You are naïve, Reya. I heard the women talking in the kitchen this morning." He crossed his arms, a barrier against the pull of her presence. "They mentioned the inappropriate way you look at the gardener."

And yet here she was, looking at him the way she shouldn't. The way that made the edges of his control fray.

Before he could react, Reya grabbed his shirt and hauled him into the room, the door snapping shut behind them. The force of her closeness sent a sharp jolt through his veins—a battle cry of want and restraint. The lavender fragrance lingering on her skin, the heat of her breath, the fire in her grip.

"What do *you* want, Ashur?" Her words were a challenge, her eyes burning into his.

You. The answer was instinctive, undeniable.

But it wasn't the right answer. It wasn't the answer their people needed.

"What I want is not the best thing for our people." He forced the words past the weight in his chest, ignoring the way his pulse throbbed when she didn't step away.

"But you do want me." Reya's gaze drilled into him.

The words struck like an arrow, precise and undeniable. Ashur clenched his jaw, forcing himself not to give in—to the pull, the temptation, the raw need threatening to take root. If he were wiser—stronger—he would dismiss it. He would counter with reason, remind her of their duty, of the fractures already splintering beneath them. But instead, he held her gaze, letting the statement settle between them.

"Would you have even considered me back at home?" The question carried more weight than he had intended. His voice was rougher as the edges of restraint frayed. He forced himself to stay still, to keep his hands clenched at his sides rather than act on the temptation—the unrelenting need—to slide his hands over her silky skin, tracing the warmth of her pulse with his fingers. To know if she would melt against him the way she did with her magic. The mere notion of it had no place here. Not when duty and reason demanded he keep his distance.

Reya's expression hardened, but she didn't retreat. "Look around you, Ashur. There is no longer a fae realm. You are almost as powerful as I am. Your magic feeds us and binds our enemies. Your magic helped me build these walls and this palace. It works seamlessly with mine. Or did you not notice?"

She stepped into his personal space, and the heat of her closeness licked at his control, testing him, taunting him.

Ashur pressed his lips together, exhaling slowly. He noticed. By the gods, he noticed. When they had woven the walls together, her magic had slid against his like a dance—one too intimate, too evocative, too much like desire. It had curled and stretched, folding into his power like a lover's touch, leaving a whisper of sensation that had lingered long after. He had felt her presence through the stones, even when she was nowhere near him. It had left him buzzing long after the stone had solidified beneath their hands. And the lingering hum of her magic hadn't faded. And that was dangerous.

Reya stabbed her finger into his chest, a sharp punctuation to the thoughts spiraling through him. "You have not once questioned my authority or given me shit like Quinn has done multiple times since we stepped through the portal."

"You are my queen." The words were meant to reaffirm the barrier between them. Instead, they felt like something else—like a confession, like surrender.

"Exactly."

Ashur clenched his jaw. She didn't understand.

She thought power meant alignment, that their magic weaving together meant they belonged together. But it wasn't that simple. He could feel it—the way she looked at him, the trust she had in him—but trust was dangerous. Trust meant opening himself up. Trust meant falling.

Something shifted. The invisible current flowing between them crackled, charged with meaning deeper than mere words. Ashur's eyes narrowed, and he leaned forward, letting his presence press against hers.

"If I were your equal, I would not blindly follow orders, My Queen." His words were deliberate, each syllable a challenge. "I would provide you with alternative ways of thinking that you may not like."

Then, before reason could win, he pulled her against him, his grip firm, heated, a betrayal of all the restraint he had fought to maintain.

"I have a mind as sharp as my magic, Your Majesty."

And then he kissed her.

Hard, hungry, desperate.

Every ounce of pent-up frustration, longing, and defiance poured into the act, into the fire burning through his veins. She tasted of power, of battle, of something he could never let go of once he allowed himself this moment.

But gods help him—he had stopped trying to resist.

CHAPTER 37

R EYA'S WORLD NARROWED TO the warmth of his lips, the way they moved with a deliberate hunger that sent shivers through her. Time splintered around them, dissolving into the rush of sensation—his breath against her cheek, the firm yet careful pressure of his hands as they squeezed her waist. A trembling exhale escaped her as heat curled along her spine, sinking deep into her chest. Everything about him—his scent, the steady rhythm of his heartbeat against her—wrapped around her like a silent promise, leaving her breathless with the quiet intensity of it all.

Reya's fingers fumbled over his stubborn shirt buttons, frustration threading through the haze of warmth curling in her chest. Her breath hitched as she tugged at the fabric, the fine stitching resisting her unsteady hands. He let out a quiet chuckle—a deep, knowing sound that sent a shiver through her.

"Here," he said, his hands covering hers, steadying the frantic pace of her movements. His touch was gentle, guiding her fingers over the first button until it slipped free. Embarrassment flickered across her skin, but his gaze was unwavering, patient, as if savoring the moment, the way her need pressed against her hesitation.

As she finally slipped the last button from its loop, the shirt parted, revealing the warmth of his skin beneath. The tension in her melted into quiet relief, though the intensity in his eyes reminded her that the moment had only just begun.

Reya's breath stilled as she traced the expanse of his newly bared skin, warmth radiating from him like an invitation. Her fingertips skimmed over the contours of his chest, hesitant yet drawn forward by an inexplicable pull. A shiver rippled through him at the feather-light touch, his own hands steady against her waist.

The tension between them deepened, charged with something fragile yet undeniable. Each movement felt deliberate—his fingers pressing gently against her lower back, the slight shift in his stance as he pulled her closer. The world outside the embrace dissolved, leaving only the heat pooling between them, the silent exchange carried through touch and breath.

Reya's pulse pounded, a deep, insistent rhythm that seemed to echo the tension crackling between them. Every movement weighted with anticipation—the slow drag of his fingers along her spine, the way his breath fanned over her skin, igniting sparks that surged through her veins. She could feel the hesitation in his grip, the quiet restraint that only heightened the urgency curling in her chest.

Her hands skimmed his shoulders, tracing the firm lines of his frame with reverence, as if committing the sensation to memory. Heat coiled low in her stomach, stealing the air from her lungs. His gaze met hers, dark and consuming, sending another wave of electricity through her body. The silent exchange between them stretched taut, a delicate balance of longing and control—neither willing to surrender fully, yet both lost in the moment's gravity.

Ashur undid the clasp holding Reya's dress together, and the fabric slipped from her shoulders, the whisper-soft sensation sending a shiver across her skin. Ashur's gaze pressed into her, reverent yet searching, as though he was committing each detail to memory. Vulnerability coiled within her chest, an ache that teetered between anticipation and uncertainty.

Her breath came uneven, snared in the magnitude of the intensity simmering between them. Ashur's eyes met hers, holding her in place—anchoring her as much as unraveling her. There was no judgment in his expression, no hesitation—only a quiet, steady admiration that made warmth bloom beneath the surface of her skin. It wasn't just desire—it was understanding. A silent exchange that held everything she hadn't yet spoken aloud.

Ashur stripped the bloody blanket from the bed and gently pushed Reya onto her back. His eyes sparkled at the prospect laid out before him, and he licked his lips before a heated smile spread across his face, bringing forth dimples Reya had rarely seen.

Her heart drummed against her ribs as he unthreaded his pants until his well-endowed length slipped from the fabric, standing at attention. Ashur's cheeks flushed, and he slid his boots off and kicked his pants away before he crawled onto the bed.

Ashur's lips brushed over hers, a fleeting, taunting whisper of touch that sent a shiver through her. Heat curled low in her belly, spreading like fire beneath her skin. He was deliberate, measured in his movements, as though savoring the moment before claiming it.

His breath fanned against her cheek, the warmth sending a tremor through her spine. "What would you prefer first, My Queen?" His voice was a hushed promise, roughened by restraint. "My hands, my mouth—perhaps something more?"

The words weren't just spoken; they settled into her like silk, smooth and dangerous. Reya's pulse stammered, caught between surrender and the intoxicating weight of his presence.

His mouth traced the delicate line of her jaw, each kiss a lingering imprint, a whisper of possession. The tender hush that bridged them thickened. The scent of him—cedar and pine and warm ocean breezes—filled her senses, drowning her in the inevitable.

Her hands uncurled against his chest, feeling the steady thrum of his heartbeat beneath her fingers. A reminder that even power could falter in the presence of desire. Her own breath was uneven now, drawn from somewhere deeper, tethered to him in a way she wasn't sure she wanted to name.

The question still lingered between them, but in the way Ashur's mouth hovered just beyond her lips, in the way his hand skimmed slow and knowing over her breasts, Reya knew the answer had already been decided.

Each butterfly kiss he traced over her throat sent a wave of chills through her. His thumbs gently caressed her breasts, tracing her nipples into hard nubs. Her breath caught as Ashur's teeth and tongue circled the sensitive flesh before he moved lower.

Reya's mind warred against itself, caught between surrender and the aching need that curled within her like a living thing. Every kiss, every whisper of touch, carried a new language, pressing against the boundaries of what she had always controlled.

Her breath faltered as Ashur moved, the heat of his skin imprinting against her own, his slow, deliberate ministrations unraveling her with a patience that both soothed and set her ablaze. He wasn't rushed. He was precise, each caress a quiet demand, testing her restraint.

The room felt smaller, the air thick with the essence of him—an ocean-side forest and something richer, something undeniably him— until the world narrowed to only this. Only them. Every brush of his mouth left a lingering trail, not just of sensation, but of something deeper. A tether forming, one she wasn't sure she had the will to sever.

The shift in Ashur's expression—his slow, knowing smile—only deepened the tremor beneath her ribs. This wasn't simply desire; it was something more dangerous. Something real. And that, more than anything, made her pulse stutter, her fingers tighten against his skin in quiet defiance.

She had always held the reins. Always dictated the terms. But here—here—he was rewriting the rules with every lingering touch, with every breath that made her body betray the logic her mind still clung to.

She had never been touched like this. With reverence and a skill that had her unraveling with delicious ecstasy, yelling his name as she quaked under his mastery. His command over her body both thrilled and terrified her.

Once she quivered under each aftershock from the magic of his tongue, Ashur slowly made his way up her body, kissing her skin before he claimed her mouth with his. He settled between her thighs, languidly running his member over the wetness, creating shivers of pleasure through her.

He pulled away from the kiss and smiled down at her.

Reya held his gaze, her whisper barely more than breath, yet carrying something carnal and raw. "Please, Ashur."

Ashur stilled, his features shadowed with quiet intensity, eyes momentarily closing as though settling himself in the moment.

Reya's pulse fluttered in her throat. She was acutely aware of every sensation—the heat pooling beneath her skin; the tension coiling in her limbs; the slow, deliberate pressure of him pressing forward. Her body ached with anticipation and something more—something fragile, tangled in trust and uncharted surrender.

Ashur's voice, when it came, was steady but edged in something rougher. "You've never done this before, have you?" It was not a question—it was a realization, spoken low, curling around her like smoke.

"No." The admission settled between them, stripping away every mask of distance she might have worn. And yet, beneath the pressure, she found a quiet clarity. She was not afraid—not when it was him. Not when his every movement was careful, reverent in a way that stole the air from her lungs.

When he hesitated, when the lines between his brows deepened in restraint, she moved. Her legs curled around him, pulling him closer—needing to bridge the space between control and surrender. The sharp crest of sensation rippled through her, pain and pleasure entwining, and the cry that tore from her lips was not just from the physical—it was from everything this moment meant.

It stemmed from the realization that there was no turning back.

CHAPTER 38

ASHUR'S GAZE LOCKED ONTO hers, the raw vulnerability in her eyes tightening something deep within him. The moment was a fragile threshold—one he couldn't cross without consequence, without leaving something irreversibly changed between them.

The pressure of her legs tightening around his waist sent a ripple through his control, a silent plea wrapped in instinct. He was aware—too aware—of the responsibility in his hands. Of the power in this moment, her moment. And yet, restraint felt cruel. Drawing it out would be agonizing, stretching the space between hesitation and inevitability until it became unbearable.

He inhaled slowly, deliberately—trying to quiet the storm beneath his ribs. But then, with a powerful thrust, he erased the hesitation.

Her gasp filled the space around them, sharp and sudden, and his chest constricted in response. The sound—raw, unguarded—was too much. It held weight, significance, something deeper than pleasure or pain.

He stilled. For a breath, for a heartbeat, for the eternity that stretched between them.

The crease in his brow deepened. Had he hurt her too much? His hand trembled as he brushed against her skin, a silent question woven in the warmth of his touch.

Are you okay?

She didn't speak, but her body answered—her grip tightening, her presence pressing into him, anchoring him to this, to her. His heart squeezed painfully in his chest.

When the tension in her face eased, a quiet relief settled into his chest—a release of a restraint he hadn't realized he was holding. She was letting him in, yielding in a way that was more than just physical.

Ashur rocked his hips in a slow, deliberate rhythm, each movement balanced on the razor's edge of pleasure and torment, like standing with one foot in heaven and the other in hell. Every shift of his body against hers pulled him deeper into something raw, something uncharted.

The warmth of her, the way she molded against him, stole the air from his lungs. It wasn't just desire—it was something more potent, something dangerous in its undeniability. The way she looked at him, dark lashes fluttering as each breath hitched, made his pulse pound in a way that had nothing to do with control and everything to do with her.

He wasn't sure what wrecked him more—the way her body responded to him, or the knowledge that she had given this moment to him alone.

His hand curled against her waist, fingers pressing into heated skin. Her unrestrained sounds of pleasure, the way she tilted into his rhythm, were a revelation—an unraveling of the careful restraint he had tried to maintain.

It was too much. Not enough. Everything.

Ashur fought against the tide threatening to pull him under, his restraint hanging by a fraying thread. Every tremor of Reya's body beneath him, every breathless sound that escaped her lips, chipped away at his control with merciless precision. He held himself at bay—not just for her, but for the impossible need to make this moment something more than desire.

And then, she shattered him.

Her body clenched around him, her voice—his name—tore through the still air, reverberating off the cold stone walls. It wasn't just sound; it was possession; it was everything he hadn't known he needed.

His grip tightened, fingers pressing into the heat of her skin as he let go, finally surrendering to the force of it—the inevitability of her, of them. The world blurred, his pulse a thunderous rhythm against hers, and for the first time in too long, he wasn't thinking. He wasn't guarding himself. He was only feeling—falling into her, into the wreckage of restraint that had once held him together.

He breathed her in, the scent of warmth and lingering ecstasy wrapping around him like something sacred. His mouth found the curve of her shoulder, a quiet reverence in the way his lips traced over flushed skin. This moment—this woman—was his undoing.

And he welcomed it.

CHAPTER 39

REYA DOZED IN ASHUR'S warm embrace, his steady heartbeat a gentle rhythm against her cheek, anchoring her. The scent of him—cedar and pine—lingered on her skin, a quiet reminder of all they had endured together. His arms, firm yet tender, wrapped around her as if shielding her from unseen dangers, offering a sanctuary she hadn't known she craved.

But even as the warmth of his body lulled her into the softness of sleep, doubt stirred beneath the surface. The fae would not accept him easily—perhaps not at all. Especially Quinn, who thought his place was ruling over everyone, including her. Doubt curled at the threshold of her mind like a whisper in the dark, threading through the refuge of his embrace. She pressed closer, as if the sheer force of proximity could silence the worry gnawing at her.

A distant breeze rattled the leaves outside, a striking departure from the even cadence of Ashur's breath. For now, they were safe—wrapped in something momentary and fragile. But the world beyond his arms was waiting.

The scent of roasted meat and spiced wine curled through the air, coaxing her out of her satiated stupor. The aroma pulled her from the fog of sleep before her mind caught up. Warm embers and Ashur's skin still clung to her senses, but the richness of the cooking meal was insistent, curling its fingers around her awareness. She inhaled. The notes of rosemary and slow-burned broth weaved through the room.

Ashur stirred beneath her, his breath shifting as his hold loosened. For a fleeting second, she considered staying—letting the shelter of his presence delay the inevitable. But her people would not wait. Neither could they.

She sat up, the silken sheets whispering against her bare arms. Ashur followed, stretching as he ran a hand over his face, the remnants of sleep lingering in the way his movements were slow, deliberate. His eyes found hers in the dim light, searching, as if gauging the storm waiting beyond the door.

"They're making sure we move," Reya said with a voice rough with sleep.

Ashur huffed a quiet laugh, blinking against the soft glow of the wall sconces. "Then we should oblige." Though the comfort of lingering was tempting.

Reya rose from the bed and gathered her clothing. The scent of warm bread—crisped at the edges, soft at the center—sealed her determination. Their meal was waiting.

They dressed in silence, though the hush between them was not empty. It was thick with all that was coming—the quiet was necessary, a space to gather themselves before stepping into what waited beyond the door.

Reya smoothed the fabric over her arms, the cool silk a blistering contrast to the lingering warmth of Ashur's touch. The evening air carried traces of fire-smoke and distant rain, threading through the chamber, mingling with the scents of the meal—roasted meat, crushed herbs, the rich sweetness of baked fruit. It calmed her, even as restlessness gnawed at the boundaries of her thoughts.

Ashur fastened the last of his buckles, his movements deliberate, steady. The way his shoulders squared, the way his breath deepened, as though gathering something within himself. The rest of the fae would watch him. Measure him. Judge him. And she knew without question that he understood that better than anyone.

She stepped to his side, threading her hand through his, and together, they moved.

The grand hall stretched wide before them, columns rising into vaulted ceilings, their carved surfaces catching glints of amber light. The dinner spread before them was decadent—bowls of golden fruit, plates of smoked venison, goblets filled to the brim with mulled wine. Yet despite the beauty of it, the tension lingered, thick as the scent of burning herbs in the air.

The demand of expectations pressed against her ribs, but she did not falter.

Reya caught the brief flicker of uncertainty in Ashur's stance before he squared his shoulders, his expression settling into something composed, something kingly. She stood beside him, ready.

Let them see. Let them judge.

Tonight would decide everything.

CHAPTER 40

ASHUR SCANNED THE ROOM, his jaw tightening as he took in the long table—more than just the fae were gathered. The humans had been seated among them, their presence an unsettling confirmation of the shifting tides. Even Malek and Janine were here, placed deliberately, their positions chosen with careful intent. Malek sat beside the queen's left—a place of honor. But the seat at her right, the seat meant for her consort, was occupied by Quinn.

Reya's body stiffened beside him, her fingers a sudden vice around his as she dragged him forward. Ashur let himself be pulled, though the heat rising in his chest made every movement feel heavier. The air was thick with roasted meats, spiced wine, and charred herbs, but beneath it, there was something sharper—a barely contained tension suffocating the space.

"I believe you are in Ashur's seat," Reya said, her voice smooth as steel.

Quinn briefly glanced up, his nose wrinkling as if Ashur were something unsightly, something unwanted. "Ashur is your guard. He eats after we do."

The blood in Ashur's veins slowed, hardened. The way Quinn looked at him—it was not simply dismissal. It was disgust. As if he were filth clinging to Reya's side, something to be scraped away and forgotten.

"Ashur is my chosen consort. And you are in his seat." Reya's voice did not waver, but the pressure of her grip tightened against his skin.

Quinn's smirk was a blade twisting deep. "He is not of royal descent. You were betrothed to my cousin, and since he is not here, the duty falls on my shoulders."

The words struck with the precision of an arrow, lodging deep where reason had no place. Duty. His place. His absence. Ashur knew the game, knew the cruelty behind it, but it did little to temper the fire burning beneath his ribs.

"I never agreed to the arrangement; otherwise, I would have already been married to that ass." Reya's nails dug into Ashur's palm.

Quinn flinched. "It matters little what you want, princess. I was sent here to make sure our royal line endures." He grinned, slow, deliberate. "You and I were meant to produce an abundance of heirs."

Ashur's world narrowed. The scent of wine turned bitter on his tongue. The flickering candlelight dulled, overtaken by the sharp pulse of rage curling in his gut. He pulled his hand free from Reya's grasp, barely registering the loss of warmth before his fingers twisted in Quinn's shirt. The fabric bunched beneath his grip, the strength in his arm effortless as he hauled the smug noble to his feet.

"If you ever speak that way to your queen again," he growled, his voice low, rough, deadly, "I'll take your head and put it on a pike for all to see."

The words cracked over the table, reverberating through the hall, silencing the breath between them.

But Ashur did not release his hold.

Quinn had tested him. And now, Ashur would make sure he understood exactly who he had challenged.

The silence in the hall stretched taut as a drawn bowstring. Ashur kept his grip firm on Quinn's shirt, the pulse of fury steady beneath his skin. He could feel every gaze on him—fae, human, queen. Judging. Calculating. Waiting.

But it was Malek's stare that cut through the haze first.

Ashur caught it—the flicker of interest, sharp and discerning, behind Malek's otherwise composed expression. He sat beside the queen, his fingers loosely curled around the stem of his goblet, his posture relaxed. Yet his eyes were keen, watching the exchange with an intensity that was anything but passive.

Malek was taking stock.

Measuring.

Not merely amused by the display, but studying its fractures, its weaknesses.

Ashur released his grip on Quinn, shoving him back into his chair with a controlled force that sent the goblets rattling against the wood. The noble straightened his collar with an indignant huff, but he did not rise again. The message had been received.

Reya did not flinch as Ashur pulled out Reya's chair for her. Once she was settled, he grabbed an empty chair and set it next to hers at the head of the table, acting as a barrier between Quinn and Reya. He settled beside her, though he felt the subtle press of her hand against his thigh beneath the table—a quiet tether, centering him. He exhaled through his nose, forcing the breath past the fire still simmering low in his blood.

Malek took a measured sip of his wine, his gaze flicking between Ashur and Quinn before settling on Ashur alone. His lips curved—not a full smirk, but something knowing. Intrigued.

A test. A calculation.

Ashur met his gaze.

If Malek wanted a glimpse into the battle brewing beneath the surface, he had gotten one.

Now the real question was—what would he do with it?

"Asher will lead by my side. If you take issue with that, you are welcome to leave our sanctuary." Reya's voice cut through the weighted silence like tempered steel, sharp enough to carve through bone. Around the table, the fae sat frozen—wide-eyed, mouths parted, caught between disbelief and reluctant admiration. Even the candle flames seemed to still, the air thick with something raw, something undeniable.

Ashur breathed in shallow pulls. His pulse slowed, heavy, pressing against his ribs as he studied the faces before him. He had spent years being overlooked, dismissed, treated as less. But here, with Reya's unwavering declaration ringing across the hall, there was no mistaking what had just been done.

She had bound him to her.

Not as a shadow at her side, not as a mere protector, but as an equal. As her chosen.

It was a strange thing—how something so simple could unravel the years of doubt that had buried themselves beneath his skin. He had come into this hall prepared for war, for judgment, for battle waged in words and posturing. But Reya had chosen a far simpler, far deadlier path.

She had silenced them with certainty.

She lifted her goblet, the deep red of the wine catching the light, but her gaze was sharper than the liquid's gleam as it passed over the stunned faces at the table. "And if you leave and attempt to harm the humans," she continued, her voice cold, resolute, "I will hunt you down and gut you myself."

Ashur exhaled slowly, forcing the breath past the slow burn of emotion curling in his chest. A quiet admiration hummed beneath his skin, tangled with something deeper, something that threatened to unsettle him.

This was Reya.

This was the woman Quinn had tried to contain, to shape, to control.

And this was the moment where she proved he had never truly understood her at all.

CHAPTER 41

REYA TOOK A SLOW sip of her wine, the dark liquid rich and spiced, coating her tongue like silk. She let it settle, savoring the quiet weight of it before placing the goblet back onto the polished wood of the table. The metal rim of her ring tapped softly against the glass—a sharp contrast to the heavy silence hanging over the room.

"But your majesty. This is not how things are done," Petal's voice cut through the stillness, its delicate lilt laced with displeasure.

Reya turned her gaze on the pink-haired fae, noting the way Petal's fingers curled around her goblet, knuckles pressing white. She looked so much like Quinn—with those same delicate features, that same aristocratic sharpness—but there was something softer beneath it, something uncertain.

Reya leaned forward, slow, deliberate, allowing her words to settle before she spoke. "This isn't up for discussion," she said. "Our world crumbled under the goblin attacks. We are all that is left."

The truth of it sat heavy in her chest—a relentless ache, a wound that would not heal. She had seen the destruction firsthand. Had walked through the ruins, smelled the blood thick in the air, felt the ghost of her parents' touch before they passed their crowns to her.

She inhaled deeply, the scent of roasted venison and mulled spices curling around her senses as she forced herself to remain steady, unwavering. "Now, unless you want to challenge me, I suggest you get used to a new rule—where there is no caste system. Ashur and I will rule, and everyone else here is on equal footing."

The words rang out, final, a declaration carved from steel.

Malek shifted in his chair, his green eyes sparkling with amusement as he glanced around at the chattering fae. "What's involved in a challenge?" he asked, the edges of his lips curving, as if he were enjoying the dissent brewing around the table.

Reya met his gaze, unblinking. "Hand-to-hand combat to the death," she answered, spitting the words out like venom.

A hush rippled through the room, and she followed it with her eyes. Tension curled in the air, thick and potent.

She did not move, did not flinch, as she let her words settle like stone. "And most of the fae at this table are fully aware of my skills. After all, I've been training with the King's elite security force since the day I was old enough to wield a weapon." Her gaze flicked to Malek, sharp and unwavering. "Thus, the lack of challenges."

Silence stretched between them, but it was not empty—it was crackling, waiting.

Quinn narrowed his eyes at Reya, the dim candlelight flickering against his sharp cheekbones, shadows slicing across his tense expression. With a deliberate flick of his wrist, he threw his napkin onto the table, the crisp fabric crumpling into a heap. His voice carried through the heavy silence like a blade unsheathed.

"I challenge you."

Petal gasped, the sound sharp and breathless, like a flower torn from its stem. Her fingers flew to her mouth, trembling against her lips, but her wide, panicked eyes pleaded—pleaded—for her brother to take the words back.

The moment froze, stretched taut as Reya inhaled, slow and measured, forcing the breath past the flare of heat igniting in her chest. The scent of roasted meat and spiced wine clung to the air, nearly choking. Her grip tightened around the edge of the table, nails pressing hard enough to leave crescent-shaped imprints.

She pinned Quinn with a glare that cut colder than steel. "As you wish."

Quinn's grin slashed across his face, jagged and victorious. He placed a hand on the back of the human's neck beside him, fingers curling with possessive ease.

"And my human here will be my proxy."

Reya stilled. A cold coil of fury spiraled through her veins, so sharp it almost stole her breath. Centuries of law and blood pressed against her ribs, against her heartbeat hammering in a slow, dangerous rhythm.

With deliberate precision, she leaned her elbows on the edge of the table, the polished surface cool against the heat rising beneath her skin. "There is no proxy clause when challenging the crown."

The words landed like a death knell, and Quinn paled in an instant. His throat worked as he swallowed, his confidence cracking at the edges. He blinked rapidly, as if grasping for an escape—one that did not exist.

"You have five minutes to say your goodbyes. I'll meet you in the courtyard."

Reya slid her chair back, the legs scraping against the stone floor with a low, grating drag. The sound cut through the thick silence, final in its intent. She rose to her full height, shoulders squared, expectation pressing into every deliberate motion.

"If you are not outside in that time, you will forfeit."

Her voice carried like tempered steel—sharp, cold, unquestionable. With that declaration, Reya turned on her heel, her skirt snapping at her calves as she strode toward the door. Her boots struck hard against the floor, each step precise, the rhythm a warning of her resolve. As she passed through the archway, a gust of air followed in her wake, rustling the flames in the lanterns lining the walls. The door swung shut behind her with a heavy thud, sealing her departure like the slam of a gavel.

CHAPTER 42

QUINN GROWLED, THE SOUND raw and guttural, thick with contempt. His palm cracked against the human's cheek with a sharp snap, the impact sending a tremor through the heavy air. The human flinched, their breath hitching as red bloomed across their skin. A shudder ran through their shoulders, as if they were fighting the instinct to recoil further.

"What good are you if you can't die in my stead?"

Quinn's voice dripped with disdain, curling around the words like venom. He raised his hand again, fingers twitching with unchecked rage, the sinew in his forearm tightening. The table had frozen—no one moved—except for Ashur.

A cold, biting clarity cut through his shock, fury unfurling in his chest like a wildfire. His pulse pounded in his ears, a steady, roaring beat. Before Quinn's hand could descend, Ashur surged forward, fingers closing around his wrist like iron. The heat of Quinn's skin burned beneath his grip, his pulse frantic beneath Ashur's hold. He could feel the raw tension coiled in the man's muscles, the twitch of resistance before realization dawned.

The moment hung suspended, charged with quiet threats. Ashur's grip tightened, not enough to break—but enough to warn. His breath was controlled, measured, though the fury curling behind his ribs threatened to spill over.

"They are not here for you to take your misguided rage on." Ashur's voice was sharp, cutting through the charged air like tempered steel. His fury simmered just beneath the surface, contained but palpable. He took a measured step forward, the scent of overturned wine and seared meat thick in the room, clinging to the tension that had settled like a storm cloud.

"Now either slink back to your room and forfeit your challenge or get out there so my queen can take your life."

His tone was icy, devoid of patience, pressing like judgment itself. Without hesitation, Ashur's hand shot out, fingers locking around Quinn's arm with crushing precision. The heat of his skin burned against Ashur's palm, his muscles tensing beneath the grip. A flicker of shock flashed across Quinn's face before Ashur yanked him from the chair, the legs scraping against the floor with a protesting shriek.

Quinn stumbled, his balance stolen in an instant, his breath leaving him in a startled huff. Ashur didn't give him a chance to recover—shoved him forward, forcing him toward the door with unrelenting force. His palm slammed against Quinn's back, sending him staggering, boots scuffing against the stone in a graceless attempt to stay upright.

The door loomed ahead, its presence final, unmoving. Ashur's heart hammered, but his expression remained unreadable—resolute, unwavering, a force that would not bend.

He had witnessed Reya's training—had watched her move like a predator, every motion precise, every breath controlled. Beneath that soft-hearted exterior was a force carved from war, tempered by fury and resilience. He could still hear the rhythmic pound of her boots against the dirt, the sharp inhale before a strike, the muted thud of bodies hitting the ground in defeat.

That was how she bested the man who tried to take her.

Ashur remembered the moment with chilling clarity. She had fought with the wild desperation of survival, not just technique but instinct, raw and unrelenting. Her hands had been brutal, her grip vice-like as she twisted away from his grasp. The snarl that had ripped from her throat had been more animal than human, a warning edged with lethal promise.

She had bitten—hard—blood bursting from the wound, igniting her power. And when she had wielded her magic, it had been over.

If she had steel or an arrow in her grasp, she was unstoppable.

Ashur had seen it—the sheer certainty in her movements, the way she wielded death like it was something familiar, something necessary. And yet, beneath it all, there was something else—a fire that refused to be extinguished, a will that no one, not even the gods, could break.

Ashur's gaze swept across the table, his steel eyes cutting through the dim candlelight like embers in the dark. Fae and human alike sat stiffly beneath his scrutiny, their postures rigid, expressions unreadable—but he could feel it. The tension pressed thick against the air, a wariness curling at the edges of their silence.

"The humans are not here to be abused. Understand?"

His voice was more than a growl—it was a warning, low and edged with quiet fury. The words settled heavy in the shadow-laced ether they didn't cross, sinking deep like iron into flesh. His hands rested against the polished wood of the table, fingers flexing, coiled with restrained force. He was ready to act should anyone dare challenge his decree.

"They are only here to aid us with our magic, and if I find any of you doing harm to them, I will deliver justice to you in the same manner that you have treated them."

The murmured flicker of breath, the shift of weight—small tells of misgiving rippled through the gathered company. Some averted their eyes; others held still, deliberate in their refusal to react. Ashur exhaled slowly, controlled, though the raw heat of his anger simmered beneath his ribs.

Then, his focus locked onto Malek, sharp as the edge of a blade.

The tension between them thickened, charged with something dangerous.

"That does not mean my people cannot defend themselves against an attack."

Malek stiffened, scarcely perceptibly, but Ashur caught it—the twitch of his jaw, the way his fingers curled against the armrest. He did not look away, did not flinch, but Ashur knew he had heard him. Felt him.

"If that is to happen, then whoever is responsible will be executed."

The finality of the sentence landed like stone, sealing the moment in something unshakable. The firelight flickered in the silence that followed, the scent of wax filling the space, but no one spoke—no one dared.

CHAPTER 43

REYA SHED THE LIGHT dress, the soft fabric whispering against her skin as it slipped to the floor. She pulled on the leather pants—worn to a supple fit over years of training—and fastened them securely at her waist. The tunic Lily had stashed away smelled of aged wood and the wild roses that crept along the castle walls, a lingering imprint of the life she had left behind. The leather creaked as she adjusted her stance.

With deft fingers, Reya gathered her long locks, smoothing them back as she began weaving the strands into a tight battle braid. Her scalp tingled under the firm pull, the tug of each twist sharp but familiar—a ritual of readiness.

The thick plait coiled against her spine, weighty and secure, the dark strands catching the glow of the nearby candlelight. Loose wisps framed her face, teasing against her skin as if resisting containment.

She reached for the queen's crown, the cool metal grazing her fingertips before she lifted it. The filigree edges pressed lightly against her palms, the weight heavier than she remembered, or perhaps that was just the burden it carried. She fit it onto her head, adjusting until the gilded frame settled against her brow. The delicate grip of the metal against her temples was a silent reminder of what she had built, what she had fought for.

She turned to the bureau, where her father's crown gleamed under the candlelight, its intricate filigree catching in the flickering glow. The metal was cool against her palm as she lifted it. She clenched her fingers around it, inhaling sharply, as if bracing herself against the storm gathering in her chest.

Stalking to the courtyard, she stepped onto the earth that had once been nothing but barren stone—a place she had imagined into existence, sculpted with sheer will and magic. The scent of distant bonfires filled her senses. The night breeze teased strands of her hair free as she moved to the center.

She faced the grand doors, towering and carved with ancient sigils, the entrance through which Quinn and the rest of the fae would soon emerge. Her pulse thrummed steadily, but deep beneath it coiled an edginess she refused to name. She tightened her grip on the crown.

Ashur was the first through the door, his presence slicing through the whispers that swelled behind him. His gaze locked onto hers, sharp and unrelenting, like steel finding purchase against stone. Shadows flickered in the depths of his piercing eyes, darkening as they swept over her, reading the set of her shoulders, the tension in her stance.

Behind him, every occupant of the dining room spilled into the courtyard, their eager footsteps scuffing against the pristine ground, their hushed anticipation thickening the air. The scent of spilled wine and roasted meat clung to them, remnants of a meal abandoned for something far more intoxicating—the promise of blood.

Ashur halted before her, the breath between them taut with unuttered words, his eyes begging her not to lose this fight. Reya inhaled slowly, willing her fingers steady as she raised the king's crown. The metal was cold, heavier than it should have been, its weight pressing into her palm like judgment itself.

She lifted it.

For the briefest moment, she hesitated, the sight of it in her grasp splintering through her. It had belonged to her father once. The man who had ruled, who had bled—who was gone. And now, she perched it atop Ashur's head, fitting it to him like a blade to its sheath.

The crown gleamed under the firelight—an emblem of power reclaimed, a symbol of what was to come. Reya forced her breath to remain even, though something coiled tight within her chest.

Archer lifted an eyebrow but said nothing. He did not remove the crown she had placed upon his head, its gilded edges catching the glow of the torches lining the courtyard. The weight of it did not bow him; did not make him hesitate. The silence pressed in around them, thick and expectant, a force unto itself.

"Are you sure?" His whispered question was a knife's edge, drawing the breath straight from her chest.

"Yes."

The word was steady, but her fingers tingled as if the act had left something behind—an imprint, a fracture, a choice she could not undo.

The crowd had stilled, their excitement tempered into something quieter, more dangerous. Some looked to each other in silent calculation, the language of shifting loyalties playing across tense expressions. Others could not hide their astonishment, their gazes flickering between Ashur and the crown that now sat atop his head. The gleaming proof of power passed from one hand to another.

A murmur rippled through them, hushed but unmistakable, like the first tremor before an earthquake. The scent of burning wood filled the air, mingling with the sharpness of anticipation. She could see it in their eyes—their understanding of what this meant, of the storm it would bring. Some wore smirks, relishing the inevitable clash. Others swallowed hard, wary of the weight that had just settled upon their world.

Ashur seemed to consider her answer, then shifted—his steps slow but deliberate—as he came to stand beside her. The movement was simple, but to the watching crowd, it was everything. A declaration. A reckoning. A line drawn in the sand.

Quinn stepped into the courtyard, his stride deliberate, shoulders squared with purpose. His sister followed, smaller in presence despite the striking sharpness of her gaze. Petal wrung her hands, her fingers twisting in tight, nervous knots, the movement betraying the tension she tried to swallow down. Reya caught the subtle tremble in her posture, the way her breath hitched too shallowly, a quiet admission of fear.

But Quinn... Quinn was something else entirely.

His sneer sharpened the moment his gaze landed on Ashur, the sight of the crown atop his head igniting something primal in him. The expression twisted, a slow, curling revelation of teeth—a predator catching the scent of an unexpected foe. His features tightened, the muscles in his jaw clenching hard before his words rasped through the thickening air.

"Is he your proxy?" The growl was low, raw, laced with the insult of it, the accusation that she was too weak to stand alone.

Reya did not flinch.

The heat coiled in her chest, slow and unrelenting, but she refused to let it rise, refused to let it scorch her restraint. Her fingers reached up, unthreading the crown from her hair, the metal catching briefly against the tangles of loosened strands before she freed it. It settled in her palm, cool and certain, a reminder of who she was, what she had fought for.

She stepped forward, meeting Quinn's gaze with unwavering steadiness.

"No." Her voice was calm, smooth like tempered steel. "He is my king, and you challenged me—not Ashur."

She turned, pressing the crown into Ashur's waiting grasp. The silent exchange held something final, something immovable. Ashur's fingers curled around it, solid and sure, as if there had never been a question at all.

The watching crowd held its breath.

Let Quinn reckon with that.

CHAPTER 44

ASHUR STOOD AT THE edge of the courtyard, the crown a solid weight in his grasp. His fingers curled around its cold metal as he watched Reya and Quinn circle each other. The energy between them crackled like the charged air before a storm, sharp and unavoidable.

Quinn lunged first. A blur of muscle and precision, he struck out, aiming for Reya's ribs. She twisted just in time, evading the hit with a sharp pivot, her boots skimming the dirt in a near-silent slide. Ashur caught the flicker of satisfaction in her gaze—quick, deadly. She was reading Quinn's movements, dissecting them as they came, and already adjusting before he even landed a second strike.

Their fists clashed in a furious exchange, each impact resounding through the courtyard. Reya was fast, impossibly fluid, her body bending to the rhythm of battle as though it had been carved into her bones. But Quinn had weight, brute force, and a coiled rage that drove every strike harder than the last.

The crowd tightened around the brutal fight, breaths held, anticipation thick in the air. Every grunt, every shift of their footing, every snapped movement built upon the charged silence like a song played in clenched fists and narrowed eyes.

Then came the opening—brief, nearly imperceptible. Quinn overextended on a punch meant to knock Reya off balance, and she was already moving before the mistake had fully formed. She ducked, twisted into the gap, and slammed her palm into his sternum with the force of a hammer. Quinn staggered back, breath hitching, frustration flaring in his eyes.

Ashur smirked, just enough for himself. Reya was proving what he already knew.

She wasn't just a warrior. She was something far more dangerous.

CHAPTER 45

REYA DIDN'T LET THE moment slip away. Quinn staggered back, breath uneven, frustration flashing like a blade behind his eyes. She could feel the shift in him—the fleeting crack in his control as she pressed forward.

The courtyard was alive with the tension of their fight. The scent of churned earth mixed with the underlying tang of sweat. The whispers of the gathered crowd hushed but brimmed with anticipation. Her heartbeat thundered in her ears, but her mind remained sharp, calculated.

Quinn adjusted his stance quickly, shaking off the misstep with a sneer. His movements became heavier, more deliberate. He wasn't just fighting to win—he was fighting to remind her of his strength, his authority, his claim over their world.

But she wasn't a subject to be cowed.

He swung, but she caught the motion in his shoulders before the strike even landed, twisting away just enough to let his knuckles graze past her ribs instead of making full impact. She pivoted, dipping low, her muscles coiling like a spring before she surged upward, slamming her forearm into his chest in a brutal counterstrike.

The breath left his lungs in a sharp exhale.

Their gazes locked, a heated battle raging just as fiercely as the fight itself.

The crowd sensed it. This wasn't simply a match of skill—it was a clash of wills, a war over who would dictate the balance of power.

Reya refused to falter.

Quinn adjusted too quickly. Reya saw it in the shift of his weight, the taut coil of muscle before his next strike—except this time, it wasn't aimed directly at her. His feint was flawless, forcing her to anticipate a different trajectory, and when his true blow came, she had just pivoted, but not far enough.

Pain erupted across her side.

The impact sent her staggering, breath stolen from her lungs as fire bloomed beneath her ribs. The crowd gasped—some in satisfaction, others in shock—but she hardly heard them over the ringing in her skull, the pulse of raw sensation rippling through her body.

She gritted her teeth.

Her vision blurred at the edges, but she forced herself to straighten, refusing to let the weakness settle. Her breaths came short and sharp, the effort of pulling air back into her lungs a battle unto itself. Every motion sent fresh pain slicing through her torso, but she locked it away, burying it beneath sheer will.

Quinn prowled forward, sensing the shift, but Reya refused to give him the satisfaction of hesitation. Instead, she braced herself, setting her stance, her body screaming in protest as she prepared to meet his next attack head-on.

Pain was a lesson. And she had learned how to wield it.

Quinn pressed the advantage, closing in fast, his strikes relentless, forcing Reya to keep moving despite the fire threading through her ribs. Each impact sent fresh pain reverberating through her bones, but she refused to yield.

Pain was temporary. Power was permanent.

She saw it—the mistake, the fraction of hesitation as Quinn adjusted for his next hit, assuming she was slowing, assuming she would fold beneath the intensity of his aggression.

She twisted, using his own momentum against him.

His fist sailed past her shoulder, and in the heartbeat where his center of gravity wavered, Reya struck. A brutal heel to his knee sent him stumbling, and before he could recover, she drove her elbow into his jaw with enough force to snap his head back.

The crack of impact silenced the courtyard.

Quinn hit the ground hard, his breath torn from him as he struggled to rise, but Reya was already standing over him, her pulse thunderous, her body protesting every motion even as she ignored it.

She exhaled, sharp and unwavering.

"It's done."

The crowd knew it. Ashur knew it. And most importantly, Quinn knew it.

Victory belonged to her.

The silence in the courtyard pressed against Reya's ears, heavy with expectation. Quinn lay before her, blood seeping from the split in his lip, his chest rising and falling in uneven breaths. The old ways demanded that she end him—that she draw her blade and let it decide his fate.

But she didn't move.

Her fingers curled into fists, not around a weapon, but around restraint. The echoes of the past whispered to her, urging her forward, reminding her of all the warriors before her who had stood in this place and made the choice that history expected.

No, she would not be history's puppet.

Reya lowered herself, slow, deliberate, until she met Quinn's gaze directly. His body was bruised, battered, and yet the defiance in his eyes had not dulled.

She could take his life. She could silence him forever, rid herself of his challenges, his threats, his opposition. But what would that truly prove?

"You are defeated." Her calm voice was unwavering. "I will not take your life. Not when there are so few of us left. That is a mercy you will remember."

A ripple spread through the crowd, protests of confusion, of disbelief. Quinn's gaze flickered, something unreadable shifting beneath the raw edges of his fury.

She stood. Let him rise, let him feel her mercy in his bones, let him know that power was not simply who could strike the hardest. It was who could choose when not to strike at all.

Ashur stepped forward and handed the queen's crown to her. He stood beside her in silent solidarity. The choice had been made.

She had won.

Not just the fight—but the right to decide what kind of ruler she would be.

CHAPTER 46

REYA WALKED OUT OF the courtyard with Ashur by her side, the cool night air pressing against her sweat-damp skin. The scent of crushed leaves and smoldering torches clung to the air, mingling with the iron tang of dried blood still on her hands. She kept her stride steady, her head high, even as exhaustion gnawed at her control. The itch of unseen eyes pressed against her back—whether from wary observers or figments of her own paranoia, she couldn't tell.

Only when the door to her room clicked shut did she allow herself to falter. Her knees buckled, breath hitching as the last vestiges of adrenaline abandoned her body. Ashur caught her instantly, his arm firm around her waist, the warmth of his touch steadying her against the cold numbness creeping into her limbs. The scent of him—cedar, pine, and soft ocean breezes—grounded her.

"Let's get you cleaned up," he said, his voice low, rough with concern. His hold on her was gentle as he guided her toward the bathing room, the promise of warm water and sanctuary beckoning through the haze of exhaustion.

Ashur guided Reya through the bathing room's threshold, his grip steady but careful, as though he feared she might unravel completely if he pressed too hard. The scent of damp stone and lavender-infused water curled in the air, coaxing her toward something resembling relief. Steam rose in slow, curling tendrils, softening the harsh edges of the chamber, casting the golden lantern light in wavering halos.

She let him help her sit on the cushioned bench beside the basin, the marble cool against her palms as she braced herself. Her limbs felt leaden, her fingertips trembling with the last vestiges of spent energy. Ashur crouched before her, his presence solid, unwavering. He dipped a cloth into the warm water, wringing it out before pressing it gently to her face. The warmth seeped into her skin, chasing away the lingering chill, though the ache beneath it remained.

She closed her eyes, letting the rhythmic motion of his careful hands lull her into stillness. He worked in silence, wiping away the dirt, the dried blood, the smudges of something more intangible—something she wasn't ready to name. When he reached her hands, he hesitated, his thumbs brushing lightly over the cuts along her knuckles, the raw skin where battle had left its mark.

"You're shaking," he said, a hair louder than the trickling water.

"I know," she whispered back, her voice thinner than she intended.

He didn't ask more—didn't press her for words she wasn't ready to find. Instead, he continued, his touch patient, methodical, the care in it nearly unbearable. As if he saw the pieces of her slipping and refused to let them scatter.

Reya hardly registered the gentle scrape of Ashur's fingers as he worked, the cloth tracing over her hands with deliberate care. Warm water seeped into the shallow cuts along her knuckles, the sting sharp but fleeting. She let herself lean into the rhythm of it—the quiet, the patience—as her exhaustion pressed heavy against her ribs.

Ashur shifted, his movements careful, as though he feared breaking the silence would shatter whatever fragile control she still held. He soaked the cloth again, wringing it out before running it down her forearm, chasing away the grime and dried sweat. The warmth soothed where the tension remained knotted deep in her muscles, and she exhaled slowly, forcing the stiffness in her shoulders to ease.

The room held an almost sacred stillness. Only the occasional drip of water and the rustle of fabric broke the quiet, the soft glow of lantern light casting elongated shadows against the stone walls. Steam curled from the basin, lending the space a muted warmth, as if insulating them from the rest of the world.

Ashur's touch slowed when he reached the inside of her wrist, his thumb brushing over the pulse point there—a ghost of contact, but enough to make her shiver. Not from cold, but from something deeper.

She forced her eyes open, meeting his gaze. His brow furrowed, though he said nothing. He didn't need to. The concern on his face, the quiet patience in his touch—it said enough.

"You don't have to do this," she said. Her voice was thin, fractured.

Ashur exhaled, shaking his head once. "Yes, I do."

He continued, his motions unhurried, steady, as if to remind her that some things didn't require urgency. That care—true, unwavering care—could exist in the spaces between survival and duty.

Her fingers grasped the edge of the cloth where his hand lingered. She wasn't sure why—perhaps to hold on to the warmth, the steadiness, the proof that she hadn't unraveled entirely.

Perhaps just to hold on to something.

CHAPTER 47

ASHUR WATCHED REYA'S FINGERS curl around the cloth, her grip tentative, as though she was unsure whether to hold onto him or the moment itself. He let her, didn't pull away, didn't rush her. Some wounds required pressure. Others required patience.

She was unraveling, but not in a way that was visible to anyone else—not in a way she'd allow to be seen. He could feel it in the subtle tremor of her breath, in the way exhaustion softened the sharp edges of her presence. Her control had carried her through the courtyard, past the silent gazes of those who had seen what she'd done, what she'd endured. But here, in the solitude of warm water and low lantern light, it was slipping.

He shifted, kneeling fully before her, the stone floor pressing into his knees—a discomfort easy to ignore. His eyes traced over the fresh bruises blooming along her forearm, the cuts along her knuckles where her fists had met flesh. He knew the story of each wound without her telling him.

Carefully, he reached for the pitcher, refilling the basin with fresh, warm water. The steam rose again, carrying mists of lavender through the air, curling between them like a barrier against the world outside this room. He dipped the cloth once more, wringing it out before pressing it to her collarbone, just beneath the dried streak of blood trailing toward her shoulder.

She barely flinched.

"I'll be quick," he said, though he had no intention of rushing. His movements stayed steady, methodical—a promise that she didn't need to brace for anything else. That for now, she could just exist in the quiet.

As he worked, her exhaustion became more apparent. Her shoulders, usually rigid with control, eased by degrees. Her breathing slowed. He felt it when she exhaled—like she was letting go of something too heavy to carry alone.

Ashur wasn't foolish enough to think this moment would mend anything. Some wounds were deeper than flesh. Some lingered long after the blood was washed away.

But if she would allow it—just for tonight—he could hold some of it for her.

"You need blood." His voice was low and edged with something that wasn't quite hesitation but lingered close to it. Reya stilled, her fingers tightening around the edge of the basin, the damp cloth forgotten in her grip.

The lantern light flickered, casting wavering gold against the steam curling through the room, blurring the sharp edges of reality for a moment. He didn't need to say more—she knew exactly what he meant. To tap into the healing magic in her blood, she needed to replenish it. And that meant facing what neither of them particularly wanted to discuss.

"We haven't figured out the logistics of that with Malek yet." Her voice was quieter now, but not weak. Just tired. Her eyes, shadowed with exhaustion, met his, searching for something— perhaps reassurance, perhaps resolve.

"They have a healer with them." He kept his tone even, practical, though something in him bristled at the idea of relying on outsiders. But this wasn't about pride. It was about necessity.

She exhaled, the sound mixing with the slow drip of water from the cloth. For a long moment, she didn't speak, only held his gaze as if weighing the options in silence. Then, finally, she gave him a small nod.

"As soon as we finish here."

The tension remained. The silence threaded between their gazes. But for now, it was enough— they had settled the matter, if only temporarily. Ashur shifted, adjusting his grip on the cloth, forcing himself back to the quiet task at hand.

CHAPTER 48

REYA STOOD BEFORE THE mirror, the dim lantern light casting uneven shadows across the marred surface of her skin. Her reflection stared back at her—grim, exhausted, but steady. The bruises stood in stark contrast against her complexion, blooming in deep blues and sickly yellows along her cheekbone, a harsh reminder of the night's toll. She dabbed the spot, testing the depth of the ache. A sharp, pulsing sting answered, radiating down to her jaw.

Her split lip throbbed in time with her heartbeat, the slow ooze of blood seeping into the damp cloth she pressed against it. The cool fabric was a slight relief, but it did nothing to dull the deeper pain beneath—the kind that settled in bone, in memory.

She inhaled, slow and controlled, and let her gaze drop lower. The mirror offered no mercy. Her torso bore the worst of it—her left side a mottled mess of purples and reds, the kind of bruising that suggested Quinn hadn't held back. She gingerly traced the edges of the discoloration, biting back the hiss that threatened to escape when her fingers ghosted over her ribs. Pain flared, deep and sharp, confirming what she already suspected. A crack, maybe two.

Her reflection wavered as the steam thickened in the room, softening the harshness of reality for a brief moment. But she didn't look away. She needed to see it—to measure the damage, to calculate what she had left to give.

Distant footsteps echoed beyond the chamber, reminding her she wasn't alone. Ashur was fetching Malek, handling the logistics of her survival while she stood here taking stock of her brokenness.

She winced as she eased the fabric over her shoulders, the soft linen catching briefly against the tender bruises lining her ribs. The dress, loose and mercifully forgiving, draped over her aching frame like a whisper, offering relief where every other option would have been a fresh agony.

She exhaled slowly, fingers tracing the edge of the neckline, the material cool against her overheated skin. The scent of it—clean, carrying the faintest hint of cedar and something distinctly Ashur—lingered as she pulled it into place. It wasn't just the practicality of it that made her throat tighten. It was the thoughtfulness behind it. The quiet understanding that she wouldn't have asked for help, but that he had given it anyway.

She could have cried at his kindness, but she bit down on the feeling, swallowed it before it could take root. She couldn't afford sentiment now. Any other outfit would have been suffocating, pressing against the deep bruising along her ribs, carving pain into every breath, dulling her focus. And she needed all of it—all her wits, all her sharp edges—to face Malek.

She rolled her shoulders, testing the limits of movement, letting herself find steadiness. The dress was a small mercy, but it was enough.

The door swung open, its hinges groaning in protest, and Ashur strode inside, his grip firm around Malek's arm. Reya caught the subtle resistance in the human's posture—the tensed shoulders, the barely checked irritation in the set of his jaw—but he did well to bite his tongue. Wisely so.

Malek's clothing was rumpled from the handling, dust settling unevenly over the folds of his shirt as if he'd been dragged through more than just a hallway. His expression shifted between indignation and forced neutrality, his lips pressed into a thin line, but his jade eyes flickered with protest. The lantern light cast a wavering glow across his face, illuminating the crease of irritation on his brow. He had the look of someone balancing on the edge of frustration, but not foolish enough to let it tip into defiance.

Ashur released him with little ceremony, the sudden absence of force making Malek stumble half a step before he righted himself. His gaze flicked to Reya, scanning her, assessing—but she stood unmoving, spine straight despite the ache threading through her ribs. The dress Ashur had chosen still felt like the only barrier between her pain and the world outside of it.

She let the silence stretch just long enough to remind Malek who held control here. The steady drip of water from the nearby basin was the only sound, slow and rhythmic, counting the seconds as tension thickened the air.

"I assume you understand why you're here," she said finally, voice smooth despite the exhaustion pulling at its edges.

Malek's jaw twitched, but he nodded, his movements clipped. He still hadn't spoken—not yet.

Good.

Malek straightened, brushing the creases from his tunic in a deliberate motion, as if reclaiming some semblance of control. But his silence told Reya everything—he knew better than to test her patience.

She studied him with quiet scrutiny, the dim lantern light casting sharp shadows across his face. His posture was stiff, bracing against the words left unsaid. She could sense his reluctance, the way his fingers twitched at his sides as if itching to push back, to argue. But Ashur's presence at her flank, solid and unmoving, was enough to keep Malek's tongue in check.

Reya shifted, pressing into the ache along her ribs, the deep soreness radiating through her side like a slow burn. The pressure was a reminder— a force against the exhaustion threatening to pull her under. She was still standing. Still in control.

The lantern light flickered, casting uneven shadows across the stone walls, the heat of the room mixing with damp linen and a tinge of old blood. Her fingers curled at her sides, nails pressing into her palm, a small focus point amidst the swirling tension.

"Considering we never discussed how your process of blood collection would occur, we will need to improvise." Her voice remained steady, though the words settled thick upon the light breeze swirling through the room.

Malek grunted, a sharp exhale of irritation, his glare cutting through the dim haze of the room. His posture was stiff, shoulders squared like he expected a fight, even though he knew better than to start one here. He offered nothing—no argument, no cooperation—just his silence, taut and simmering.

"I assume you can heal from a simple cut. Correct?" Reya's voice was steady, measured, though exhaustion brushed up against her control. The flickering lantern light cast uneven shadows across Malek's face as he gave a curt nod, his expression tight with restraint.

She turned her gaze to Ashur, the silent understanding between them passing without the need for elaboration. "Clean his arm, please."

Ashur didn't hesitate. The air carried the scent of damp stone as he strode toward the washroom, his steps firm, purposeful. A moment later, he returned with a rag, water darkening the fabric as it dripped in slow rivulets between his fingers. Without preamble, he grasped Malek's wrist, the grip efficient rather than gentle, and pushed his sleeve up past his forearm. The exposed skin was mottled from old bruises, the sheen of sweat clinging to it.

The cloth met flesh with a muted drag, wiping away the dust and grime that clung to Malek's arm. The water's coolness sent a shiver over his skin, though he didn't flinch. The quiet scrape of fabric against flesh filled the silence, an oddly rhythmic sound that seemed to punctuate the charged air between them.

Reya watched, absorbing the details—the tension in Malek's posture, the irritation in the tightness of his jaw, the controlled efficiency in Ashur's movements. All of it was a prelude to what was coming next.

Reya's fingers curled around the hilt of the knife, the cool metal pressing against her palm. The blade gleamed under the dim lantern light, catching the flickering glow as she lifted it from the table. The weight of it was familiar, balanced, steady in her grasp.

The room held a charged stillness, the quiet punctuated only by the rustle of fabric as she moved. The air carried the lingering scent of damp stone and burned wick, a muted backdrop to the tension coiling in her chest. She took slow, measured steps toward Malek, the sound of her footfalls barely audible against the worn floor.

His gaze followed her approach, guarded yet unreadable, though she didn't need to see his expression to know his thoughts. The charged air pulsed between them, stretched thin with expectation.

The knife sat easy in her grip.

She stopped in front of him, the dim light casting long shadows between them. Without preamble, she slit the blade across his exposed skin.

Malek hissed air through his teeth, the sharp sound cutting through the tense silence between them. Reya met his gaze, absorbing the brief flicker of discomfort in his expression, but she refused to let it sway her. The instinct to apologize pressed at her resolve, but she shoved it aside, burying it beneath necessity.

Her fingers curled firmly around his forearm, the heat of his skin pulsing beneath her grip. She could feel the tautness in his muscles, the barely restrained irritation simmering just beneath the surface.

His pulse thrummed beneath her fingertips, steady but tight, his breaths measured, controlled. The tension lingered, a quiet war between restraint and resistance. But Reya didn't waver.

She dipped her mouth to the cut, drawing blood into her mouth. The bloom of magic surged through her veins, hot and electric, chasing the coppery tang of iron that coated her tongue. As she forced the mouthful down, a shiver traced the length of her spine, the raw essence latching onto her like an unseen force. She drew one more breath, deeper this time, the taste of Malek's lifeblood burning against her senses. Then, with a sharp exhale, she pulled away, wiping her mouth with her trembling hand as she stepped backward, putting precious distance between them.

Malek's gaze burned into her, his fingers pressing against the wound as if trying to contain what had been taken. The crease in his forehead deepened, a question forming in the gap that held their silence—one laced with wariness, with something that bordered on understanding, yet stopped just short. The air between them thickened, charged with a gravity neither dared to acknowledge aloud.

CHAPTER 49

ASHUR STARED BETWEEN THEM, his breath caught somewhere between his chest and throat as the pit in his stomach yawned wide, threatening to swallow him whole. The sight of Reya's lips—soft, parted—pressed to another man's skin sent a white-hot pulse through his veins, jealousy burning so fiercely it bordered on pain. His fingers curled into fists at his sides, nails biting into his palms, but the sharp sting did nothing to ground him. It was necessary. He knew that. He knew. And yet, knowing did little to keep the darkness at bay. It crept in, slow and insidious, coiling through his ribs like smoke, feeding on the part of him that wished, irrationally, that her touch had been meant for him alone.

The pause that settled between them charged with something unspoken, something that pressed against his lungs as he fought to swallow it down. His jaw locked as he forced himself to remain still, to not flinch, to not let the betrayal—no, not betrayal, but something dangerously close—register on his face. But his body betrayed him in other ways. The tightness of his throat, the heat flushing beneath his skin, the way his vision sharpened on Reya with a hunger he couldn't afford to name.

Ashur forced himself to breathe, slow and measured, though each inhale felt shallow, ineffective against the weight pressing against his chest. Reya's gaze flicked toward him, something unreadable passing through her expression—guilt, hesitation, resolve. He couldn't tell which, and maybe it didn't matter.

Malek let out a slow exhale, adjusting his grip over the cut, his jade eyes scanning her with quiet calculation. The lingering traces of magic sparked along Reya's fingers, curling in the air like embers before fading.

Ashur's jaw tightened. "Is it done?" His voice came out rougher than he'd intended, edged with something he couldn't quite smother.

Reya swallowed, her throat working against the remnants of Malek's blood still coating her tongue. She nodded, but she didn't speak, and the silence scraped against his patience, raw and grating.

Malek glanced between them, his expression unreadable. "For now." He dragged his hand away from the wound. The cut had stopped bleeding, but the open wound was still raw enough to need a bandage.

The bruises on Reya's face faded as the magic did its work, yet Ashur could feel the lingering charge in the air, the way it clung to Reya like an unseen weight.

She stepped back again, distancing herself from both of them this time, her fingers twitching at her sides. Her shoulders tensed, and conflict flickered behind her eyes. The darkness that had crept into him whispered insidious things—how easy it had been for her, how natural—and he hated that it spoke to the worst parts of himself.

But she looked shaken. Unsettled. The act hadn't come without a price, and maybe that was enough to appease him.

Ashur exhaled sharply, the breath leaving him in a sharp, uneven rush as he forced his hands open, the tension locking his muscles refusing to fully release. His glare landed on Malek, sharp as a blade, but it did little to ease the fire clawing at his ribs.

"Then you can leave," he ground out, the words rough, edged with a force he didn't bother to temper. He didn't know if he said it for Reya's benefit or his own—either way, it rang hollow in the wake of the beast roaring inside him, unsatisfied, unchecked.

Malek didn't argue. Didn't hesitate. He spun on his heel, footsteps heavy against the floor, and strode toward the door. The scent of blood and magic clung to the bridge between them, making Ashur's stomach tighten as Malek wrenched the door open.

The slam echoed like a gunshot, reverberating through Ashur's bones, leaving behind the unsettling quiet of an emptied room and too many unsaid things. The absence of Malek should have been a relief, but it only sharpened the tension pressing against his chest. The air still held the remnants of Reya's breath, the charged weight of what had just happened settling deep into his skin, refusing to let go.

His pulse still raced. His jaw ached from clenching. And Reya—she was still there, standing just far enough away that the distance felt intentional. He could feel her gaze on him—uncertain, waiting.

But for what?

Ashur inhaled, but the breath was shallow, ineffective against the fire still burning beneath his ribs. Whatever had been unsaid between them before had now settled into something worse—something that couldn't be ignored.

And neither of them seemed ready to confront it.

He turned to Reya, his breath uneven, the adrenaline of the moment still crawling under his skin like static. She stood motionless, her fingertips danced on the edge of control, as if the remnants of magic still lingered there, clinging to her like an unseen force.

The scent of iron remained in the air, sharper now that Malek was gone, mingling with the musk of skin and sweat. It made his stomach twist. Not because of the magic. Not because of the necessity of it. But because of how easily her lips had parted, how naturally they had pressed against Malek's arm, how it had burned to witness it.

Ashur swallowed, jaw tight, and forced his arms to cross over his chest as if that could make the feeling go away. "I didn't like that." The rough words scraped from somewhere deeper than he meant to reveal.

Reya's gaze flickered to him, hesitant. "I know."

The simplicity of her answer didn't soothe him. If anything, it made the tension worse. The moment still stretched between them like a taut wire, vibrating with all the things he couldn't say. She hadn't enjoyed it either—he could see that in the way she rubbed the heel of her palm against her mouth, as if she could wipe away the lingering taste—but it didn't erase the fact that he had seen it. Felt it.

"I know it was necessary," he continued, though even to his own ears, the words sounded hollow. "But watching you—" He cut himself off, inhaling sharply through his nose. "I didn't expect it to feel like that."

Reya's fingers curled, tension coiling through her shoulders. She looked away, shifting from foot to foot, the discomfort threading through her body as if she had nowhere to put it. That was the worst part—how they both felt it, neither knowing what to do with it.

A silence settled between them, heavier than before, stretching into something that might have been unbearable had it not been for the way she finally—finally—spoke.

"I didn't like it either," she admitted, voice quiet, but edged with honesty.

That admission, slight as it was, carved through him, settling the beast inside him just enough. It didn't erase the jealousy, nor did it undo the heat that had burned through his blood. But it meant something. More than he wanted to admit.

Ashur exhaled slowly, eyes flickering toward the door Malek had slammed shut behind him. He had an irrational urge to follow, to demand that something be settled—but settled how?

Ashur looked back at Reya, his gaze locking onto hers, searching for something—confirmation, understanding, maybe even regret. He could still taste the bitter tension, like remnants of magic lingering in the room.

"So, I am officially your king?" The words came quieter now, stripped of the sharpness that had edged his voice moments before. But they carried weight. More weight than he was ready to acknowledge.

Reya nodded, a simple motion, but it did nothing to ease the pressure in his chest. The reality of it settled deep in his bones, cold and heavy, wrapping around his ribs like something alive. This wasn't just a title. It was a reckoning. A shift in power, in duty, in everything that had tethered them together—sometimes against their will.

Neither of them moved. The silence stretched between them, thick and unsettled, pressing down on Ashur like a hand at his throat. He could feel the heat of her presence, close yet distant, the ache suspended in the silence suddenly feeling too vast.

Her lips parted as if she wanted to say something. But no words came. Just that quiet, lingering hesitation.

Ashur inhaled slowly, trying to steady himself, but the breath barely scratched the surface of his anxiety. His hands twitched at his sides, itching for something—to reach for her, to step away, to break whatever strange, fragile thing had formed between them.

Even so, neither of them moved. The moment hung between them, waiting, stretching into something that felt dangerously fragile.

And Ashur wasn't sure whether he wanted to hold onto it or shatter it completely.

CHAPTER 50

THE SURROUNDING AIR PULSED with tension, thick and crackling against her skin like a gathering storm. Reya could feel it pressing in, wrapping around her lungs, making each breath shallow and incomplete. Ashur held her gaze, unwavering, yet his emotions played so clearly across his face— flashes of fear, intrigue, the flicker of something deeper, rawer. And then—acceptance.

The moment stretched, taut and fragile, and for an instant, she was caught in it, unable to move, unable to breathe. But when his lips twitched at the edges, the dam inside her cracked, then shattered completely.

She surged forward, crossing the room before she could think to stop herself. The distance between them collapsed as she threw her arms around him, fingers clutching desperately at the fabric of his shirt, pulling him to her with a force that left no room for hesitation. Her lips found his in a crushing kiss, fierce and unrelenting. A confession poured into the meeting of mouths.

Heat bloomed between them, searing through her veins, igniting every nerve. The taste of him—warm, unmistakably Ashur—sent a shiver through her body, the sensation settling deep, filling the spaces where restraint had once lived.

She pressed closer, molding against him as if she could drown herself in the moment, as if she could carve away the distance that had stretched too long between them. The scent of him—salt and pine, tinged with the remnants of blood and magic—wrapped around her, intoxicating.

His hands found her waist—firm, certain, and that certainty sent another pulse of heat through her. His heart beat, strong and insistent against her chest, and the realization struck her like lightning—this was real. Undeniable.

For once, there were no words. No calculations. No walls. Just the raw, consuming weight of everything they had held back, finally breaking free.

CHAPTER 51

MONTHS DRIFTED BY IN a fragile but welcome peace, the tension between fae and humans softening into something that resembled coexistence—perhaps even trust. Reya observed with quiet satisfaction as barriers were lowered, alliances cautiously forged in the wake of necessity. The initial apprehension had not disappeared entirely, but it no longer clung to every interaction like an open wound.

Yet amid the harmony, Reya faced her own reckoning. She had tasted what Ashur endured when she drank from Malek—had felt the strange mix of duty and discomfort coil within her like something unnatural. And when the roles were reversed, when Ashur fed upon a human woman in the same manner, the feeling was unbearable. Cold, visceral jealousy had scraped against her ribs, twisting in a way she hadn't anticipated. She had voiced it, sharp and adamant, behind the privacy of their bedroom door—just as he had.

From that night forward, they came to an understanding, not just as rulers but as something tangled far deeper. The act of drinking was necessary, but the choice of host mattered just as much as the blood itself. The boundaries they set were silent yet firm, shaped by the rawness of emotion they no longer wished to ignore.

In time, a healer among the humans devised an alternative—the draining of blood into bags to be stored and ingested later, offering a semblance of control over the exchange. But the method was flawed. Those who volunteered became pale and drawn, their bodies sluggish for days after, unable to contribute much until they fully recovered, sometimes taking weeks before they could offer themselves again.

By comparison, the direct cut-and-drink method, though riskier, proved far more effective. A wound cleaned immediately healed quickly, and those who took part found themselves recovered in mere hours instead of days. More surprising still was the quiet intimacy it fostered—a closeness between fae and their chosen human that transcended mere survival. Some had grown attached enough to refuse rotation at the end of the month, opting instead to stay. Bonds had formed in ways none had expected, reshaping the dynamic of their uneasy alliance into something deeper. They saw possibility among the fae. A life.

A future. Reya had noticed the shift—more laughter between them, shared meals, whispered discussions of what could come next.

Reya watched it all unfold with a quiet, wary sort of hope, keenly aware that peace was as delicate as a thread pulled too taut, ready to snap under the uncertainty. Trust was not given freely; it was shaped, tested, reforged in the fires of hardship. Yet, for now—this moment—stability held. It was a fragile thing, but something neither she nor Ashur could afford to take for granted.

Still, she couldn't shake the unease coiling in her gut.

Her gaze flicked toward Malek, observing the way he stood apart from the others, his posture rigid, his expression carved from stone. His people had adapted, weaving themselves into the fabric of the stronghold, finding purpose beyond survival. They spoke with the fae, shared meals, built alongside them with something that almost resembled ease. But Malek did not join them. He lingered at the edges, watching with cold scrutiny, his sharp eyes never softening, never yielding.

A bitterness clung to him, thick as smoke from a dying fire. Each month, when the exchange of people occurred, he lingered by the gate, his eyes searching. And when the last of the trade had finished, his shoulders dipped in defeat.

And Reya knew he had never truly forgiven her. From the moment she brokered the peace arrangement, his ire calcified into resentment that only increased tenfold the moment she fed on the blood from his arm.

She could feel it even now, curling in the spaces between them like an unvoiced threat.

Her stomach twisted violently, a slow churn of nausea rising from deep within. The scent of damp earth and cooling embers drifted through the cracked window, mingling with the remnants of breakfast—eggs and bacon—turning the once-appetizing aroma into something unbearable. She swallowed hard, turning away, pressing the back of her hand to her mouth as a sharp wave of dizziness followed.

The air inside their chamber felt too thick, laced with the tang of old wood and the cold bite of blood. A chill seeped through the stone floors, curling around her bare feet, sharp against her skin. She exhaled slowly, trying to steady herself, but the rolling sensation in her gut refused to ease.

Behind her, the soft creak of a door and the muted shuffle of footsteps drew her attention.

"Are you okay?" Ashur's voice was warm, edged with concern. He stepped out of the washroom, steam curling from the threshold, the scent of worn soap and fresh water clinging to his skin. His white hair was damp, unruly, falling over his shoulders in loose waves.

He wore jeans and a t-shirt—simple, practical, traded from the humans in exchange for food. The old leathers and tunics of their realm had become relics of a past that no longer fit. Their wardrobe had expanded alongside their uneasy alliance; boots thick enough to endure the crumbling roads, coats lined for the creeping bite of autumn.

And yet, despite the warmth of Ashur's presence, Reya could only focus on the relentless jitters twisting in her belly, a slow, rolling sickness that refused to settle. Heat prickled at the back of her neck, sweat dampening her skin despite the cool autumn air leaking through the window. She exhaled sharply, pressing a hand against the ache in her stomach, willing it away.

"I can't seem to get my stomach to settle lately."

Ashur cocked his head, his cobalt eyes narrowing, sharp with quiet scrutiny. "When was your last cycle?"

The question landed like a knife drawn clean across her thoughts. She parted her lips to answer, but found the words lodged in her throat. Slowly, her mind ticked through the weeks, tracing back over days filled with bloodshed, survival, and fragile alliances.

She only had a few cycles in this broken world. But it had been at least a couple of blood slave rotations since the last one.

She blinked at Ashur, and then the meaning of his question crashed down with the force of a hurricane, shaking her to her core. The room blurred for a fraction of a second, the floor beneath her seeming less solid, as if the realization had unmoored her.

A few of the other fae females had fallen ill with the same symptoms, only to discover they carried life within them—fragile, improbable, but undeniably real.

"Before the last rotation or possibly the one prior," she whispered, and her voice cracked, barely more than air between them. "Do you think..."

The realization came like a whisper of magic—elusive at first, then undeniable. Reya pressed a hand to her stomach, the hum of life sparking beneath her fingertips. A child. Ashur's child.

CHAPTER 52

ASHUR STOOD FROZEN. REYA'S words settled over him like an unseen force. Silence stretched between them, tense and fragile, as his mind fractured between two warring thoughts: the undeniable reality of what she had said and the sheer impossibility of it.

Then, something sharp coiled within him—fear, perhaps, or the ghost of responsibility he never thought he would bear. His gaze locked onto Reya's, searching for doubt, for hesitation, for something that might make the moment less real. But her eyes held steady.

A slow breath escaped him, heavy and measured, as his hands—hands that had wielded magic, crushed enemies, torn through fate itself—

ached with the unfamiliar urge to reach for her. To touch, to confirm, to feel their future.

"A child," he had finally said, the word tasting foreign on his tongue. A hundred possibilities had flickered through his mind—what it had meant for him, for her, for the world they had carved with blood and sacrifice.

And beneath it all—beneath the tension, the fear, the disbelief—there was something softer. A flicker of something frighteningly close to hope.

A moment of fragile wonder, delicate as the breath between heartbeats. His lips stretched into a smile so wide that his cheeks ached, a deep, unfamiliar pull ghosting along the edge of his grin. The sensation was startling—like warm sunlight on skin long accustomed to cold steel and shadows. His chest tightened, the pressure both foreign and oddly freeing, as if something within him had cracked open, letting in air for the first time.

The scent of Reya's skin—warm, familiar, threaded with something new—curled into his lungs, grounding him in the reality of her, of this impossible truth. His fingers twitched at his sides, the ghost of an instinct urging him to reach out, to press his palm against the flat of her stomach and feel for the stirrings of what had yet to exist.

A child. His child.

CHAPTER 53

"GO GET JANINE. SHE was able to tell the others were with child." Reya pointed toward the door, though her voice carried a tremor—a thread of barely contained anticipation weaving through the command.

Ashur turned, that radiant, breathtaking smile fading as he shifted toward the door. Yet even with his back to her, the echo of his expression lingered, filling her with something bright, something undeniable. The warmth of it curled in her chest, unfurling like the first touch of dawn against cool skin.

Her heart stuttered, then surged forward, excitement thrumming through her veins, too fierce and wild to contain. The sight of him—his sharp, commanding presence softened by joy, his features carved by a happiness so pure it bordered on reverence—left her breathless.

He was devastatingly handsome like this. Not just in the way his grin transformed him, but in the way it made her feel—like she was standing at the precipice of something vast and life-altering, her own emotions folding into his, amplifying, expanding.

She swallowed against the rush, fingers pressing lightly against her abdomen. Soon, they would know for certain. But in that moment, she already did.

It took only moments before Janine trailed Ashur into the room, her medical bag clutched tightly in her hand. Reya barely registered Ashur stepping aside to let the healer through—her pulse was too loud, hammering in her ears like the rhythmic beat of war drums.

"Ashur said you think you might be pregnant?" Janine asked, breathless. Her straw-colored hair was swept up in a ponytail today, wisps curling loose around her flushed cheeks, as if she had sprinted here the moment she heard.

Reya swallowed, tasting the sharp edge of anticipation in the back of her throat. "It seems I have some of the same symptoms as the others you confirmed to be with child." She tried to keep her voice even, but her hands betrayed her. Fingers tangled together, restless and twisting. The nervous energy pooled in the space between her palms like something tangible, something alive.

Janine pulled out a small box from her bag, her movements brisk but steady. The room seemed impossibly small as Reya watched her open it and retrieve a plastic stick with a thin strip on one end.

"Pee on this end, please." Janine pointed to the delicate strip, her tone matter-of-fact. "Then put this cap back on and bring it to me."

Reya stared at the object in her hand, the reality of it settling into her bones. It was so unassuming, so simple—and yet it had the power to confirm something that felt utterly world-altering. Her eyebrow lifted in disbelief, but she said nothing, turning instead toward the washroom.

Her steps were measured, deliberate, though inside she felt unsteady, as if each movement carried her closer to something irreversible. The anticipation crackled along her skin, warming her fingers, tightening in her stomach. Soon, she would know.

After following Janine's instructions, Reya emerged from the washroom, the plastic stick clutched in her fingers like a fragile piece of fate waiting to be revealed. The cool air of the bedroom pressed against her skin, in clear opposition to the warmth of the enclosed space she had just left. Her heartbeat thrummed in her ears, steady but unnervingly loud, each pulse a reminder that everything could change in mere minutes.

She handed Janine the test, her fingers tightening before she let go, as if reluctant to relinquish control over what it might reveal. The room felt smaller now, the walls closer, heavy with expectation.

"Have a seat," Janine said gently, motioning toward the edge of the bed. "This will take a few minutes. Do you mind if I examine you?"

Reya hesitated, the words catching in her throat. The idea of human hands measuring the rhythms of her body, scrutinizing the core of what made her fae, unsettled her in ways she couldn't quite name.

"I am fae, not human," she replied, her voice carrying an edge of uncertainty that she had not intended to reveal.

Janine smiled, her expression warm but unwavering. "I've found we are similar enough over the past few months. Our bodies function essentially the same—hearts beneath the ribs, pulse just a bit slower than yours. Temperatures run in the same range as ours." She offered a small shrug, a simple confidence in her assessment. "And this way I can take a benchmark of what your pulse and blood pressure are now, so later in the pregnancy, if things change drastically, we can monitor you more closely."

Pregnancy. The word lingered in the air, settling into the silence like a stone dropped into deep water. Reya exhaled slowly, feeling the moment coil through her body, sinking into her bones with a gravity she hadn't prepared for.

She flicked her gaze to Ashur, searching for reassurance, for something steady to anchor herself to. His expression was unreadable at first—a flicker of surprise beneath the surface, then something softer. A quiet nod. Not permission, not insistence—just solidarity.

The simple gesture loosened something in her chest, enough for her limbs to obey. She eased onto the chair, her movements deliberate, as if shifting too quickly might shatter the fragile hold she had on the moment. The wood creaked beneath her weight, the cool air pressed against her skin, and still, the word reverberated through her skull.

Pregnant.

It wasn't just a possibility anymore. It was real.

Janine worked with practiced efficiency, the cool press of the thermometer against Reya's lips, the firm grip of fingers at her wrist, measuring the pulse that thrummed just beneath the skin. The cuff tightened around her arm, the squeeze sharp but fleeting before releasing with a soft hiss.

Each measurement—temperature, pulse, blood pressure—was recorded in neat script in the notebook Janine carried, the scratch of pen against paper filling the silence between them. Reya sat stiffly, her breaths shallow, heart ticking faster than she knew it should. The air felt heavier now, dense with anticipation, curling against her skin like something inevitable.

Then Janine looked down.

The plastic stick was small in her hands, seemingly insignificant—until the smile stretched across her lips, soft but unmistakable. Slowly, she turned it, angling it so Reya could see.

Two clear blue lines.

For a moment, Reya could only stare, her world narrowing to that little window, that undeniable confirmation. The air thickened, pressing against her chest. A flicker of movement trembled through her fingers, not quite sure whether to reach for it or retreat.

Janine's voice broke through, gentle but certain.

"Congratulations."

The word settled into Reya's bones, slow and inexorable, reshaping the future she hadn't yet dared to embrace.

CHAPTER 54

REALITY DIDN'T EASE INTO Ashur—it struck, swift and unforgiving, like a blade to the chest. Janine's reaction was subtle— a soft smile, a quiet certainty in the way she turned the plastic stick toward Reya. But it landed with the force of a twister.

He was going to be a father.

The words didn't merely settle in his mind— they detonated, sending shockwaves through his very being. His breath hitched, his pulse hammering against his ribs, loud enough that he swore the room could hear it.

Everything around him blurred at the edges— the dim candlelight flickering against the stone walls, the scent of cooling embers and damp earth filtering through the window, the distant murmur of voices beyond their chamber. All of it faded beneath the sheer magnitude of the moment.

Reya sat still, her fingers clenched against her lap, the ghost of disbelief shadowing her expression. Ashur knew her well enough to see the tremor beneath her composure—the way her throat bobbed in a swallowed breath, the way her muscles tensed as though bracing for the world to shift beneath her feet.

And it had.

A child. Their child. In a world not built for softness, not meant for gentle things.

A surge of something fierce and protective roared to life inside him. This world was dangerous, brutal, unforgiving. But if fate had carved out this path for them, if this life had found them amidst the ruin—then he would fight. He would give everything he had to shield what was theirs.

Slowly, carefully, he reached for Reya's hand, threading his fingers through hers. He felt the warmth of her skin, the tremor in her grip, and squeezed gently.

No words passed between them—none were needed. A quiet, steadfast happiness took root in his bones, settling deep and unwavering, but even as it did, a shadow of foreboding lingered at the edges. Peace, after all, was never more than an illusion.

CHAPTER 55

DUSK SMOTHERED THE HORIZON in bruised tones of violet and ash, the sky bleeding into the earth like a wound stretched open. Then came the first cries—sharp, desperate, clawing through the quiet like the sound of a dying animal.

Ashur's pulse kicked hard against his ribs. They came in waves, pouring over the barren landscape on foot and in carts, their bodies hunched with exhaustion and fear.

Vander's voice split through the chaos, urgent and raw. "Open the gates! We're being hunted!"

Ashur stepped forward, his breath tight, scanning the flood of bodies from his perch at their bedroom window. It wasn't just a handful of refugees. It was Malek's entire village. They surged toward the obsidian walls, tripping over uneven ground, clutching children to their chests, their eyes wide with terror.

And behind them, the monsters came.

Metal beasts rolled forward in unnatural silence, their exteriors gleaming beneath the fractured sunset, the barrels of their guns glinting like predatory eyes. Then—fire. Thunder. A deafening crack split the air as bullets tore through the earth, erupting in bursts of dust and stone, sending villagers stumbling, screaming, falling.

Ashur's jaw clenched. These fools had led death straight to their doorstep.

He turned to Reya, but he already knew—they had no choice.

Their stronghold would not survive if they hesitated.

The castle steps echoed beneath Reya's swift descent, her voice cutting through the chaos with surgical precision. Ashur felt the charged energy in the air—the sudden movements, the hurried footsteps against slick flagstones, the desperate murmurs of both fae and humans scrambling for weapons.

Skylark, his second-in-command, stood at the entrance to the armory, wind shifting around him with restless energy as he shoved weapons into waiting hands. The touch of steel was cold in Ashur's palm, reminding him of the grim reality of what was to come. Through the high castle window, the approaching threat loomed—dark forms shifting at the edges of vision, their unnatural stillness making his pulse pound against his ribs.

They would need more than fae magic in this fight. The human weapons, crude and inelegant, might be the difference between survival and annihilation.

"Open the gate!" Malek's voice rang out, raw with urgency, cutting through the tense air as he came to stand beside Reya and Ashur, his sword gripped so tightly his knuckles had gone white.

"If we open the gates, we will be overrun." Reya's tone rang sharp against the wall. She lifted her hand, and the obsidian wall rippled like a liquid shadow before solidifying into glass-like stone.

Ashur's breath hitched as the scene beyond sharpened into view. The chaos outside slammed against his senses—cries thick with desperation, the dull, rhythmic pounding of fists against the barrier, the guttural sound of terror crawling into voices that were quickly losing hope. The scent of sweat and dust mingled with the distant iron tang of blood, thickening in the air as the sea of unarmed people swelled against the walls like a storm surge before collapse.

Malek's finger jabbed toward them, his chest rising and falling with barely controlled fury. "Those are my people out there, and if you hadn't noticed, they are unarmed."

Ashur's stomach tightened. He could see it now—the hollowed expressions, the soot-smudged faces, the way hands grasped at one another as if sheer grip alone might keep them from being swallowed whole by the darkness closing in.

The decision weighed against his ribs, pressing deep. If they opened the gates, their sanctuary would be torn apart. If they didn't, those outside would perish.

A choice, edged in blood.

CHAPTER 56

REYA DIDN'T FLINCH, THOUGH the air throbbed with distant concussions—the mechanical beasts were closing in, their deafening blasts rattling against the obsidian walls, sending tremors through the stone beneath her feet. The scent of burning metal thickened in the air, layering with the acrid sting of smoke that curled from the battlefield beyond.

"Reya, we need to help them." Ashur's voice was a quiet plea, threaded with urgency, meant only for her ears. "We can't watch them gunned down knowing we could have done something."

She held his gaze. His words pressed against the already suffocating tension. The unrelenting machine fire, the cries of terror from those outside—it gnawed at her control. But then her eyes shifted to Malek, and the heat of mistrust sharpened into something ice-cold in her chest.

"I swear." Each word was edged with steel. "If your people harm ours, the truce is over. We will slaughter every last one of you. Understand?"

Malek swallowed; the rigid nod barely masked his own desperation.

Reya turned to the barrier, the smooth surface cool beneath her palm. She inhaled, slow and steady, forcing herself to focus despite the whirlwind of uncertainty thrumming beneath her skin. The obsidian pulsed once under her touch before shuddering apart, cracking open like a fissure in the night.

The moment the gap was wide enough, the flood came. People surged forward, breathless, wide-eyed with terror, their feet stumbling over one another in their rush to escape the slaughter beyond the walls.

Ashur dropped to a knee, his hands pressing to the earth. The pulse of his magic rippled through the ground in a silent command—thorns erupted from the soil, twisting into an impenetrable wall behind the refugees. The barricade rose in a ruthless sprawl, black and sharp, shielding them from the crawling metal horrors beyond.

As the last of Malek's people flooded through the opening, the tension in Reya's chest remained coiled, refusing to ease. The air was thick with sweat and dust, the scent of fear sharp enough to taste.

Then—movement. A flash of dull green against the chaos.

She barely had a second to register the battalion of soldiers slipping through the blind side, their boots scuffing against stone, their rifles raised in a seamless, calculated motion.

Gunfire erupted.

The crack of bullets split the air, biting into the walls with deafening, concussive force. Reya's pulse slammed through her veins. She didn't hesitate—her palm struck the obsidian barrier with a fierce slap. The impact sent a shock of energy through her arm as she willed the gate to seal.

The rock groaned, shifting, slamming shut in a grinding cascade—too late. The damage was done.

Screams of the fallen tangled with the acrid scent of gunpowder and the metallic sting of blood curling into the air. The ground beneath her feet felt unsteady, as if the earth itself recoiled from the violence that had wormed its way inside their sanctuary.

This wasn't just a breach. It was a betrayal.

The scent of gunpowder and blood twisted in the air, thick enough to choke her. Screams clashed against the ringing of gunshots, reverberating through the stronghold like the echoes of a dying world. Reya didn't have time to process—only to act.

She raised her hands, power thrumming at her fingertips, lashing outward like a storm unfurling its wrath, turning guns into useless piles of melted metal. The humans were relentless, pulling sharp weapons from underneath hidden fabric. Their crude weapons were no match for fae magic, but they had numbers, and numbers could erode even the mightiest defenses.

Blood slaves and fae fought side by side—an unlikely alliance forged in survival—but they were faltering.

Her magic surged again, forming a barrier that slammed into the advancing humans in camouflage, sending them flying backward in a violent crash of limbs. But the effort burned through her reserves too quickly. Her breath caught in her throat. Power waned.

Ashur fought beside her, his movements swift and precise. Magic wove through his strikes, but Reya could feel his exhaustion. It clung to him like the dying embers of a once-roaring fire.

A blood slave let out a guttural cry as a blade sliced into their leg. A fae rushed forward to shield them, taking the next hit in their stead. Reya's heart twisted. They were not warriors—they were survivors, just barely clinging to the scraps of hope they had left.

Another human lunged for her. She countered, twisting out of reach, sending a burst of energy toward his chest. He crumpled with a harsh gasp, but not before his blade nicked her arm. Blood beaded against her skin.

And then, as swiftly as it had begun, it ended with a targeted flash of lightning that hit every predator within the walls, striking them down, leaving an electrical scent mixed with blood hanging on the air.

Victory was bitter on her tongue. The battlefield was littered with bodies—some fae, some human, all paying the price of desperation. She stood amid the carnage, panting, eyes sweeping over the broken remnants of their people.

She turned to Ashur. Their eyes met.

Her magic was spent, and from how the other fae staggered through the battlefield, she wasn't alone. The last tendrils of magic drained from their bodies, leaving them raw and vulnerable.

And Malek was watching.

CHAPTER 57

ASHUR'S GLARE WAS SHARP enough to cut. His breath slowed, measured—holding together the fraying edges of control. The humans huddled like prey, their wide, shell-shocked eyes darting between the bodies strewn across the stone. The scent of blood hung thick in the air, mingling with sweat, fear, and the acrid sting of gunfire residue still clinging to the battlefield.

Vander stood before them, arms outstretched, a shield against the inevitable reckoning.

The human in Ashur's arms choked out a final, shuddering gasp, their body twitching before falling limp. Their warmth was already fading, the slick crimson pooling between his fingers, cooling in the night air. Ashur's jaw tightened, the sensation defending him against the encroaching tide of fury. He put the body down with deliberate precision and licked the blood from his palm—iron-salt tang sharp against his tongue. His magic flared in response, a searing pulse that crackled through his veins, demanding retribution.

Thorns erupted from the ground, twisting into an impassable cage around the remaining humans. The sharp brambles gleamed under the low, flickering torchlight, their dark points glistening with stray droplets of blood. Let them cower. Let them understand that survival was a borrowed mercy.

His gaze swept across the battlefield, searching. Malek. The traitor should have been here, among the fallen, but his form was nowhere in sight. Had he escaped? Slipped into the chaos before the gate had sealed?

Beyond the thorny barricade, the mechanical beasts still prowled, their relentless, unnatural hum vibrating through the earth. Ashur pressed his hand to the ground, his fingertips sinking into the dirt, feeling its pulse beneath his touch. It was thin—his magic waning, stretched to its last reserve—but rage sharpened his focus, narrowed his will into something precise, lethal.

The ground convulsed.

A cavern tore open beneath the machines, the stone swallowing them in one violent collapse. The roar of magma surged upward, churning in furious waves as the metal units plunged into the abyss. Heat licked at the edges of the fissure, casting eerie shadows against the walls before, with one final exertion of will, Ashur slammed the earth shut. A resounding clap of thunder split the air, sealing their fate.

The battlefield stilled, but inside him, the storm raged on.

CHAPTER 58

REYA STRODE FORWARD, THE fallout from the bloodshed pressing against her skin like an iron brand. The air thickened with the tang of copper and churned earth, heavy with the raw stench of sweat and fear. Ashur's thorny prison loomed ahead, twisting brambles forming a jagged cage around the humans—its spiked edges gleaming under the flickering torchlight.

She stopped before Vander. The vines cast shadowed slashes across his face. His expression was taut—defiance and resignation locked in battle behind his dark-rimmed eyes.

"Whose idea was this attack?" Her demand cracked like a whip through the tense, smoke-laden air.

Vander held her gaze, unflinching, though his grip on the vines betrayed the tremor in his fingers. "The army found us." His voice frayed at the edges. "And we ran to the only place we knew was safe."

Safe, Reya almost laughed at the bitter irony. Her eyes narrowed, cold and slicing.

"And yet you struck the fae with that knife." She pointed to the blade still clutched in his grasp, blood dripping from its edge, staining the dirt beneath his feet in slow, deliberate drops. Her stomach twisted—not with hesitation, but with fury. "I am not as gullible as you and Malek think I am."

The taste of anger was sharp on her tongue. She wet her lips, voice lowering to something dark, final. "And I told Malek that if this was a double-cross, I would slaughter every single one of his people."

Vander's face drained of all color, his breath halting as realization crashed down upon him.

Reya's gaze dragged over the prisoners, their forms hunched, trembling, some pressing into each other as if proximity alone could shield them from her judgment. Their shallow breathing was erratic, their eyes darting between her and the thorns that caged them.

"You will sustain us for a long time," she said, her voice laced with quiet cruelty.

She turned back to Vander, holding his stare in a suffocating grip. "Executions will start at sunrise."

A sharp inhale, a desperate grasp at the vines—his plea tumbled forth, cracking under his dread. "Please. They didn't know. They just thought we were being attacked by the army. They didn't know we had made arrangements with them before fleeing our home."

Mercy. He begged for mercy now.

Reya's laugh was hollow, cutting, devoid of warmth. "You declared war." She stepped back, surveying the battlefield beyond the wall of thorns—the fae tending to their wounds, the blood slaves who had fought beside them, battered but standing. "And now you want my mercy?"

She did not grant them the dignity of an answer. Instead, she turned, stepping away from the makeshift prison, their judgment already settling into her bones. The cool night air did little to chase away the suffocating scent of blood clinging to her skin like unseen chains. Her boots pressed into damp earth, each step deliberate, forcing down the coil of fatigue winding through her limbs.

She reached Ashur and the rest of her people, her gaze sweeping the battlefield—ashen bodies, broken weapons, the remnants of a fight that should never have happened. Two fae lost. The price of another senseless battle.

Her voice was steady, cutting through the stillness with the precision of a blade. "We will bury them with dignity along with the loyal humans who fought beside us. Burn the rest after you harvest what little blood is left within their broken forms."

The fae moved swiftly, their expressions grim, the air thick with grief. The crackling torches cast restless shadows over the fallen, illuminating the lifeless forms with brief flashes of gold before they were swallowed by the darkness.

Ashur stepped forward, and the warmth of his presence was immediate, shielding her against the tide of exhaustion pressing at the rim of her vision. His blood-soaked fingers lifted, slow, deliberate, tracing the curve of her cheek. The touch was warm—sticky with battle, with loss, with something private in his gaze.

"You look tired," he said.

She closed her eyes, just for a breath. Just long enough to feel the rupture of everything settle in.

But there was no time to linger in weariness.

Not yet.

CHAPTER 59

ASHUR'S LIMBS ACHED WITH an exhaustion that seeped into his bones, dragging at his movements like lead. His fingers were raw from digging, caked with the bloodied earth that smelled of decay and regret. Every shovel of dirt he threw over the fallen felt like a whisper of their last breaths, a chorus of voices he would never hear again.

The scent of death clung to Reya, though she bore it with the stubbornness that had always made her formidable. He knew she needed blood—could see it in the pallor of her skin, the tremor she tried to hide in her fingers. Yet she refused, allowing the others to drink the little they could salvage. Her resolve was maddening. He wanted to force the blood to her lips, to strengthen her, to take away the slow unraveling he could see in her eyes.

With the last grave filled, they returned from the graveyard. Ashur's throat was dry as dust when Reya turned to the pile of dead traitors. Her fury burned through her grief. She met his gaze, the fire in her eyes igniting something just as dark inside him.

"Burn them."

Ashur turned to Bella, watching her slow, deliberate flick of the fingers as flames consumed the heap of bodies. The crackling of burning flesh was sickening. The air thickened with greasy smoke, the acrid stench clawing at his lungs. It smelled of betrayal. It smelled of regret.

Reya did not flinch.

Neither did Ashur.

He forced himself to breathe through it, swallowing down the bile rising in his throat, suppressing the part of him that whispered they had once been allies. Now, they were just charred remnants of what had been.

With the castle looming ahead, Ashur took Reya's arm—not to guide her, but to steady himself. The others disappeared into the cottages, their silence heavier than words. Ashur stepped forward, the heat of the fire still burning at his back, and he wondered whether it would ever leave him.

Ashur closed the castle doors behind them, the distant crackle of burning flesh still clinging to the air. The scent of charred bodies mixed with the stone-cold dampness of the hall, but it was nothing compared to the dismay curling in his gut.

"I am not sure I am comfortable with you fighting now that you are pregnant," he said as they stepped inside. The words felt heavier than he intended, dropping between them like a stone into deep waters.

Reya halted so suddenly that Ashur nearly stumbled. She turned. Her sharp stare cut through the dim torchlight, searching his face for weakness, for control—perhaps for something she could strike down.

"All of us are needed when there is an attack." Her voice was steady, but tension laced each syllable.

He inclined his head, holding her gaze despite the storm brewing in her eyes. "I know. I'm just telling you, I am not comfortable with it."

The space between them seemed to shrink, yet the distance had never felt greater. The silence wasn't empty; it bristled with unexpressed fears. He could feel the pressure building. The argument uncoiled like a beast waiting to strike. The flickering light from the torches sent shadows across her face, highlighting the fatigue in her eyes, the tightness in her jaw. And yet, she was unwavering.

Ashur resisted the urge to step closer, to reach for her, to break the simmering tension with touch alone. But he knew better—Reya was not one to yield simply because he asked. And he, for all his concerns, was not sure whether he wanted her to.

She crossed her arms, the movement sharp and deliberate, a shield between them that Ashur could not break. The torchlight flickered, casting restless shadows across her face, highlighting the tightness in her jaw, the defiance in her stance.

"What would you have me do instead?" Her voice was edged with challenge, yet beneath it, he could hear something quieter—something tired.

Ashur chuckled, though the sound came out more like an exhale, a release of tension he knew would never truly leave him. He took her arm, his fingers pressing gently against her skin, held still by the warmth she radiated.

"I'd erect a barrier between you and anyone who wished to harm you," he admitted, his voice softer now, his worry settling between them. "But I know that's just my need to keep you and my child safe. It's not something you would ever allow me to do."

The thought lingered, his fears curling like mist in the dim corridor. He could feel the pulse of her determination beneath his fingertips—a reminder that she would always fight, no matter how much he wished she wouldn't have to.

CHAPTER 60

IRRITATION PRICKLED AT REYA'S skin, hot and restless, like embers beneath her flesh. It coiled in her gut, tightening with every breath, every flicker of torchlight casting shifting shadows along the stone walls. The castle's air was thick with the remnants of battle—blood, sweat, the horrid stench of burning bodies still clinging to her senses.

She had fallen for Ashur, an ache she had not expected, a comfort she had allowed herself despite the war pressing in from all sides. But love did not mean surrender. The thought of relinquishing control over her fate, of being shielded when she was meant to stand, unsettled her more than the scars lining her arms. She had fought for this place, for these people—for survival.

Her fingers curled into fists, nails biting into her palm as if to anchor herself. She was one of the strongest fighters among them, and though their numbers dwindled, she refused to be treated as fragile. Not by Ashur. Not by anyone.

Ashur's fingers brushed against Reya's stomach—a whisper of warmth. The touch sent a ripple through her, not of fear, but of something deeper, more uncertain.

She exhaled, her breath shaky, her pulse a steady drum against the chaos in her chest. Could the life growing within her feel it? The turmoil, the battle, the unrelenting push and pull between duty and survival?

Her fists, still clenched with the remnants of her defiance, slowly unfurled. The tension in her fingers eased, though the storm inside her did not. She glanced at Ashur, finding something in his eyes that steadied her—something unshaken despite the fire, the blood, the war. His touch had been brief, yet the warmth lingered. A silent promise. A quiet tether to a future she wasn't sure she could hold on to.

Reya let out a slow breath, the tension in her shoulders loosening, though not entirely fading. She stepped forward, her boots scuffing against the worn stone floor of the castle corridor. The flickering torchlight cast shifting shadows along the walls, distorting the past victories and wounds carved into the stone itself. The smell of blood and fire still clung to her, thick and suffocating, testing her resolve.

Ashur walked beside her, his presence steady, but his uneasiness crackled between them. He was waiting for her to speak, to tell him she understood his fears. That she would take caution. But the words wouldn't come—not because she didn't care, but because caution had never been an option.

She turned to him, catching the sharp lines of his face in the dim light. His slate eyes searched hers, trying to read beyond the silence, beyond the rigid set of her jaw.

"I know you're worried." Her voice was quieter than she had intended. "But I can't afford to step back. Not now."

Ashur's expression flickered, something unreadable passing through his gaze. He nodded, though it wasn't in agreement—it was simply acceptance.

"I won't stop worrying," he admitted, his voice rough. "But I know better than to ask you to change."

Reya reached for his hand, curling her fingers around his own. It was a small gesture, a fleeting acknowledgment of the space they shared—the love they carried, even in the midst of war.

The battle wasn't over. Their burdens weren't lessened.

But, for now, they walked forward together.

CHAPTER 61

THE DOOR GROANED UNDER Ashur's touch, the sound splitting the silence like a whispered warning. Shadows slithered along the walls, stretching and distorting as if alive, feeding on the absence of light. The room was suffocating in its stillness, the air thick with something waiting.

He stepped forward, and agony erupted in his side—a white-hot bolt that stole the breath from his lungs. His vision swam, the pain sharp and brutal, cutting through muscle and bone with merciless precision. The world tilted, and his knee hit the cold stone floor with a sickening crack.

The warmth of Reya's hand was torn from his grasp, leaving behind only the ghost of her touch.

Her gasp cut through the dark, laced with alarm, sending chills racing down his spine. The air shifted—no, it ignited. The torch flared in an instant, flooding the room with harsh, blinding light. Ashur blinked rapidly, his body protesting as the shadows recoiled, exposing the jagged edges of danger lurking just beyond his reach. He clenched his jaw, forcing himself to move, to push past the pain and rise.

Ashur's breath came in shallow, ragged rasps as he pressed a trembling hand to his side. Warm blood seeped through his fingers, thick and slick, spreading over his palm as a dull roar filled his ears. His vision blurred for a heartbeat, the pain twisting deep, stealing his balance.

Then Reya's gasp cut through the fog.

He turned, every muscle locking into place, and the world narrowed to the sight before him.

Malek.

The knife gleamed in the flickering torchlight, its edge pressed against Reya's throat, so close he could see the indentation it made against her skin. Her chest rose and fell in controlled breaths, but her eyes—fierce, wild—burned with restrained fury.

Ashur froze, his own injury forgotten, drowned beneath the flood of panic that gripped his lungs like a vise. He could smell the iron tang of his own blood, feel the sluggish pulse of his heartbeat hammering in his chest, but none of it mattered.

Malek twisted his hand in Reya's hair, dragging her back with a brutal jerk.

"Let my people go, or she dies," Malek growled, his voice a guttural, vicious threat that scraped through the heavy air.

Ashur's pulse spiked, his body screaming for movement, for action—but one wrong move and that knife would slice. He forced himself to breathe, to steady the storm clawing at his throat.

Not Reya. He couldn't lose her.

Every instinct screamed at him to charge, to tear Malek apart, to rip that blade from his hand. But Malek wasn't reckless—he was calculated. A single mistake, a single misstep, and Ashur would watch the life drain from the woman who had become his reason to fight.

His fingers twitched at his side, curling into the bloodied fabric of his shirt as he fought against the suffocating fear, trying to think past the rage blinding him.

Reya was strong. But even the strongest warriors could fall to a blade at their throats.

And Malek knew it.

Ashur swallowed hard, forcing the tremor from his voice. "Let her go, Malek." The words were low, deliberate—but the raw edge of desperation clung to them.

Malek only smirked, tightening his grip.

Ashur had to act. Had to do something—before the next breath was Reya's last.

"Take down the cell walls you raised, and when my people are set free from this hellscape, I'll release your precious queen," Malek snarled with impatience lacing every word.

Ashur's breath rasped in his throat, the taste of iron thick on his tongue. His wound pulsed in time with his frantic heartbeat, every throb a brutal reminder of his own failing body. He could feel the warmth of blood pooling beneath his fingers, seeping into the fabric of his shirt, but the pain barely registered—not when Reya stood on the edge of oblivion.

The torchlight flickered, casting fractured shadows across Malek's twisted sneer. The knife trembled against Reya's throat, a gleaming promise of destruction. Ashur's stomach coiled tight, a sickening weight dragging him under.

"I can't. Not without blood. Please…she's with child." The words spilled from him, raw and pleading—an admission of vulnerability he never wanted to make.

Silence.

Malek's knuckles whitened around the hilt. His breathing hitched, uneven, wavering—but the blade did not move. Hesitation flickered in his eyes, a war of conflicting thoughts Ashur couldn't decipher. Was it doubt? A moment of wavering humanity? Or simply the cold calculation of a predator savoring its kill?

The room pulsed, heavy with danger, suffocating in its intensity. Ashur wanted to move, to lunge, to rip Malek's hand away—but his body refused, caught in the impossible balance of desperation and futility. He had nothing left to give. No power to do as Malek demanded. No leverage.

The torchlight dimmed, shadows thickening around them, stretching like waiting jaws.

Malek inhaled sharply, and his grip shifted. His blade hovered, a heartbeat away from sealing fate.

And the world held its breath.

The End
Stay tuned for Book 2: Curse of the Fae coming
soon!

About J.E. Taylor

Reading books never felt so dangerous!

Explore a world of chilling suspense and fantasy with books that come alive as you read.

J.E. Taylor is a USA Today Bestselling Author, a publisher, an editor, a manuscript formatter, a mother, a wife, a grandmother, a retired business analyst, and a Supernatural fangirl. Not necessarily in that order.

She sat down to write her first book in February of 2007 after her daughter asked:

"Mom, if you could do anything, what would you do?"

From that moment on, she hasn't looked back.

She publishes supernatural suspense, urban fantasy, paranormal romance, and fantasy romance that isn't for the faint of heart.

You can find J.E. Taylor at the following places:

Website: https://JETaylor75.com

Facebook reader group:
https://www.facebook.com/groups/jetcryptkeep
ers

LinkedIn:
https://www.linkedin.com/in/JTaylor8

Bookbub:
https://www.bookbub.com/authors/J-E-Taylor
Twitter/X: https://twitter.com/JETaylor75

Instagram:
https://www.instagram.com/JETaylor75/

TikTok: https://www.tiktok.com/@JETaylor75

If you enjoyed MAGIC OF THE FAE, you may also enjoy the FIRE AND FAE DUET:

WHISPERS OF FIRE & FAE and KINGDOM OF FIRE & FAE

Enemies by birth, allies by fate.

Experience the sizzling tension between Lanae, the fierce fae, and Draven, the city's last dragon, in "Fire & Fae Duet". Can love defy centuries of contempt?

393

Find these books and more at
HTTPS://JETaylor75.com!